"Forgive me," Gabriel muttered. "I promise you... it won't happen again."

Stunned and humiliated, Miranda sat on the muddy grass, her clothing plastered to her body.

What am I supposed to do now? she wondered miserably. Go home and simply forget La Caridad? I can't bear to be around him after this. Yet she couldn't desert her people. She'd promised them.

"I want to tell you how sorry I am," Gabriel said. "For us to get involved would be a mistake. I have a country to think about. And you're here only temporarily. Your life is waiting for you back in the States. We'd just be asking for heartbreak."

Despite everything, a thrill of optimism seized Miranda. He was telling her she was the kind of woman that, once bedded, he'd want to keep.

If she even hinted at her thoughts, he'd push her away. His dedication and his decency would take precedence. Yet she'd made up her mind. She wouldn't leave La Caridad without tasting his kisses again. And more.

Dear Reader,

One of your favorite authors is on tap for this month: Nora Roberts. It's been a while since she last appeared in the line, but I think you'll find *Unfinished Business* well worth the wait. I'm a particular fan of stories that reunite past lovers, so I was really rooting for Vanessa Sexton and Brady Tucker, and I think you will be, too.

The rest of this month is pretty exciting, as well. Ann Williams is back with *Without Warning,* a complex tale of greed, revenge and—of course!—passion. Hero Michael Baldwin was reported dead years ago, but as Blair Mallory discovers, the reports of his death were greatly exaggerated! In *True to the Fire,* Suzanne Carey uses her lush island setting to full effect as she spins a tale about a woman trying to carry on her father's legacy and the handsome revolutionary who wins her heart. Finally, welcome Blythe Stephens to Silhouette Intimate Moments. In *Wake to Darkness* she grabs your attention right on page one and never lets go. I found myself completely involved with heroine Yvonne Worthington's search to regain her memory—and find love.

In coming months, keep your eyes out for more great reading from Silhouette Intimate Moments. We'll be bringing you books from favorite authors such as Marilyn Pappano, Paula Detmer Riggs, Joyce McGill and—very soon!—Linda Howard. You won't want to miss a single one of the books we have scheduled for you.

Yours,
Leslie Wainger
Senior Editor and Editorial Coordinator

SUZANNE CAREY

True to the Fire

SILHOUETTE·INTIMATE·MOMENTS®
Published by Silhouette Books New York

America's Publisher of Contemporary Romance

If you purchased this book without a cover you should be aware that this book is stolen property. It was reported as "unsold and destroyed" to the publisher, and neither the author nor the publisher has received any payment for this "stripped book."

SILHOUETTE BOOKS
300 East 42nd St., New York, N.Y. 10017

TRUE TO THE FIRE

Copyright © 1992 by Verna Carey

All rights reserved. Except for use in any review, the reproduction or utilization of this work in whole or in part in any form by any electronic, mechanical or other means, now known or hereafter invented, including xerography, photocopying and recording, or in any information storage or retrieval system, is forbidden without the permission of the publisher, Silhouette Books, 300 E. 42nd St., New York, N.Y. 10017

ISBN: 0-373-07435-2

First Silhouette Books printing June 1992

All the characters in this book have no existence outside the imagination of the author and have no relation whatsoever to anyone bearing the same name or names. They are not even distantly inspired by any individual known or unknown to the author, and all incidents are pure invention.

®: Trademark used under license and registered in the United States Patent and Trademark Office and in other countries.

Printed in the U.S.A.

Books by Suzanne Carey

Silhouette Intimate Moments

Never Say Goodbye #330
Strangers When We Meet #392
True to the Fire #435

Silhouette Desire

Kiss and Tell #4
Passion's Portrait #69
Mountain Memory #92
Leave Me Never #126
Counterparts #176
Angel in His Arms #206
Confess to Apollo #268
Love Medicine #310
Any Pirate in a Storm #368

Silhouette Romance

A Most Convenient Marriage #633
Run, Isabella #682
Virgin Territory #736
The Baby Contract #777
Home for Thanksgiving #825
Navajo Wedding #855

SUZANNE CAREY

is a former reporter and magazine editor who prefers to write romance novels because they add to the sum total of love in the world.

Chapter 1

Was she the kind of woman who enjoyed a man?

The thought stole into Gabriel's consciousness, wafting, perhaps, on the soft night air with its haunting aroma of cereus blooms. He tried to dismiss it and found he couldn't. Like the breeze that stirred so seductively against his skin, it was subtle but persistent, reminding him that more than a year had passed since he'd made love to anyone.

He couldn't afford to get involved with Miranda Burton. She might be the daughter of Juan Almeida, martyred hero of the island of La Caridad's 1968 revolution. She might be sexy in the elegant, casual way he liked, if her publicity photographs were any indication. But she hadn't given them a firm commitment. She'd simply promised to do what she could during her sabbatical from the concert circuit. In practical terms, that might translate to exactly one week of her help and support.

Shifting his position against the thatched wall of a farm worker's abandoned shack, Gabriel consulted the illuminated dial of his watch. It was almost time. He'd be able to satisfy his curiosity about Juan's daughter soon enough.

As if on cue, he heard the growl of what he hoped was their borrowed jeep's engine. Getting to his feet, he drew his *pistola* just in case.

He couldn't help smiling as he pictured the sheltered American women in a vehicle that was lurching over the pitted crushed-shell-and-dirt road. Her aunt and traveling companion, Pilar Guzman, lived in Mexico now; she'd be used to such roads. But though Miranda Burton had been born in La Caridad, she'd spent most of her life in that lap of luxury, the United States.

The moon took cover amid luminous trade-wind clouds. A moment later, the jeep came into view. Gabriel's second in command, Father Félix Hill, was at the wheel. He'd switched off the headlamps. Braking in front of the shack, he left the motor running.

"¿Quien es?" Gabriel challenged softly, observing their usual precautions.

His angular features barely discernible in the darkness, Félix returned the password. *"Somos amigos."*

Thrusting the pistol back into his belt, Gabriel detached himself from the shadows.

For the first time, Miranda Burton got a look at him, though she couldn't see him well.

Like the priest-activist who'd met them at San Juan Airport, he was tall and he wore casual clothing. But that was where the similarity ended. Whereas Félix Hill was lanky and in his late forties, the man she knew to be revolutionary leader Gabriel Sánchez Luna had a compact, muscular physique. Despite his position of responsibility, she doubted if he'd reached forty.

Before she realized what he intended, he'd stepped onto the jeep's tiny fender skirt and caught hold of the windshield. Hard as the wood of the ceiba tree, his thigh pressed against her shoulder as Félix shifted gears and they moved forward, bumping without illumination down a soft dirt track and turning into the pineapple field he'd told them to expect.

Something sweet, a whiff of some exotic flower she didn't recognize, drifted to Miranda on the moist velvet air. Beneath it, she caught a faint but unmistakably masculine fragrance. Little shivers of a difficult-to-define emotion skidded down her arms.

"I'm Gabriel," the newcomer said, leaning over so that his head was level with theirs and his voice was audible. "Happy to make your acquaintance, ladies. Many thanks for coming. If you don't mind, we'll save the rest of our conversation for when we're in the air."

Miranda's aunt Pilar Guzman, sister to the martyred revolutionary hero whose magnetism Gabriel and his friends hoped to revive in the person of his daughter, murmured something in reply. Miranda said nothing. The moon reappeared, easing out from behind a cloud. By its silvery light, she could see the small, somewhat battered-looking plane that stood ready at one end of a rough-cut, grassy runway. Seconds later, they were stopping beside it. A small wooden crate had been positioned to make a step.

"It's best if we hurry," Félix urged, starting to unload their luggage as Gabriel jumped down and offered Miranda his hand. "There are many drug patrols. And, though the authorities wouldn't find any contraband aboard, we'd have a lot of explaining to do if they caught us."

The need for a timely departure couldn't be questioned. Yet as Miranda stepped to the ground and stood there looking up at Gabriel, neither of them moved.

Surely the firm grip of his fingers meant nothing. It was a mere courtesy extended to prevent her from stumbling. So why should she feel as if an electrical current had passed between them? Or that she'd been invited to share the secrets of her soul? She didn't even know what kind of man he was—whether or not he merited her admiration and trust.

Gabriel was struck by similar contradictory emotions. Though he'd agreed to seek Miranda's help, he still had mixed feelings. He didn't want to succumb to raging hormones before reason could sit in judgment. Yet that was just what he seemed about to do. *She's even more attractive than the camera made her look,* he admitted reluctantly, *more moved by meeting her than he'd been by anything in years.*

"*¡Vámanos!*" Félix urged, throwing them a worried look.

Hurriedly Miranda and her aunt scrambled aboard and fastened their seat belts. While Félix stowed their bags, Gabriel started the engines and made a rapid check of the instrument panel. The priest had barely assumed his place when they were heading for takeoff, hurtling down the crude excuse for a runaway as if hell-bent for destruction in a looming tangle of trees.

At the last possible moment, Gabriel pulled back on the stick and the plane rose sharply. Shuddering with protest at such deliberate abuse, it continued to climb at an acute angle, then leveled off, well below the altitude that would make it visible on radar screens as they headed for Puerto Rico's northwest coast.

Swallowing hard, Miranda ordered her heartbeat to resume its normal rhythm. After her hours of practice as a recently licensed pilot, she couldn't help but admire Gabriel's steady nerves. Personally she wasn't ready to perform such daredevil stunts.

More quickly than she might have supposed, the lights of the shore were beneath them, a glittering, irregularly set necklace of yellow diamonds. Ahead lay the black expanse of water that separated Puerto Rico from La Caridad. The die of her adventure was cast.

Checking their heading once more, Gabriel settled back for the ride. Almost as closely attuned to what Miranda was thinking and feeling as he was to the multiple facets of his duties as a pilot, he acknowledged her composure and grace under pressure. She hadn't stirred or made a sound when they'd taken off, though her aunt had gasped and held tightly to the seat in front of her. Did that mean Miranda possessed the cool nerves and daring that would allow her to be of real use to them?

Only time would tell.

Unbidden, his personal speculations about her reasserted themselves, though his more practical side would have preferred not to give them thought. So far, all he knew was the few details *Vanity Fair* had printed about her in its article highlighting a new generation of classical performers. But that lack of knowledge was changing rapidly. By itself, the elusive presence of her perfume in the cockpit was altering his view of her. Though he suspected her of being politically frivolous, everything in him wanted to renew their physical contact.

Wouldn't it be ironic if we became lovers? he thought. He couldn't imagine a more ill-advised, unnecessary complication. Yet the potential was there. He knew it as surely as he sensed her silent questioning of him and his motives. To translate it into reality would be a mistake. He had a motherless daughter to care for. And a government to overthrow. A past that had made him wary. Yet he'd been without a woman too long. And that made him vulnerable. Though she was an unknown quantity, he couldn't deny the idea of romancing her fired his blood.

Attracted to Gabriel though it violated every maxim of practicality and common sense, Miranda was asking herself some comparable questions. She found it stunning that the mere touch of his hand could excite her in a way her sometime escort Tony Braithwaite's heartfelt kisses had failed to do. Though she liked Tony and genuinely cared about him, she'd always felt something was lacking in their relationship. Now she knew what it was. With Gabriel Sánchez, she guessed, it would be all too easy to experience the headlong passion that so far had eluded her.

If only she could get a better look at him.

As if he'd picked up on her wish and decided to grant it, he glanced over his shoulder. Revealed in three-quarter profile by the greenish glow of the instrument panel, his features were firmly sculpted. More arresting than handsome, they spoke of sensitivity toughened by adversity and determination. She'd never known a man whose eyes beckoned with such alluring depths.

"Forgive me, ladies, if I've been a little brusque," he said after a moment. "Your safety had to be my first consideration. I imagine Félix has told you a little more about the situation in La Caridad. If you like, I'll be happy to elaborate."

* * *

The trip from takeoff to landing took less than twenty-five minutes. Mesmerized by Gabriel's soft, deep accents as he described the Santos regime's repressive measures and economic failure, Miranda was startled when he interrupted the flow of their mostly one-way conversation to inform them La Caridad lay just ahead.

"We'll approach the coast north of Gerónimo, circle the Juradas Peaks of Las Montañas, and come in from the west," he explained, taking for granted she and Pilar knew the island's geography.

Fascinated, Miranda pressed her face to the glass. Already the distant glow of Gerónimo, a major port active in the shipping of sugarcane, molasses and tobacco, could be seen off their left flank.

Once they were over land, she spotted only a few scattered lights, as if from isolated ranches or farms. Soon the mountains Gabriel had mentioned were hulking shapes in the moonlight. It appeared that, in seeking a remote area to obscure his comings and goings, he'd chosen well.

Pilar was looking apprehensive. "This airstrip..." she asked finally. "Is it anything like the one we left behind?"

Gabriel grinned. Despite his reservations, he was beginning to enjoy himself. "A little less forgiving of pilot error, perhaps. It's not exactly carved out of a pineapple field on level ground."

A moment later, he was activating the radio and signaling his compatriots. *"Manuel, Manuel, tengo la mercancia. ¿Comprendes?"* I have the goods. Do you copy?

"Sí...no hay moros," a man's voice answered, drowning in static.

The coast was clear. A row of lights switched on, illuminating a narrow landing strip hacked out of jungle-like terrain in a fold between two steep ridges. Gabriel dropped the landing gear into place.

"Here we go," he said, addressing Pilar again as they began to lose altitude. "Maybe you should shut your eyes."

For her part, Miranda refused to do any such thing. Far from certain she was sufficiently committed to La Caridad and its welfare to play even a small part in its current troubles, she'd agreed to investigate the possibility out of respect for her father's memory. Now that she was actually approaching its soil, excitement gripped her. She wanted to drink the cup of experience to the dregs.

Her stomach did somersaults as Gabriel brought them in hard and fast and neat. The plane barely wobbled as they touched down and he slowed their forward progress. As they jolted over the rough ground toward what was probably a makeshift hangar, a jeep ran alongside, older and more derelict in appearance than the one Félix had borrowed to meet them in San Juan. It contained a teenager and two grown men, all carrying machine guns.

Maneuvering the plane into the hangar's camouflaged, vine-clad womb, Gabriel cut the engines. Quickly he and Félix helped Miranda and her aunt from their seats.

They were immediately greeted by a small band of men. Everyone spoke English, it seemed. "Greetings, Miss Burton, Señora Guzman," said a balding man of medium height who introduced himself as Manuel Roa, the man Gabriel had communicated with by radio. "La

Caridad is proud to welcome the daughter and the sister of Juan Almeida.''

"As is another member of the Sánchez family."

Surprised, Miranda turned toward a man who looked as if he might be Gabriel's brother if not his twin. A moment later she realized they were really quite different. An inch or two shorter and perhaps two or three years younger than Gabriel, he was better-looking in a conventional way. She guessed that he hadn't acquired much of Gabriel's daring or formidable strength. Perhaps his charm and amiability compensated for the lack.

Obviously aware of the comparison she must be making and seeming accustomed to provoking that reaction from people he met, he took possession of her hands. No electrical charge was forthcoming.

"Angél Sánchez Marin, at your service," he murmured, lifting her fingers to his lips. "I'm Gabriel's cousin. I hope you'll allow me to help make your stay here a more pleasant one."

The amenities observed, they didn't linger. While Gabriel put the plane to bed and Félix transferred the luggage, Manuel, Angél and the teenager who had accompanied them, dragged a screen of netting and branches into place. Within minutes, the plane was effectively hidden from all but the most inquisitive eyes.

"Let's go," Gabriel exhorted them.

With seven people and the luggage crammed into it, the jeep was terribly crowded. Miranda ended up on Gabriel's lap while Gabriel's cousin drove and Manuel leaned into them from the passenger side. Miranda's aunt, Félix and the youth were squeezed in back. The luggage was everywhere—strapped on behind, piled beneath their feet.

"My violin..." Miranda asked with sudden concern as they left the airstrip behind. Though music was as necessary to her as light and breath, she wondered if she'd been a fool to bring it.

"Don't worry," Félix assured her. "We have it. We're looking forward to a private concert."

There wasn't any road for several kilometers, just a rough track defined by occasional use. Following it, they cut through overgrown vegetation, narrowly missing a number of massive tree trunks half-obscured by monstera and strangler fig. With every jostle and bounce, Miranda grew more conscious of Gabriel's body pressing against hers. How hard he was, how lean, as if from years of regular physical exercise. She caught his scent again, intriguing and a little musky. Guiltily she drank it into her nostrils.

Never had a man excited her so much. Never had one made her long to throw caution to the wind in quite the same way that he did. Incredibly, she was in La Caridad, the land of her birth, a hard-line Communist country in the Cuban mold that had long since severed relations with the United States. She was descending toward its more heavily populated coast through lush, tropical woods and hip-deep fields studded with royal palms. Yet all she could think about was Gabriel's solid, masculine presence, the feathering of his warm breath against her neck. Keenly aware of his cousin's speculative gaze, she tried not to betray even an inkling of what she felt.

Once they'd reached what passed for a highway and turned onto its semipaved surface, their contact wasn't quite so intimate. Gabriel found himself regretting the absence of so many jars and bumps. He'd been alone too long and now he was paying the price. The warm, delicious weight of Juan Almeida's daughter on his lap was making him think of smooth skin and rumpled sheets, the sweet forgetting that was only possible in a woman's arms.

How tempting it would be to pull her closer, guide her mouth around to his and sample its crushed-petal sweetness. If the barriers ever come down between us, he realized, struggling not to tighten his hold on her, I'm going to want more than a taste.

A yard light had been left burning at the *finca* of Gabriel's aunt, Josefina Roa, which would serve as home base during the visit. At the jeep's approach, a dog barked and someone silenced it. Seconds later, a door opened, spilling forth a yellow triangle of illumination.

"Están aquí," a man's voice called out.

The house was relatively small, though it boasted several outbuildings. Miranda noted pale stucco walls, carmine-stained shutters. An arcade of native coral stone supported a second-floor balcony. The roof was paved with old, somewhat damaged barrel tiles. The country estate was extremely modest. Her mother's description of how La Caridad's upper class had lived twenty-four years earlier had led Miranda to expect something far more grandiose.

A tall, thin woman in her early seventies, dressed in tan jodhpurs and a snowy shirt, Josefina came out to greet them. She was accompanied by three men and two women—all members, Miranda guessed, of the insurrectionist group Gabriel had called La Cábala. The word meant "intrigue." I'm glad it isn't an exclusively male club, she thought, conscious of her status as a liberated American female in a Spanish-speaking country where, traditionally, men had been dominant.

Josefina embraced her and Pilar when Gabriel introduced them. "I thank you from the bottom of my heart for coming, *mis hermanas,*" she said, styling them sisters. "Please...enter. Such as it is, my house is yours. We'll celebrate your arrival with a toast."

Josefina's *sala,* comprising the shallow space defined by the stone arcade, ran nearly the full width of the house. It had thick stucco walls, a dark beamed ceiling and a floor of terra cotta tiles. The furniture, mostly Spanish Colonial and primitive pieces devoid of excessive ornamentation, was charmingly mismatched. Several rather shabby upholstered chairs as well as most of the lamps, pillows and ashtrays contributed to a dated, late sixties' ambience.

A dashing older man who gave his name as Ruben Camargo volunteered to open the champagne. There were several bottles—a rare luxury in La Caridad under the Santos government, as Miranda quickly learned. Everyone laughed, including Ruben, when one of the corks blew prematurely, releasing foam down the front of his shirt.

The other women were also wearing trousers. One of them, a severe-looking, dark-eyed beauty in her midthirties, looked at Gabriel with longing. From what Miranda could tell, he was totally oblivious to her interest.

The room was fairly well lit and Miranda seized her first real opportunity to study him. Clad in a black polo-type shirt and faded khaki bush-style trousers, he exuded a sense of being at perfect ease, in both his body and his surroundings. By now, his strong, firmly chiseled features were familiar to her. But she hadn't guessed his skin and medium-to-dark brown hair would be so bronzed—almost gilded—by the powerful Caribbean sunlight. Or noticed the small, wry groove that tugged at one corner of his mouth.

His cousin Angél might be better-looking in a moviestar sense. But when it came to sex appeal, Gabriel easily had it over him. Any man who can land a plane like that without breaking a sweat knows exactly who he is and what he's doing in the world, Miranda thought. And to me, that's sexy. The passion and deep caring for others that had filled his voice as he'd spoken of his country's problems during their flight from Puerto Rico had only confirmed that estimate of him.

Words were cheap and she couldn't let them disarm her skepticism of him in a political sense. Yet, though they'd barely met, from a personal standpoint she'd begun to view him as someone special, the kind of man most women only dreamed about.

She gave her emotional self a little shake. She hadn't come to La Caridad to get mixed up with someone. She had a life—and a career—in a different world. As enticing as he was, Gabriel Sánchez could never be for her.

With a courtly little flourish, Angél handed Miranda a glass of bubbly. She thanked him. Face it, she thought. You don't have a thing to worry about. Gabriel Sánchez isn't interested in you as a woman. Just in what you can do for his cause.

The object of her thoughts chose that moment to meet her eyes. For her, it was as if they'd physically touched again. She could feel the pull he exerted from across the room.

"Is everything all right?" Angél asked, giving her a quizzical look.

"Yes, fine," she answered, smiling up at him casually as she could. "I'm just a little unsettled from all the excitement. Our flight from Puerto Rico wasn't exactly like taking the bus."

Watching their exchange without appearing to pay them any undue attention, Gabriel longed to walk over and stake a claim. What's the matter with you? he taxed himself. Miranda Burton probably has half a dozen men dangling on the end of her chain back in the States. Besides, you can't afford to get mixed up with a spoiled *norteamericana* whose long-term interests lie outside the country you're trying to liberate.

As for a marriage of expediency—like the one Félix and several other members of La Cábala had recently suggested—he'd sworn off such lunacy years ago. He planned to make his decision stick. The fact that Miranda was an even more attractive proposition than he'd bargained for couldn't be allowed to undermine his resolve.

Still, he couldn't seem to stop staring at her. One look and he'd been forced to admit her photographs didn't lie. Yet in the half-light of the plane and during their jeep ride from the airstrip it hadn't occurred to him that tiny freckles might cover her skin like gold dust. Or that there'd be more flecks of the same rich color suspended in the irises of her large hazel eyes.

Her dark hair was a mass of ringlets—clean, sweet-smelling and natural, reaching well below her shoulders. His libido spinning out of control, he imagined himself lifting it by the handful. All too easily he could guess how it would look spread out like a halo on his pillow. Or falling about his face as she lowered her mouth to his.

By now, everyone was holding a glass of the best black-market champagne he'd been able to locate, and they were waiting for him to offer a toast. Consigning his fantasies to the scrap heap, Gabriel raised his glass.

"To Juan Almeida. And to his daughter and sister," he said, his gaze seeing Miranda first and then traveling past her to Pilar. "May we all be true to the fire he started a quarter century ago until our homeland is free again."

Chapter 2

The bedroom Josefina Roa assigned to Miranda later that evening had a dark, beamed ceiling. Its floor, made of wide mahogany planking, was worn but well polished and strewn with round straw rugs in patterns as delicate as lace. Other than the walls, which had been painted a pale salmon tint, there was no color. The intricately carved four-poster bed's headboard was reminiscent of the altarpiece in a Spanish church. Canopied and swathed in translucent white mosquito netting, the bed had been painstakingly fitted with smooth, neatly mended white sheets and a white-on-white embroidered cotton spread.

Thanking her hostess and bidding her aunt a fond good-night, Miranda washed her face and hands in the tiny bathroom at the end of the hall before returning to her private quarters to put on her nightgown. Through the open, floor-to-ceiling French doors that led to the upper balcony she could smell the salt tang in the air, though they were too far from the ocean to hear the pounding of the surf. Mild and soft, a capricious breeze stirred the bed curtains.

I'm really here, in La Caridad, she thought. Gabriel's real. I'm not just dreaming this.

Outside a jeep started up, disturbing the night's lush tranquillity and causing several tropical birds to screech and flap their wings in protest. Was Gabriel about to take his leave? That evening one of the men had mentioned that Gabriel's ranch, Las Brisas, The Breezes, was situated on the coast. He'd added that Gabriel, a widower, lived there with his eleven-year-old daughter. No doubt the man who'd impressed Miranda so much felt a responsibility to return home as soon as he could. She couldn't help frowning at the thought that he regularly placed himself in danger. At the same time, she didn't understand how he and his coconspirators could enjoy as much freedom as they did. Weren't insurgents usually subject to privation? And in danger of arrest?

According to Pilar, the answer had something to do with Las Montañas's traditional isolation and the enormous difficulty the Santos government was having, just keeping order in the rest of the country. As a refuge of high-born planters who'd fled to their summer homes in the breeze-swept north during the Santista revolution a quarter century earlier, Las Montañas might be a breeding ground for violence. But it wasn't a violent place. Historically, the worst trouble had always been in El Panal, the southern province heavily populated by the farm workers and laborers who had once been Juan Almeida's power base.

So far, La Cábala and the other like-minded groups its members sought to incorporate into a more cohesive front had chosen the path of demonstrations, general strikes and increasingly frequent commando raids in preference to all-out civil war. La Caridad didn't have a rebel army equivalent to the contras who'd inspired so much controversy in Nicaragua.

For someone raised in the United States with its two-party system, the situation was frustratingly complex. As she brushed her hair before the oval mirror above a petite, old-fashioned dressing table, she couldn't keep her thoughts from returning to Gabriel. Lord, but it was difficult not to let them run wild when the man attracted her like a magnet. She'd never met anyone like him, both sexy and deeply protective, though it was clear he expected a woman to stand on her own two feet. His seeming courage and decency were almost more than belief could handle. In retrospect, she didn't find it too surprising his friends in La Cábala hoped someday he would be their presidential candidate.

I'm here for Papa's sake, not his, she reminded herself, getting up to extract a worn and faded scrapbook from her duffel bag. When her Aunt Pilar had arrived from Mexico City for a Christmas visit to Miranda's home in Fort Lauderdale and relayed La Cábala's invitation to visit the land of her birth, the scrapbook's contents had helped her decide what course of action to take. Usually so dutiful and willing to please, she'd gone against her mother's wishes and her stepfather's strong, well-meaning recommendations because of Juan and her half-perceived responsibility to him.

She didn't remember him well. She'd been just five years old when he died of gunshot wounds a few feet from the front door of their boxy little house in the island town of Batey Venus. The fatal burst of lead had been administered by a hit man acting for Leander Santos, whom Juan had originally admired and supported, and whom he ultimately turned against. Miranda had been playing nearby when it happened, digging in the dirt with a toy pail and shovel while Juan had smoked a leisurely after-dinner cigarette. Of that terrible scene, she recalled just two painful snippets: her wrenching fear at the rat-tat-tat-tat of gunfire and screaming "Papa!" as he fell.

A neighbor with a small box camera had recorded the aftermath. Mercifully, though she knew of their existence, she'd never seen the resulting snapshots. Aside from the trauma of that day, which still had the power to turn her dreams into nightmares, she retained only a kaleidoscopic panorama of lesser images. She and her mother, who'd taken her away from La Caridad at once and remarried within two years of her husband's death to become Célia Burton, rarely talked of Juan. Miranda knew him best from newspaper clippings and photographs.

By now, the scrapbook's pages were almost falling apart. The clippings between its covers had turned brittle and yellow. Curling up at the foot of the bed, Miranda handled them with care. In sum, they represented the adult life and brief political career of the former field boss on a sugarcane plantation who'd become Santos's confidante and right-hand man in the salad days of La Caridad's 1968 revolution, before it had been perverted by Communist influence. She knew exactly which clipping she wanted. Locating it, she studied the crude dot pattern on cheap newsprint that had captured her father's youthful and somehow vulnerable features as they'd appeared on September 10 of that year, three days before his death.

Wearing one of the typical straw hats that shaded the eyes of his beloved *guajiros* as they toiled in the fields, the man universally hailed as Juanito was standing *beside* the comrade in arms who'd already ordered his execution. But he hadn't stood *with* Leander Santos any longer, and Miranda was very proud of that. Disillusioned by what he'd described to her mother as the emerging dictator's sellout of the revolution to pro-Castro elements, Juan had already been working behind the scenes to remedy the situation.

As always, gazing at her father's photograph evoked a haunting sense of familiarity. In his face, Miranda saw the man who'd carried her about on his shoulders at a country fair, promising her a *helado,* ice cream. She also saw herself. We're very much alike, she thought. It's as if we were created in the same mold.

Yet in one way she and Juan were very different. He'd known what he believed in, and she didn't. Yes, she embodied the usual American principles and prejudices, but from the time Miranda had been very young and displayed unusual musical ability, Célia had insisted she think only of her professional future and avoid life's grittier aspects.

True, she frequently donated her time and talent to good causes, playing without compensation for this or that worthwhile charity or benefit. But she'd never gotten personally involved, or taken the time to embroil herself in politics. Lately, as she'd traveled more in her career, she'd begun to see her dearth of experience in that area as a blank spot, a shirking of communal responsibility. She wondered if it wasn't time she got her hands dirty. Took a stand. Laid her comfort and safety on the line for the sake of something more important than herself.

She wasn't sure if Gabriel and his cohorts merited her support. The idea of democracy was a heady one, but did it mean equal opportunity for everyone, including the *guajiros*, or a return to the former gangster-ridden regime?

What Gabriel and the rest of La Cábala wanted *her* to do was simple: court the workers of the El Panal region. They hoped the cane cutters and stevedores would see her. Remember Juan. Connect him with their movement. And rise up in their support. There wasn't much doubt Leander Santos's grip on La Caridad had been weakened as a result of their efforts. Yet unless they could unite the laboring class's strength in numbers with their own strategic and managerial ability, Santos and his regime might continue to prevail.

What do you think I should do, *papacito?* Miranda asked.

Though a photograph couldn't speak, the answer wasn't that difficult to figure out. Dead for twenty-four years, Juan still had unfinished business in the land that had nurtured them both. The workers he'd championed continued to suffer from hardship and exploitation. If she was to help Gabriel and his friends, she had to make sure they had the workers' interests at heart. She couldn't allow herself to pledge allegiance solely on the basis of her strong physical attraction to a man she'd just met.

Gabriel hadn't left for Las Brisas as Miranda thought. Despite the bodyguards he'd posted in shabby vehicles at the nearest crossroads, he was unwilling to leave the American visitor alone on her first night in the country, when she'd come so far in response to their invitation. His daughter, Raquelita, had been fast asleep on a cot in her Great-aunt Josefina's room since before Miranda's arrival.

As Miranda put away the scrapbook, switched off the lamp beside her bed and nestled between breeze-scented sheets, a meeting of La Cábala's prime movers and shakers was taking place around Josefina's dining room table. A suggestion that Miranda and Gabriel develop something other than a strictly political relationship was being discussed.

"As I understand it, Miranda Burton has taken a leave of absence from the concert circuit to write a new concerto for violin under a grant from the National Endowment for the Arts," Félix was saying. "She's agreed to give us one-third of her proposed six-month hiatus if we can convince her to help us. That isn't enough."

"Aren't you jumping the gun?" Ruben asked. "We don't even know yet if her presence will have the desired effect."

"Trust me. It will." Félix was adamant. "But for that effect to do us the most good," he added, "she must remain longer than two months. If we can pressure Santos into calling a free election, we must make certain of winning it. That's why it would be better if you married her, Gabriel. As your wife, she'd naturally see the process through. Pablo Escobar and his lieutenants would be assured of a permanent advocate."

Gabriel frowned at the name of the labor boss, whom he disliked though he frequently had to deal with him. As for the suggestion he marry Miranda, he'd heard it before. "I told you," he said quietly. "That's asking too much."

"Not when you consider what's at stake."

They'd gone over the same ground in early December, when the idea of inviting Juan's daughter to return to La Caridad had first arisen. Wary of repeating past mistakes, Gabriel had turned thumbs-down on the proposal. He hadn't changed his mind since, though he had to admit it would be easy, from a purely pleasurable standpoint, now that he and Miranda had met.

Throughout La Caridad as well as among their co-conspirators, Félix was listened to with respect. If he hadn't been a priest, firmly dedicated to reestablishing the faith after Santos's ouster, he would have made an excellent candidate to head the next government. Gabriel would have been off the hook.

Glancing around the table, he saw most of his compatriots agreed with the priest-activist. With each strike and demonstration, each bomb blast directed at a government building, Santos came closer to toppling. Yet unless they could provide an alternative who would be readily accepted by all the people, their striving could come to nothing.

Gabriel would have liked to think he could fuel the loyalty and political will of the laboring classes just by being the man he was. But he didn't delude himself. He'd committed the unpardonable sin of springing from La Caridad's upper class. For all his personal fire and daring as a guerrilla, he was that dreaded thing known as a gentleman. Assuming the mantle of Juan Almeida would give him clout where he needed it most. Despite his reservations, he'd concurred in the decision to seek Miranda's help.

But for them to *marry?* He wouldn't tread that path again. Nor did he suppose the notion would interest her, considering what she'd have to relinquish. As if in reply, a gust of wind caused the flames inside the hurricane lamps to shudder and dance. The breath of prophecy, Gabriel thought, then discarded the fanciful notion.

Though he was attracted to Miranda he suspected her of having accepted their invitation on a whim. She didn't owe them anything. In the unlikely event she became emotionally involved in freeing La Caridad, he believed she wouldn't be able to stay the distance.

"I tell you, it's impossible," he said. "She's an American. And though she's only twenty-nine, she's gained some renown as a violinist on the classical stage. Why would she choose to give that up... devote her life to a man she doesn't know? And to a country that, compared with the United States, is only a dot on the map?"

"Your mother was American," Ruben reminded him. "And she was happy here. She was very committed to ending Communist rule."

"Even so."

Briefly, silence filled the airy, cream-painted room with its tall, shuttered windows, scarred but well-polished dining table and collection of ancestral portraits.

"She's not bad-looking," Angél remarked, quirking one handsome brow.

The somber, coercive mood around the table lifted. Several of the men chuckled. The aristocratic features of seventy-one-year-old Josefina Roa relaxed in an indulgent smile.

"He's right," said Manuel Roa, Josefina's nephew by marriage and one of Gabriel's closest advisers. "I know your mind's made up. But you might not find it such a terrible sacrifice."

That night, every bed in the house was taken. Following the meeting, Gabriel walked outside and lay down in a hammock under the trees. Lacing his fingers behind his head, he stared up at the lovely, hurrying trade wind clouds. You're at a dangerous crossroads, he acknowledged with a little shake of his head. If you get mixed up with Miranda Burton, everything you've worked so hard to achieve will be up for grabs. It was a bad idea, staying here with her tomorrow while Ruben and Angél drive in to Gerónimo and try to influence the dockworkers.

He could see the necessity for talking with her in detail about what they wanted her to do and assessing her ability to do it. He even agreed that the task should fall to him. It was just that she'd gotten under his skin. The more he saw of her, the more he wanted her. If La Cábala were to realize their goal in bringing her to La Caridad without his compromising his principles, he'd have to get hold of himself.

Drifting off to sleep, he was prey to restless dreams. He awoke, as usual, several times. When he ultimately rose it was barely light. He remembered with a pang of hunger that he hadn't eaten the night before. Josefina would have bread. Coffee. And grapefruit. Quietly, so as not to disturb the household, he entered and went into the kitchen. He was standing at the sink, picking out grapefruit seeds with a serrated spoon, when he caught a movement in the fields outside the window.

Paying sharp attention, he noted another. And then a third, a little way apart. There were men in the sugarcane, advancing on the house!

Where the hell were Pepe and Armando?

As far as he knew, he was a man alone, charged with the care of sleeping women. A man with only a pistol in his belt against what might be an army. With the speed of the trained guerrilla, he raced for his serious gun.

Seconds later, he was taking the stairs two at a time to Miranda's room.

They'd come for *her*, of course. As Juan Almeida's daughter, she was dangerous. He knew it wouldn't trouble the Santistas to kill her if they thought they could do so with secrecy and dispatch. Somehow, he had to prevent it. And what about his child? And the other women? Their safety was important, too.

Pepe... Armando... *for God's sake!* he thought.

Miranda's door was partly open. She was awake, standing at the window in her nightgown, watching the silent men approach. Sensing his presence, she turned, seeming innocent of the tantalizing picture—or the inviting target—she made in her semitransparent batiste and lace.

"What's going on?" she asked in puzzlement. "There are *guajiros* coming toward the house. When they reach the yard, they just stand there, looking up at the windows."

Her eyes widened when she saw his gun.

In a flash, Gabriel was beside her, his fingers biting into the flesh of her upper arm as he drew her back behind the shutters. "This isn't the United States!" he whispered hoarsely. "Surely you have more sense...."

The words trailed off as he noted in surprise that the men weren't armed. It was as she said. They were standing and looking up at the house, as if with great respect. Chills rippled over his skin when he realized what was actually taking place. Somehow, laborers who were old enough to remember Juan Almeida, as well as many who'd only heard of him, had learned of his daughter's presence. They'd come to pay a silent tribute.

Gabriel struggled to suppress the lump in his throat. It was the way he'd wept, ever since he was small.

"Forgive me," he said, letting go of her and wincing as she rubbed the red finger marks his hand had left. "I was mistaken. Those men mean you no harm."

Miranda stared. "Who are they?"

"Men who supported Juanito. Men who honor him. They've come to pay you homage in his place."

She was the one who shivered abruptly and fought back tears. For the first time, she'd encountered the full power of her father's legend, which resonated with all the force and energy he'd possessed. Juan was dead. But not to these *guajiros*. They still loved and honored him, remembered his efforts to save them. Now, it seemed, they expected something of her.

"What must I do?" she asked, suddenly afraid of the burden they might wish to thrust upon her shoulders.

Just then, Josefina, Pilar and Raquelita came into the room. They, too, had seen the men. From their faces, Gabriel could tell they'd guessed the truth.

"Put on a robe," he answered, suddenly embarrassed to be caught standing next to Miranda given her state of undress. "Go out on the balcony and show your face. Speak to them if there's something within your heart that must be said."

For several seconds, she didn't move, frozen by the weight of a responsibility that collided with her memories and half-buried fears. What had she been thinking of, to come to La Caridad the way she had? Raise the hopes of these people just by setting foot in their country? She wasn't her father and she had nothing to offer them. No magic way of solving their problems. Or even a sense of how to go about trying.

She was an American who'd taken freedom and democracy for granted since she was five years old. A musician, more conditioned to the concert hall than to harsh political reality. Measured by the needs of his constituency, Juan Almeida's daughter was nothing much.

Like them, she loved and honored him. If he'd been standing there, she would have wanted to make him proud of her. "All right," she said, snatching up her white eyelet robe from a nearby chair.

As Gabriel and the other women watched, Miranda brushed out the tangles sleep had knotted in her dark-brown curls. He could tell she was shaking inside though she was determined not to show it. A moment later, barefoot, barelegged, her face devoid of makeup, she stepped through one of the open floor-to-ceiling French doors onto the narrow balcony, where she stood looking down at the *guajiros* in the yard.

At first, the only sounds were the usual morning racket sent up by the birds and the breeze sighing in a windbreak of Australian pines. A wave of excitement passed among the poorly clad men who stood clutching their hats in front of them. Then a single voice, that of a *viejo* with grizzled hair and a dusky complexion, took up the famous chant.

¡Juanito!

Within seconds, it rose like thunder from every throat. Fresh chills raced over Gabriel's skin. Tears were streaming down Pilar's cheeks.

On the balcony, Miranda was crying, too. She lifted her hand to brush the tears aside, then let it fall. There was no shame in letting others see what she felt.

"*¡Sí...Juanito!*" she replied, gazing with love at their upturned faces.

Gradually the men quieted. They seemed to be waiting for something. With a little stab of fatalism, she remembered what Gabriel had said. With her heart so full, it wouldn't be difficult to do as he'd suggested.

By now the first rays of intense Caribbean sunlight were splashing against the wall of Josefina's house. Taking another step forward, Miranda rested one hand on the balcony's wrought-iron railing. Her Spanish, with its pronounced Cariño accent, was perfect as she spoke.

"Friends of Juan Almeida, I share your memories, though when my father died I was only five years old," she told them, her voice husky with emotion. "As he knew, better than anyone, you deserve to be free! To determine your own destiny and enjoy the fruits of your labors. God willing, it will soon be thus. I will do... whatever I can to help."

The cheering set off by her promise didn't stop until she lifted her hand in parting and stepped back into the room. To Gabriel, her eyes looked glazed, unseeing, as if she'd just run a very exhausting race. She almost stumbled as Pilar enfolded her in her arms.

Standing there in the grip of his own powerful sentiments, he wished he could be the one to comfort her. As he'd lain in his hammock the night before, he'd tried to think of ways to persuade her and to gauge her strength. He'd never dreamed she'd snatch his arguments from his mouth this way, eliminating the need for calculation.

Yet what had she demonstrated, really? That she was an accomplished speaker who knew how to handle herself in front of a crowd? Her working life was conducted on a stage. She was used to interviews, dealing with the press. Plus she'd obviously inherited some of her father's legendary talent for swaying his listeners by touching the deepest chords of their emotions.

On reflection, Gabriel realized her words to the *guajiros* hadn't been a promise at all—just an offer to do what she could. That might turn out to be anything. Or nothing. The choice was hers to make.

"Admirably done," he applauded when at last she turned to him with a question in her eyes. "You're very like Juan in some respects, I think. By the way, this is my daughter, Raquelita. *Mi vida,* say hello to Miss Miranda Burton."

Shyly the eleven-year-old girl, who looked only a little like Gabriel, held out her hand. *"Mucho gusto en conocerle, señorita,"* she said.

For the first time since he'd entered her bedroom, Gabriel saw a slight curve soften Miranda's mouth. Evidently she liked children. A little of the tension she so plainly felt appeared to drain out of her shoulders.

"I'm very happy to meet you, too, Raquelita," she replied.

It was time to dress and eat. Allow the heart to beat in its natural rhythm for a while. "Come, *chiquita,*" Gabriel directed, lightly touching his daughter's shoulder. "We'll help Tía Josefina with the breakfast... and allow Miss Burton and Señora Guzman some privacy to bathe and dress."

By the time Miranda came downstairs, a small table had been set on the patio outside the dining room. The scene was an inviting one, with the leafy shade of a bougainvillea trellis overhead and tame finches singing in an antique wire cage. Someone had piled oranges in a blue bowl. The coffee smelled rich. An omelet, cooked with potatoes, had been done to perfection.

Feeling as if she'd been infected by Raquelita's shyness, she took a chair. As it turned out, she'd chosen a seat directly across from Gabriel. In the strong dappled morning light, he was more compelling than ever.

He'd obviously found time to bathe and change before helping out with the kitchen work. His hair was damp and freshly combed. The short-sleeved black polo shirt he wore with clean khaki trousers strongly emphasized the golden tan of his muscular arms. Though his mouth was serious, his dark eyes were affectionate as they rested on his daughter.

Upstairs, when she'd come in from speaking to the *guajiros,* Miranda had sensed mixed emotions on his part, but he'd quickly hidden them.

A barrier has gone up between us, she thought. Yet he's thanked me several times for coming. And he seems to want my participation.

Drawn to him, she vowed she wouldn't let herself be tugged toward doing what he wanted out of a need to prove herself. She'd told the *guajiros* she'd do what she could. And, God help her, she meant it. She wasn't sure how to carry out her pledge or if she ought to support Gabriel's efforts. Before committing herself to him and La Cábala, she needed answers.

Josefina joined them and, after a moment's grace, they helped themselves to food and drink. Conversation was casual throughout the meal. Finally, having eaten his portion of the omelet and peeled himself an orange, Gabriel leaned back in his chair.

"First, I'd like to apologize for the panic drill we went through earlier," he said. "It never should have happened. I stationed men several kilometers in either direction from Josefina's gate, where they ought to have noticed any unusual movements in time to alert us. I myself spent the night outdoors in the hammock. As I'm a light sleeper, I felt certain I'd hear if anyone approached.

"By the time the *guajiros* arrived, I'd gone into the kitchen. Our sentries didn't notice them because they cut across the fields. I promise... in future we'll be more careful."

Miranda stared. The full impact of the real danger she was in hit her full force. Her American sense of invulnerability had led her to believe that her secretive arrival had been necessitated by La Caridad's lack of diplomatic relations with the United States, not by any undue risk inherent in the situation. Given the peace of the surrounding fields, the soft, uninterrupted chirping of the birds, it was still hard to believe that she'd have to be careful. "There's no need to apologize," she replied. "Everything turned out all right."

"In that case, I have a question. Did you mean what you said on the balcony a little while ago? About doing what you can to help?"

Miranda had been expecting the question. And, despite the haunting memories she was afraid it would evoke, she'd do her best to help him if he truly had the *guajiros'* interests at heart.

"Yes, in principle," she answered at last, aware of Pilar's and Josefina's silent regard. "I'm not sure about the particulars."

Gabriel allowed a small silence to lengthen between them. So she's backing out already, he thought. Is there really any need to continue this charade? A moment later, he regretted his harsh judgment of her. He couldn't help but wonder if it had originated in his unwilling attraction to her.

He could hardly blame her for being a desirable young woman. Unless she proved herself to be a lightweight who gave her word but didn't keep it, he owed her the benefit of the doubt.

"All right," he said at last. "I agree that we need to talk. What do you say we take a little drive—away from civilization so we won't attract too much attention?"

Miranda consented. Though Gabriel invited Pilar to accompany them, she elected to stay behind, complaining she was still tired from their journey. They were off in the jeep a short time later, passing fields of sugarcane, tobacco and coffee, weathered huts roofed with tin, the occasional *finca* in a state of repair similar to the one where Miranda had taken up temporary residence. Unlike anything she'd seen at home in the States, the soil was a loamy, reddish-gold color.

Gabriel didn't say much except to point out the homes of several people she'd met the night before. As they began to climb, via a rough dirt road like those they'd traversed during their journey the night before, she got the strong feeling they were headed for a particular destination.

"Where are we going?" she asked.

His beautiful eyes were an enigma behind his sunglasses as he glanced at her. "I know a place that's perfect for our discussion," he replied. "If you'll permit me, I'll take you there."

Chapter 3

Miranda noticed a distinct drop in the temperature as the road ascended a series of jungle-clad slopes, twisting and turning to follow the bed of a narrow stream. Even the fluffy white clouds, floating in the sky's impersonal blue, seemed close enough to touch. They'd left all trace of human habitation behind by the time Gabriel turned onto a hidden track so wild and overgrown the jeep brushed aside vines and overhanging branches as they passed.

At first she couldn't place the sound that lay ahead. Then she realized what must be causing it. "Is that a waterfall I hear?" she asked.

He nodded. "La Cascada de los Angeles. Every country with mountains must have at least one Angel Falls. This is ours."

As they approached, the roar intensified, drowning out the birds' cacophonous song and the growl of the jeep's engine. Abruptly they entered a small clearing.

Miranda could see the torrent, a slender white ribbon of water that fell perhaps two hundred feet down a sheer cliff face into a rock-rimmed pool below. The air around it was charged with ionization and mist. Ferns and vines grew everywhere, taking advantage of the plentiful moisture. A damp, mossy film glistened on the surface of the rocks.

Parking a short distance from the spray, Gabriel switched off the ignition. "We've had a lot of rain for this time of year," he said. "Sometimes in January, it's just a trickle."

"It's very beautiful."

She'd be in La Caridad for two months at most. Yet she kept wanting to know him better. *Last night he wasn't so distant, so reserved,* she thought. *He actually seemed to be enjoying himself. Today, it's as if he'd rather be somewhere else. Maybe if we did something spontaneous, I'd see a lighter side of him.*

It was worth a try. Swinging her legs over the jeep's open side, she started to take off her boots. Immediately he laid a restraining hand on her arm.

"Wouldn't you like to go wading?" she asked. "I don't see how you can resist."

Did she think this was a vacation? "Maybe in a little while," he replied, suppressing a flicker of irritation. "But picturesque as it is, *la cascada* isn't why I brought you here. I hope you won't mind something of a walk."

Dropping his keys into his pants pocket, he came around to the passenger side and held out his hand. Hesitantly she allowed him to draw her to her feet. Her pretty hazel eyes were full of questions.

Gabriel wanted to kick himself. She was his guest. And a product of her environment. Growing up in Florida as she had, and touring from one concert hall to another, she'd probably never seen a real waterfall. At least she'd agreed to help.

Again it struck him that most of his annoyance probably stemmed from the way she looked in her crisp, long-sleeved safari shirt, full-length trousers and hiking boots. She was positively delectable—more enticing in her casual clothes than most women would be in their negligees. He wished to hell he wouldn't keep noticing—and wanting to do something about it. It was an effort just to keep from touching her.

"If the clouds aren't too low," he added, unconsciously softening his approach, "from where I want to take you we'll be able to see the coast. Maybe even Gerónimo Bay. It's what I call a 'power spot.' I do some of my most effective thinking there."

She sensed the change in him at once. Like the track that had brought them to the falls, the trail that led upward from its basin rose at a precipitous angle. It was dense with underbrush. Willingly she let Gabriel help her over the rough places. She felt cared for, even cosseted as he held back runners and branches so they wouldn't whip across her cheeks.

His power spot was nearly at the top, an uneven outcrop of rock that jutted over the valleys and foothills below it like a shelf. Above it rose even more vertiginous peaks, their green summits lost in the soft underbellies of clouds. In the distance stretched the mighty Atlantic. A thin, white line indicated the creaming of breakers. To the south, she could pick out the barely discernible smudge of a city. Reduced to specks on the horizon, freighters inched to and from its ports.

Gabriel pointed. "My *finca* is that way, between the place where the road dips toward the coast and the tiny fishing village of Cinco on your left."

The island was his home. Every leaf and blade of grass, every distant vista was an integral part of him. No wonder he cared about it so much. *I hope he'll take me to see Las Brisas while I'm here,* she thought.

By tacit agreement they sat on a sun-warmed boulder, close but not touching. Miranda drew up her knees, hugging them with her arms. By now she had a fair idea why they'd come. From their vantage point, they could see one whole corner of La Caridad spread out in relief. He'd wanted her to get a feeling for it as an entity. Begin to sense her birth connection to it grafting into her bones.

Turning to pose a question, she realized he'd shifted position slightly. Instead of the view, he was watching her. So demanding and expressive, his deep brown eyes were near enough to drown in. She could almost distinguish the penumbra of his breath.

With a stab of something heated that could only be desire, she contemplated the fact that they were alone—isolated on a mountain peak, miles from anyone. Anything could happen. Though she trusted him, she wasn't sure she could trust herself. Some men, Tony Braithwaite included, had accused her of being detached, even stingy with her affection. Yet she found it difficult to keep from slipping her arms about Gabriel's neck.

A ripple of longing spread through her as she tried to imagine how it would feel to have the hard, superbly conditioned weight of him pressing against her. His scent was already hauntingly familiar to her, and so was the callused texture of his fingertips. He had beautiful hands—strong, neat and capable. She pictured him trailing them down the curve of her throat and reaching lower, to unbutton her shirt.

It was all Gabriel could do not to take her in his arms. Granted, it had been a long time. But he hadn't forgotten how to read the signals that passed between a man and a woman. Though by now he'd convinced himself Miranda Burton was strictly off-limits, he found her utterly desirable. In his opinion, she could have any man she chose. For some reason, at the moment she wanted him. The chance to crush her mouth with his, part her lips with his tongue and probe the moist sweetness they guarded was almost too tempting to resist.

His situation would change, and not for the better, if he let nature take its course. Given his priorities, it would be hell, making love to her and finding out it was as earth-shattering as he'd expected. He'd invested almost ten years of his life in his cause, and all his energies might become secondary to him. Simply by looking at him, hazel-eyed, sexy Miranda threatened to make him forget everything but her.

Torn, he drew back from the brink. Freeing La Caridad had to come first. Since any commitment she might make to its liberation was bound to be temporary, she could never be for him.

"What is it?" he asked with scarcely a hint of the inner battle he'd fought.

"I was just wondering how far are we from Asunción, the capital?"

He shrugged. "About three hundred kilometers, more or less. Not far. I know what you're thinking. This spot seems so far removed from civilization we could be in another world."

Miranda couldn't remember Asunción, but she'd seen photographs. She hoped they wouldn't provide her only look at what she'd heard had once been a very cosmopolitan city. After the way Gabriel reacted this morning, I wonder how much of the country I'll get to see, she thought. I can't do his cause any good if I stay hidden away at Josefina's house.

"Did you really think I was in danger this morning?" she asked.

Gabriel took his time about answering. He didn't want to alarm her unnecessarily. But it was only fair to tell her the truth.

"Actually, yes," he confessed. "There's little doubt Leander Santos will perceive your presence as a threat. Just the memory of your father is enough to add fuel to a fire that's already burning. Until it's generally known you're back in the country, it would be all too easy for him to have you killed and pretend it never happened. It's our job to keep you out of harm's way until we can spread the news to Juan's constituency. Once the *guajiros* know, there's not much he can do. If he touched a hair on your pretty head, he'd have a full-scale rebellion on his hands."

Thoughtfully Miranda digested the information, putting his compliment on hold. "Pilar says the authorities don't bother with Las Montañas much," she observed. "And that you're pretty much left alone by them."

A shadow crossed Gabriel's face, as if at a painful memory. "Not quite," he said. "But it's true...in the past they shut one eye to my infractions if I didn't push too hard. That's because when I was twenty-five, I married Raquel Ruiz, the only daughter of 'Mad Dog' Hector Ruiz, chief of police and the man who replaced your father as Santos's second in command."

Miranda couldn't hide her shock and aversion. One of Ruiz's men had pulled the trigger when her father was killed. "Why someone like that?" she asked in a small voice. "Were you in love with her?"

He shook his head. "I was young. And as guilty as the next man of sowing a few wild oats. We had a fling. Later, I discovered she was a narcotics addict. And possessed the morals of an alley cat."

"Yet you married her. I don't understand."

"Ruiz threw my parents and Félix into prison on a treason charge. There was going to be a trial. And, to tell you the truth, there was some very solid evidence against them. They would have been convicted. My family was considered respectable and Raquel wanted to marry me. Her father made me an offer I couldn't refuse."

She was silent a moment. You had a baby with her, she thought. You can't have hated her that much.

"It's true," Gabriel admitted, almost as if she'd spoken. "We slept together a few more times. But that part of our relationship ended long before her death. Though I treasure her as if she were my own flesh and blood, I'm fairly certain my precious Raquelita is another man's daughter."

They sat in silence for several minutes while the sun disappeared and then emerged from behind a cloud.

"I don't want you to conclude from what I've told you that I lead a charmed life," Gabriel said finally. "Or that we have nothing to worry about. Far from it. Hector and I have had a truce for Raquelita's sake. After all, I'm raising the man's granddaughter. And she loves us both. I haven't hesitated to take advantage of it, and in recent months, the truce has been increasingly strained. It could be shattered in a heartbeat with you involved."

No free rides, then, Miranda thought. Oddly enough, the danger he spoke of only firmed her resolve to help him if he merited it. "Guess I'll have to watch my back, huh?"

Gabriel inclined his head at the American expression. She had guts. It gave them a starting point. "I'll be watching it, too," he promised. "If and when we take you south into El Panal, you'll have extra bodyguards."

"About that—"

"Yes. I imagine you'd like to hear what we're hoping you'll do for us."

Not answering for a second, Miranda lifted her hair with both hands to let the breeze cool the nape of her neck. She wasn't wearing a bra and the movement caused her breasts to strain momentarily at the front of her shirt in a sensuous, highly provocative gesture. Gabriel doubted she was aware of its effect.

Switching from temptress back to schoolgirl, Miranda rested her chin on her knees. "I think I'd like to hear your plans to help the *guajiros* first."

She was silent, painstakingly attentive as Gabriel described his commitment to La Caridad's working class, both in terms of feelings and step-by-step objectives. Words are easy, she reminded herself. Especially the right ones. It's deeds my father's people need most. Yet he'd seemed sincere. Having come this far, she could give him a chance.

"What is it you want me to do?" she asked when he fell silent.

"My friends in La Cábala feel you can help unify the former planters of Las Montañas with the laborers of El Panal and the shirtless ones of Enredadera simply by lending your appeal to our movement."

"You don't agree with them?"

"I wasn't sure. After what happened this morning, it appears they were right. Having seen you interact with the *guajiros,* I think it would be very helpful if you could address your father's people whenever possible... as soon as we feel it's safe. If you're willing to help us, I propose we start with a trip into El Panal just to give the workers a glimpse of you. Say day after tomorrow, following my daughter's twelfth birthday celebration."

"You mean... the two of us? Traveling together?"

He nodded. "Plus your bodyguards."

Emotionally, it was a risky proposition. Yet when Manuel and Josefina had spoken of the need for Juan Almeida's former followers to connect her with him, he'd seen the wisdom in their thinking.

For Miranda, it was the moment of truth. Now that it was upon her, she shrank from making a too firm commitment. At the same time, she knew she'd always regret it if she didn't do her best—and take advantage of the opportunity to spend some time with Gabriel.

"Tell you what," she proposed. "I'll make the trip. And we'll see how it goes. If I'm able to make a contribution, and I perceive your concern for the *guajiros* is real, we can take it from there."

Her answer was yes, with strings attached. All things considered, Gabriel realized it was the most they could expect.

"Fair enough," he replied. "I can't help but wonder what your mother thinks of all this."

Miranda rolled her eyes as she thought about what Célia Burton's reaction had been. "She was livid Aunt Pilar would suggest it."

"It can't have been easy for you to accept our invitation, then."

"You're right. It wasn't."

"I'm curious why you did."

"I suppose my reasons were...and are...a little complex. My mother and I rarely talk about Juan. She's discouraged any interest I might have taken in politics. I have a feeling that's because those things are painful for her. Though she loves my stepfather, Tom, what happened to Juan and to her, in losing him...is like a scar that disfigures her happiness. She doesn't want anything bad to happen to me. Or for me to be scarred like she was."

Gabriel didn't, either. Though they'd just met and he'd been all too ready to dismiss her as frivolous, he realized he'd fight to keep tragedy and hardship from her door. "You're explaining why she didn't want you to go," he pointed out. "Not why you decided to go against her wishes."

"In a way I am. When I was seven, my stepfather adopted me. My surname was changed to his. Maybe because I've lacked connectedness with Juan, I've felt a greater debt to him. My memories of him have inspired deep love. And admiration."

How quickly they'd penetrated each other's defenses and touched the core of each other's private thoughts. Amazed because he hadn't let anyone see into him that way for a long time, Gabriel got to his feet and suggested they start back down the mountainside.

As they negotiated the precipitous slope, sliding on vines and decaying leaves, the roar of the waterfall grew ever louder in their ears. Keyed up from her provisional decision to help him, sharing some of her most intimate feelings and—let's face it, she acknowledged—his sheer physical presence, Miranda yearned for some kind of release.

"Mind if I get my feet wet now?" she asked when they reached the level of the pool again.

His mouth curved indulgently. "Be my guest."

Perching on the edge of the jeep's running board, she rolled up her pant legs and untied her boot laces.

After his fantasies on the mountaintop, Gabriel didn't think it would be wise to join her. "Be careful," he warned as she tossed her boots and socks onto the floor in front of the passenger seat. "It's cold. And deeper than you might think. The rocks are treacherous."

"Don't worry. I can swim...."

She'd barely entered the pool when she slipped. Her shriek of dismay sent birds flapping and screeching from their hidden perches as she slid, splashing and clutching for handholds, into the water. Bobbing to the surface a second later, she was dragged back down by the weight of her clothing.

Wrenching off his boots, Gabriel dived in after her. This time, they came up together, almost directly beneath the torrent. Though he hadn't expected them to, his feet touched bottom. It was like standing beneath a shower head someone had turned on full blast.

"Cough!" he instructed, helping her to firmer footing as he pounded her between the shoulder blades.

Miranda complied. They were still sunk in water to their armpits, with the cascade tumbling about them like a curtain.

With a start, he realized she was shaking with laughter. So tousled and ethereal when it was dry, her hair clung to her head, a helmet of crimped, wet silk. As she gazed up at him, her eyes were bright with the humor of the situation, her lashes stuck together like the points of stars.

Misunderstanding, he got the impression she'd merely been playing with him. "You little fool!" he exclaimed angrily, tightening his grip. "I thought you were drowning...."

Any attempt she might have made to defend herself was obliterated by his mouth. Withheld for what already seemed an eternity though they'd just met the night before, Gabriel's kiss consumed her. Forcefully he parted her lips, demanding more from her, *more*, with each uncompromising thrust of his tongue.

Already firm from the water's chill, her nipples stood up taut and aching with need. She could feel Gabriel's erection, pressing against her thigh. The realization of how much he wanted her was like pouring gasoline on a bonfire. With a moan, she wrapped her legs around him. Eagerly her tongue dueled with his.

Her unabashed hunger had him wild in seconds. He was no boy but a powerful man who'd been known to let passion rule him. Sunk in too many lonely nights, he'd needed a woman who felt and tasted exactly as she did. Now she was there, soaked to the skin and burning incandescent in his arms. The duties of a host forgotten and his determination not to get involved with her buried beneath the avalanche of her response, he pushed up her shirt to claim her breasts. They were firm but full, filling his hands with their lushness. Longing with all the force of his being to suck at them until she writhed in ecstasy, he pushed at her nipples with his thumbs.

Instantly a line of communication sprang into being between the taut volcanoes of Miranda's peaks and the deepest part of herself. She was like a well, opening to receive him. Nothing could ease her emptiness but his sweet invasion. She pleaded for it with all her strength.

By God, he'd give her a sample of what she craved. Fumbling with her waistband, he unbuttoned it. Her zipper parted by itself as he reached down the front of her trousers. Below the flat, smooth mound of her stomach, he encountered a scrap of illusion barely adequate to cover her coarse, triangular nest of curls.

Lace beneath cotton cord. The incongruity of it fired his imagination. Forgetting himself completely, he inserted one finger into her velvet folds and began stroking her to the fever pitch he felt.

Never had Miranda known such bliss. Or such incredible urgency. "Yes...oh, Gabriel! *Yes!*" she cried, throwing back her head so that her face was pummeled by the spray, though she continued to press her lower body against him. "Take me, please. I want you to...."

With a jolt, he came to his senses. You can't do this, he thought, removing his hand, though he longed to insert his fingers even deeper. She's a decent young woman, not some streetwalker in Reunión. And she's in your care. You don't have the barest hope of a future together.

"Forgive me," he muttered, half dragging, half carrying her up the slippery bank. "I don't know what I was thinking of. I can only promise you...it won't happen again."

Stunned and humiliated, Miranda sat on the muddy grass beyond the pool's verge with her clothing plastered to her body. She was the picture of dejection and frustrated desire. Gabriel lounged a few feet away. His shoulders hunched forward and his features arranged in an expression of self-loathing, he refused to look at her.

What am I supposed to do now? she wondered miserably. Go home and simply forget La Caridad? I can't bear to be around him after this. Yet she couldn't desert her father's *guajiros*. She'd promised them. Awkwardly she did up the front of her slacks and raked her hair back from her face as she tried to form some feasible plan of action.

"I want to tell you how sorry I am," Gabriel said, cutting across her thoughts.

"Oh, *please*..."

The distress in her voice was an added lash to him. In his estimation, he richly deserved it. He had to mend things between them, and not just for the cause. In addition to desiring her, he found he was beginning to genuinely like Miranda.

Perhaps the best way to alleviate her pain was to tell her the simple truth, though he'd be unmasking himself. "Maybe this would be easier if I admitted I still want you," he confessed. "That I've wanted you from the moment you placed your hand in mine, in that pineapple field in Puerto Rico."

Though she shot him a swift glance, she didn't reply. Then why did you stop us? her eyes demanded bitterly. When it's so obvious I want you, too.

"For us to get involved," Gabriel added, "would be a mistake. I have a country to think about. And you're here only temporarily. Your life is waiting for you back in the States. We'd just be asking for heartbreak."

He was telling her she was the kind of woman that, once bedded, he'd want to keep. Despite the frustrating impossibility of their situation, a thrill of optimism seized her. In less than twenty-four hours, what Gabriel wanted had begun to matter very much.

If she even hinted at her thoughts, he'd push her away. His dedication and essential decency would take precedence. Yet in that instant, she'd made up her mind. She wouldn't leave La Caridad without tasting his kisses again. And more. Even if it had to be a once-in-a-lifetime thing, she wanted to experience the most intimate pleasures his body could give.

"Maybe you're right," she acknowledged, scraping meditatively at a moss-stained patch on her slacks with one fingernail. "I admit it makes me feel better, knowing we're both to blame for what happened a few minutes ago."

To think she'd felt solely responsible! As if he'd needed proof she wanted him. Now he'd strong-armed her into seeing things his way. They could work together, yet not become lovers. Gabriel's inner man protested the bargain was an abysmal one.

It wasn't until they'd straightened their clothing, decided they were hungry and talked about returning to the *finca* for a late lunch that he realized what he'd done. The pocket where he'd thrust his keys was empty. He swore, unaware Miranda's familiarity with Spanish extended to the colloquial terms.

"What's the matter?" she asked.

"My damn keys! They must have fallen out of my pants when we were in the water!"

We're stranded miles from civilization, Miranda thought. Unless somebody comes for us, we'll have to spend the night by the waterfall. Meanwhile, she'd discovered Gabriel had a temper. At the moment, keeping a low profile would be the better part of valor, unless she missed her guess.

Clear as the water was, diving for the keys loomed as an exercise in futility. There were a thousand crevices in the rock that could have swallowed them. Nevertheless, Gabriel made the attempt after stripping to his shorts. At last he climbed out, dripping and empty-handed, to sit beside her on the bank from which she'd offered her silent encouragement.

"Angél has the spare," he said, barely conscious of his state of undress after the way they'd almost consumed each other. "He must have forgotten and kept it last night, when he and Manuel met us at the airstrip."

"Then..."

He shoved his dripping hair back from his forehead. "I'll have to hot-wire the jeep."

They weren't stuck after all. I should have known, Miranda thought. A man who organizes protest rallies and blows up power stations wouldn't let something like a lost key ring stop him. Though in one way she was relieved, she couldn't help but feel a stab of regret.

Matter-of-factly putting on his trousers as if it were the most natural thing in the world to dress in front of her, Gabriel went to rummage in the jeep's battered toolbox. He pulled out two lengths of wire. As Miranda watched, he raised the hood and attached the end of one wire to the positive terminal on the battery. As if by magic, when he secured the other end to something he called the ignition distributor, the jeep started cranking. But there wasn't any spark.

He threw her a look. "Not to worry."

Running the second wire from the same battery terminal to a green-coated wire that protruded from the starter solenoid, he caused the engine to cough and start. Miranda hopped into her seat as he slammed down the hood and got behind the wheel.

"Why not check out the glove compartment?" he asked as he shifted into gear and backed up, preparatory to leaving the falls behind.

Casting a last look at the torrent and thinking of what had almost happened beneath it, Miranda did as he suggested. She glanced at him in surprise as they started down the bumpy, vine-tangled slope.

Gabriel grinned, once again the master of his fate. "I stockpile chocolate bars," he said. "Black market. Even revolutionaries have to feed their sweet tooth now and then."

Chapter 4

As a substitute for kissing Gabriel, chocolate was woefully inadequate, despite its reputation for containing some mysterious ingredient that elevated a person's mood. Miranda had heard the high it imparted was similar to that of being in love. But she didn't put much faith in the notion. She just knew there was something incredibly relaxed and cozy about riding along in the jeep with him as the breeze whipped their hair and dried their clothing. After what had transpired beneath the torrent, even the simple act of sharing his candy bar took on a resonance all its own.

She felt extraordinarily light and free, her everyday life shed and bubbling over with anticipation as they drove into Josefina's yard. Gabriel's cousin, Angél, and Ruben Camargo, the older man who'd uncorked the champagne the night before, were already there, conferring as they hand-rolled cigarettes beside an old truck.

With a little spurt of gravel, Gabriel pulled up beside them.

"How did it go in Gerónimo?" he asked.

Angél shrugged, glancing at Miranda and then back at Gabriel with thinly veiled curiosity. The two of you are looking very friendly, his silence commented.

It was Ruben who answered Gabriel's question. "Very well...until they called out the *policia* on the pretext that we were disrupting the unloading of one of the ships. We have some new recruits, I think."

"You spoke with the men only during their break?"

"We followed your instructions to the letter."

As they spoke, Angél continued to study Miranda. "You went to the falls?" he asked after a moment.

Was the visible record of Gabriel's passionate kiss and its awkward aftermath written all over her face? Miranda wondered. At the very least, it seemed, there were clues to what had taken place. Her hair was still noticeably damp at the nape of her neck, her shirt and trousers crumpled and moss-stained.

Simultaneously, another thought took root. If Angél could guess their destination so easily, she probably wasn't the only woman Gabriel had taken there. Nor the first he'd kissed so soulfully beneath the spray. Maybe he made a habit of such trysts. If so, she wondered, had theirs been the only aborted one?

Unable to prevent it, she felt a self-conscious flush spread upward from her collar. In La Caridad, she guessed, Gabriel was well on his way to becoming a figure of adulation. No doubt a great many women were attracted to him.

"Actually, yes..." she stammered.

They were still seated in the jeep, with the motor running. Gabriel had been listening to their exchange with half an ear as he conversed with Ruben. "That reminds me," he said. "I need the spare key to this relic. Miranda fell into the water, and I had to dive in after her. Mine is somewhere at the bottom of the cascade, wedged between the rocks."

Angél's dark brows lifted a fraction at the news. "There you have it," he answered, unclipping the spare from his ring and tossing it to Gabriel.

Switching off the ignition, Gabriel got out and walked around to the jeep's passenger side. Though he stood aside while his cousin opened the door for Miranda, he surprised her by taking possession of her hand and tucking it into the crook of his arm.

"Come," he said in his mellifluous Spanish with just a hint of possessiveness. "I'll walk you to the house."

So unexpected after his earnest speech about why they shouldn't get involved, the gesture did nothing to blunt Angél's conjecture, Miranda was convinced. As she strolled at Gabriel's side toward the stone arcade that shadowed Josefina's entryway, she could almost feel the younger man staring after them.

All thought of Angél left her head when Gabriel paused beneath one of the archways to take both her hands in his.

"What is it?" she said.

"I almost forgot to ask... it would please me very much if you and your aunt could attend Raquelita's birthday party tomorrow afternoon. It's to be held at Las Brisas, of course. You can ride over with Josefina. You already know most of the other guests."

She'd have a chance to see where he lived. Observe him in his most personal setting. "I'd love to come," she answered. "And I know Aunt Pilar would, too. I'm just not sure we should intrude on a family celebration."

"You wouldn't be. While you're in La Caridad, I consider you part of my extended household... family, in a sense."

Miranda didn't know if she felt cared for or challenged by the remark. Despite the narrow focus of her life as a concert musician, she wasn't some lamb who'd strayed unknowingly into the path of danger. Nor, after the way he'd kissed her, did she feel like a relative—even an adopted one.

"Okay then, if you think it's all right. When do you want us?"

"Late afternoon. I'd ask you to come earlier but I have... something to do. With luck, I'll be back by dinnertime. As the birthday girl's father, I'm expected to help cut the cake."

Neither of them said anything further for a moment. A separate conversation was going on in the silence. Abruptly he let her go, as if reminding himself where duty lay.

"The invitation isn't a conditional one," he added, a wry half smile tugging at one corner of his mouth. "But I was wondering if you'd bring your violin."

Miranda and Pilar drove to Las Brisas with Josefina in her aging but still serviceable 1967 Chevrolet, which the older woman laughingly insisted was held together with wire and chewing gum because American-made parts were so difficult to obtain. A pile of gifts, wrapped in much folded and reused paper, reposed in one corner of the back seat. Pitted with chuckholes that could sink a wheel up to its axle, the road that led to Gabriel's ranch ran deeply between lush sugarcane and tobacco fields. The air's salt tang intensified as they neared the coast.

Dressed in flat-heeled sandals, a white cotton-lawn frock and turquoise hoop earrings, Miranda leaned forward with interest as they turned and passed between a pair of crumbling stucco gateposts. The entrance was marked with the word *Sánchez* with an inconspicuous row of hand-glazed ceramic tiles. They were partly overrun by the flame-colored bracts of bougainvillea. A red barrel-tile roof that was in marginally better repair than Josefina's gleamed at the end of a broad *allée* cut through a dense planting of coconut palms.

Like his aunt's, Gabriel's house was built of tan coral stone and cream-colored stucco with a second-floor balcony and floor-to-ceiling windows designed to catch every wisp of the prevailing coastal breeze. As they approached, Miranda noticed the air was much fresher and cooler than at Josefina's. She could hear the rhythmic hiss and boom of the surf.

During the drive from her *finca,* Josefina had switched on the car radio. Now, as they parked in front of the house and Raquelita came running out to greet them, a news bulletin interrupted the homogeneous flow of popular music and government announcements. Shy but obviously keyed up, the thin, dark-haired child thrust her head through an open window on the driver's side to peek at her presents. Like Miranda and the others, she paused to listen.

"Striking sugarcane workers in Granja have blown up a munitions dump in a flagrant act of sabotage against the people of La Caridad," an announcer in the pay of the Santos regime reported. "Reprisals by agents of the National Police were swift. At least twenty strikers have been arrested and transferred to Blanco Prison. A spokesman for Police Commandante Hector Ruiz said work stoppages and assaults on government buildings will not be tolerated...."

For one who was still quite young and, Miranda guessed, carefully protected by Gabriel from the violent world of Cariño politics, Raquelita followed every word of the broadcast with exceptional interest.

"My father was responsible for what happened," she asserted when the regularly scheduled programming resumed. "He's winning our freedom."

Pilar and Josefina glanced at each other. Gently the latter warned that, though they were among friends at the moment, Raquelita shouldn't mention her father's work to anyone.

"Particularly not to your *abuelo* when he comes to visit," Josefina emphasized. "Because of the position he holds, it's Grandfather Ruiz's duty to arrest anyone who works against the Santos regime."

As they got out of the car, Miranda suppressed a chill. Suppose Gabriel was among those arrested? Would they be able to arrange for his release? Or would the Santistas hold him and his compatriots indefinitely as a means of crushing the resistance? What terrible things might happen to them in reprisal for their activities? For the first time, she began to realize what kind of risk she'd be running if she learned to care for him.

Dread dissolved in relief a few minutes later when Gabriel drove up in a cloud of dust. They were still in the garden, admiring the January flowers that grew in a tumble of carelessly tended profusion on either side of the front walk. With a cry of *"¡Papá!"* Raquelita ran to him. Embracing her, Gabriel looked sweaty and tired, yet more fully alive than he had at any time since Miranda's arrival.

It wasn't too difficult for Miranda to guess what he felt. Unless she was very much mistaken, he was alight with the kind of high that came only from an intimate brush with danger. *His mood is positively electric*, she thought. *If we were at the falls tonight, he wouldn't have any second thoughts.*

He chose that moment to glance at her. "Hello, Miranda," he said. "You're looking very decorative this afternoon. I'm glad you and your aunt could make it."

He'd blown up the munitions dump. And he hadn't been arrested. He had a right to feel elated. But what about the men who'd helped him, and hadn't been so fortunate? Wasn't he worried about them?

Now that he was safe, she could afford to be critical. She didn't quite return his smile. "The pleasure is ours...."

Before she could phrase the question that was burning at her lips, the moment passed. Gabriel turned to one of his field hands, who was trimming dead fronds from one of the coconut trees. "Paco," he instructed, "put the jeep in the barn, *por favor*. If anyone asks, you drove it. I've been here at Las Brisas all afternoon."

The field hand nodded in understanding. Hugging his daughter again at her insistence, though he worried aloud it would spoil her dress, Gabriel let her go, excused himself and went upstairs to change. *Trust fate to send me a woman like Miranda Burton when I can least afford to indulge myself*, he thought as he stripped off his sweaty garments and stepped into an antiquated shower that only ran cold water now that heating oil was impossible to get. *She's like some lush, virginal Gypsy in that semisheer white dress.*

As always, the water temperature was a shock. But it didn't cool his inconvenient ardor. As he soaped his exercise-hardened body, something about the brisk contact with his own skin caused his preoccupation with Miranda to deepen. God help him, she smelled like lilies. He wanted to touch. And taste.

Common sense argued he'd be making a serious error. She would not stay in La Caridad. Yet after his close call in Granja that afternoon, he wanted to take from life with both hands. He wanted *her*.

Something told him she wouldn't object if he kissed her again. Or consider him outrageous for wanting to make love to her. As he rotated his head under the spray, working the day's tension out of his neck and shoulders, Gabriel pictured himself lying with her on a carpet of pine needles in some secluded place. In his imagined scenario, Miranda's skirt was pushed up to her waist. Her daintily tucked bodice was unbuttoned to the pleasures of his mouth.

She and his other guests were drinking lemonade on the lower porch when he came down again. In his ivory linen jacket, pink tie and tan trousers, with his dark hair freshly washed and brushed, he was the epitome of that supposedly outlawed species, the landed gentleman. Miranda could see immediately that he was still keyed up, incandescent.

"I suppose the clothes are black market, just like the chocolate bars and the champagne we drank the other night," she remarked when she got the chance.

"Actually, yes." He gave her an amused look. "So's the dress Raquelita's wearing."

His gaze was warm enough to drown in. Yet she couldn't help feeling torn. The cane cutters who'd been arrested were part of Juan's legacy. Didn't their plight bother him? To her consternation, Félix and Angél, both of whom had arrived while Gabriel was upstairs, seemed unconcerned by it as well.

"We heard about what happened in Granja on the radio," she prodded, deciding to have it out with him. "The twenty or so men who were arrested by the *policia*... is there nothing you can do for them?"

Something softened in Gabriel's face. "There were only three," he answered. "The Santistas always exaggerate."

"Still..."

"Not to worry, *querida*. They're probably out by now. Admittedly it's not always that easy, but the magistrate in Granja happens to be very corrupt. A hefty bribe was paid."

Before she could absorb the endearment or apologize for having misjudged him, he'd moved on to greet newly arrived neighbors. He'd be so easy to love, she thought ruefully a few minutes later as he ushered everyone into his salmon-pink dining room with its tall, shuttered windows and scarred but festively set table. *Yet like my father did before him, he takes such risks....*

Raquelita's birthday dinner consisted of *boliche*, a stuffed round of beef Cariño style, together with yellow rice, fried plantains and a wonderful salad that contained papayas, mangoes and other fruit. When they'd eaten their fill, Concepción, Gabriel's smiling, sixtyish housekeeper-cook, brought in her masterpiece, an elaborate birthday cake that earned her a spontaneous round of applause.

Allowing his daughter to try out her budding wiles by flirting gently with him, Gabriel lit the candles himself. Drawing in a deep breath, she blew them out in a single attempt. There were more cheers, a great many fond exclamations over what a young lady she'd become.

"Another year and you'll be a teenager, *mi vida*," Gabriel reminded as she kissed him on the cheek. "The boys will be chasing you."

Today's raid must have been in the works for quite a while, Miranda decided. Relief is a very big part of this celebration. Maybe the Santista land reforms and jurisdiction never quite stretched to encompass all of Las Montañas. And maybe Gabriel's former father-in-law is able to provide him with some tacit protection for Raquelita's sake. Yet for him and the others, this is surely a moment carved out of hardship and a better than nodding acquaintance with danger.

A sweet, layered confection, Raquelita's birthday cake boasted pink sugar roses and pineapple filling. When it had been consumed, the gentleman-guerrilla who'd so captured Miranda's fancy gave his daughter permission to open her presents. This is Gabriel, family man, Miranda thought in fascination, watching him from her vantage point beside a set of patio doors that had been flung open to a flagstone-paved terrace overlooking the ocean. Without doubt, the woman he chose to love would be very lucky, though she would have to steel herself against the possibility of loss.

Attempting to get a handle on her increasingly complex feelings for a man she'd met just two days before, Miranda was unaware of both the look of longing that stole over her face and that Angél had come up beside her.

"So, tell me," Gabriel's cousin asked in a low voice, "what *really* happened at the falls yesterday?"

Startled, she prayed the cool breeze off the Atlantic would diffuse the sudden color that heated her cheeks. "I don't know what you mean," she retorted. "Nothing happened. We had motives to discuss. Plans to make, as you might expect. As for falling into the water, it was my own stupid fault. Not Gabriel's."

Angél's expression suggested there was more to the story than she cared to tell. "If you have something to say," she added a trifle irritably, "I'd appreciate your getting it off your chest."

Angél's dark eyes didn't reveal his thoughts. "I just wondered," he said, "whether our dashing commando and political leader has done an about-face."

She frowned, as much at the latent hostility in his tone as in genuine puzzlement. Across the room, Raquelita was exclaiming over a silver bracelet with devotional charms Félix had given her. Pausing to smile at his cousin's child, who seemed genuinely to evoke his affection, Angél explained.

"Before you came, several of our partners in La Cábala suggested Gabriel court you. For the sake of our struggle, *tu sabes*. As Juan Almeida's daughter, you're a tremendous asset to us. If you and my cousin were to hit it off, so to speak, you might extend your visit to La Caridad... maybe even consider making it your home again on a permanent basis."

Miranda's heart constricted at his words. Seemingly so welcoming and grateful for whatever assistance she could give, Gabriel's friends had unabashedly conspired against her. How in God's name was she going to face them—or him—again?

Belatedly it struck her that Angél had spoken of an about-face. "I take it Gabriel refused," she said in a shaken voice.

"Yes, he did. But..."

The sinking feeling in Miranda's gut intensified. "You might as well tell me everything."

"He raised the possibility that he might change his mind."

Was there to be no end to her humiliation? I've got to get *out* of here, she thought. Pull myself together somehow.

Turning her back on Angél, she went out through the open patio doors. Within seconds the breeze had disarranged her hair. Several dark strands whipped across her face. Though she tried to suppress them, inevitable tears misted her vision as she went to stand by the low stone wall that marked the edge of a fifty-foot drop-off to the beach. She stared at the hypnotically crashing surf.

Facing Josefina, Félix and the others would be one of the toughest gauntlets she'd ever had to run. But it was Gabriel's cool pragmatism that had hurt her most. Every look, every touch since her arrival in La Caridad had whispered their attraction was mutual. Yet if his cousin had told the truth, the soul-shattering kiss they'd shared at the falls might have been the first step in a well-thought-out plan of seduction—one calculated to throw her off her guard. Already in over her head, Miranda prayed the whole thing was a hideous mistake. The next time she looked into Gabriel's eyes, would she have the courage to ask?

By now it was fully dark. In the house, Raquelita had finished opening her presents. "Where's Miranda?" Gabriel asked.

Nobody seemed to know except Angél. He shrugged. "I think she went out to look at the ocean."

Asking Josefina to put some music on the phonograph for their guests, Gabriel went in search of her. He didn't have to look far. A pensive figure in white, she stood with her back to him, her short, full sleeves fluttering against her slender arms.

She jumped when he rested one hand lightly on her shoulder. But she knew who it was, without having to be told. Reluctantly she turned to face him. More relaxed, though he was still a little wired, he'd removed his jacket. And loosened his tie. In the moonlight, his exquisitely laundered shirt gleamed like alabaster.

"Everything all right?" he asked.

Nothing was. But she couldn't tell him that. He might be the kind of man who would stop at nothing to win justice for his people. Yet if asked point-blank, she guessed, he'd tell her the unvarnished truth. She might not want to hear it.

"Why wouldn't it be?" she responded, evading his eyes.

He wasn't quite sure. It was just a feeling he had. He decided to take a different approach.

"Did you remember to bring your violin?" he said. "If it wouldn't be an imposition..."

No doubt he'd think her a prima donna. But she couldn't make herself perform as if nothing had happened. Just facing his friends would be bad enough.

"Yes, I brought it," she acknowledged. "But I'm afraid I'll have to beg off. I don't feel like playing tonight."

From what Gabriel had been able to determine, Juan Almeida's enchanting daughter wasn't the temperamental type. What had happened to make her withdraw that way? Tilting her chin upward with one gentle finger, he searched her face.

"What's the matter, *chiquita?* Are you homesick already for your life in the States?"

Her eyes glittering with unshed tears, Miranda shook her head. More convinced than ever that something was drastically amiss, Gabriel fought the urge to gather her close. And lost. He could think of only one acceptable excuse.

"Then dance with me."

It was an unorthodox request, at odds with the reservations he'd stated. Had he decided to inveigle her into marriage the way his friends had suggested? Or was it simply an expression of the highly charged, unpredictable mood that had seized him after blowing up the Granja munitions dump? Forced to assess the depth of his warmth and caring, she found it easy to think the latter. He was all but impossible to resist.

"Please...not here," she begged, striving to maintain some sense of propriety and equilibrium.

From the house, the strains of a well-known Spanish love song drifted out to them. "Don't you hear the music?" Gabriel coaxed, determined to force a smile from her. "I asked Josefina to put on that record just for us."

The claim, Miranda knew full well, was pure flattery—a shameless fabrication. Before she could tell him so in no uncertain terms, he'd taken her into his arms.

God, but it felt good to have him lace strong, sunbronzed fingers through hers so that the vulnerable little interstices between them were touching. Utterly magnificent to allow the pressure of his right hand against the small of her back to mold her lower body to his. From neckline to hem, she could feel his heat, his magnetism, seeping through the fabric of her dress.

It's as if, with the striking of a single match, a whole forest is set ablaze, she thought. An indrawn breath, and bonfires of passion claim us. I've lived for twenty-nine years and I never dreamed such splendor could exist.

In addition to radiating sensuality and a deep masculine appreciation of her femininity, Gabriel was a wonderful dancer. Chivalrous, powerful, he made her feel beautiful and cherished just by the way he held her. She wanted to nestle closer, move with him in that incendiary way forever, with the scent of jasmine perfuming the air and the coconut fronds swaying in their restlessness. She just hoped no one from the house was watching them.

"What's this about?" she managed at last, obliquely posing the question that lingered in her head. "A residual high from blowing up government installations? Or a change of heart?"

So close that his breath mingled with hers, Gabriel's mouth curved. He didn't appear to connect her query with any demands his friends might have made.

"What about?"

Try though she would, she couldn't seem to answer him.

"You mean... about making love to you?"

As a guess, it was far from accurate. And yet it wasn't. There was nothing that would please her better, if he wanted to know the truth. She just couldn't bear to be used by him.

Gabriel mistook her silence for assent. "My 'heart,' as you say, hasn't changed at all," he conceded softly. "I still want to, very much. The close call we had this afternoon is just one more inducement to make me forget my scruples. You realize we might have regrets...."

Chapter 5

In the end, nothing was resolved. Though she couldn't dismiss Angél's comments out of hand, Miranda decided to give Gabriel the benefit of the doubt. Every gesture, every word that had come out of his mouth since he'd joined her on the terrace suggested he deserved it.

She couldn't back out of her promise to help unseat the Santista regime, or treat Gabriel's friends the way she felt they deserved to be treated. She'd have to maintain an ingenuous front.

"Maybe we'd better go inside," she answered at last, stepping back from him, though everything that was free-spirited in her militated against it. "If we don't, people will talk."

She was right, of course. Even if the place might be appropriate someday, the time wasn't right for them. It was his daughter's birthday. He had guests. "As you wish, *querida,*" he replied, tucking her arm through his the way he had the previous afternoon.

Apparently he'd primed his friends. No sooner had they walked back into the *sala* than Félix was handing Miranda her violin. "Favor us if you will," he begged. "It's not often, as we struggle for justice and freedom in La Caridad, that we're able to attend a concert."

Sensing Gabriel was about to demur on her behalf, she silenced him with a little shake of her head. She was a professional, used to performing no matter what her mood. She'd decided she'd have to make a few concessions and besides, Raquelita hadn't done anything to offend her. The girl's large, dark eyes were bright with admiring expectation.

Taking a handkerchief from her pocket, Miranda arranged it and then tucked the instrument under her chin. A pin dropping would have resounded like an avalanche in the silence that reigned as she lifted her bow. Feinting with the dramatic opening bars of Schubert's "Death and the Maiden," she segued abruptly into a rollicking version of "Happy Birthday" that put a smile on every face. Subsequently, cajoled by an enthusiastic round of applause into playing an encore, she delighted her audience with a dizzying rendition of Chopin's "Minute Waltz."

It was hardly the concert of Félix's dreams. But it would have to suffice. When he and several of the other guests prevailed on her to continue, Gabriel stepped into the breach. "I'm sure you'll agree...Miranda's been generous with her time and talent," he said. "However, we don't want to turn the evening into a command performance. Maybe if we don't insist, she'll give us what her American compatriots call a rain check. Besides, while it's Raquelita's birthday, it's also a school night.

The school bus will be honking at our gate promptly at 7:00 a.m."

The party broke up very quickly after that, though Raquelita lodged a halfhearted protest. Sending her up to bed with a hug and the admonition that advancing age brought responsibilities, Gabriel offered to walk Miranda to the car.

"Is our trip to El Panal still on for tomorrow?" he asked when they were out of earshot.

Though she hesitated, she'd already made up her mind. "As far as I know, it is," she said.

He nodded, satisfied. "We'll be gone for several days. Don't forget to pack a bag."

As it turned out, Miranda needn't have bothered to set her travel alarm. The excitement of spending so much time with Gabriel caused her to awaken early. The dew hadn't yet burned off the grass when he came for her in the jeep. For her protection, two young men, whom he introduced as Manuel Roa's son, Raul, and his best friend, Emilio Melendez, would follow them in an old truck.

"Do you expect trouble?" Miranda asked as Gabriel helped her into her seat.

Maybe she thought the Santistas' propensity for arresting people first and asking questions later was a figment of the insurrectionist imagination. He hoped she wouldn't find out otherwise—at least not firsthand.

"Always," he replied. "Sometimes we're lucky and it doesn't find us. But we have to be ready. We don't want anything bad to happen to you."

Waving goodbye to Josefina and Miranda's Aunt Pilar, who appeared on the upstairs balcony to see them off, they headed south, descending through the vegetation-clad foothills of the Juradas Peaks into La Caridad's agricultural heartland, which had been Juan Almeida's political stronghold. Though it had been twenty-four years since she'd seen the low, rich fields of waving sugarcane and royal palms backed by distant blue mountains, Miranda found them hauntingly familiar. She had a strong sensation of coming home.

Because of the civil strife he'd helped engender in recent months, Gabriel had warned, El Panal was a province under siege. There would be uniformed police about, occasional government checkpoints. With a view to the latter, she'd been provided with false documents. According to the citizenship papers she carried, to which a recent, unsmiling photograph of her had been affixed with an official-looking stamp, her name was Isabel Antonia Cartón de Ramirez. Her address had been noted simply as Cinco, Las Montañas. If asked, she'd been instructed to pass herself off as an elementary-school teacher on the way to be interviewed for a new position at a state-run kindergarten in the south.

Despite Gabriel's raid on the munitions dump and the flurry of anxiety it had caused, the relative peace of Las Montañas had lulled her to a false sense of security. She emerged from it with a jolt when they rounded a curve in the scattered northern suburbs of Gerónimo, and one of the checkpoints came into view.

"Is that..." she began, unable to keep a slight quaver from her voice.

With his shirtsleeves rolled up to reveal tanned, muscular forearms and his mirrored sunglasses reflecting twin images of his surroundings, Gabriel looked more sanguine than she would have thought possible in the face of Santista officialdom.

He nodded. "Don't glance over your shoulder at Raul and Emilio. And don't worry about being afraid...even if it shows. Our friends in the National Police are used to that. They rather enjoy it, I suspect."

They pulled into line and settled back to wait behind a bus from Batey Unido and a farmer driving a cart with a pair of oxen. Gabriel had told her he, too, was carrying false papers in addition to his own. In the mirrored glasses, with his dark hair coiffed by the breeze, he could probably get by with using them.

There wasn't any need. Though the bored-looking officer in charge asked them a few questions and gave the jeep a desultory search, he didn't evince a great deal of interest in anything but the twenty-peso note Gabriel handed him. To Miranda's relief, they were on their way almost immediately, unhurriedly putting some distance between themselves and the little nest of police cars and barricades. Once they were out of sight, they parked on the road's grassy verge with the motor running until Raul and Emilio came into view.

The next checkpoint, on the other side of Gerónimo, wasn't so cut-and-dried. Bustling with self-importance, the scowling corporal who ran it obviously wasn't the sort to accept a bribe or leave anything to chance. Miranda could feel her neck and shoulder muscles tense as he gave her papers a thorough going over and asked her several pointed questions.

Somehow she managed to keep from flinching when a junior officer drove up, took one look at Gabriel and whispered something in the corporal's ear. Temporarily losing interest in her, he ordered Gabriel to take off his glasses. "So," he said, his obvious satisfaction fueled with what might have been a touch of embarrassment at not having recognized a known dissident, "it's you,

Sánchez. What brings you to El Panal? You won't think us rude, will you, if we ask whether you're carrying explosives?"

A moment later, he'd ordered them to step down from the jeep while it was being searched. Gabriel hadn't stashed any bombs under the seat, had he? Suppressing a wave of nervous laughter, Miranda couldn't believe he'd be that reckless. But though she hadn't seen a gun, she suspected he was well armed. If they discovered an illicit weapon in his possession, would the Santista policemen haul them off to jail?

She hadn't bitten her nails since she was six. Now she started again as the corporal and his men appeared to go over the jeep with a fine-tooth comb. The worry that was causing all manner of havoc in her stomach didn't go away when they found nothing.

They were standing a few feet from the jeep in the shade of a huge gumbo-limbo tree. Seeming determined to find some reason for making an arrest, the corporal summoned them. "What's your relationship to this man, Señorita Cartón...if indeed that's your true name?" he asked, his beady dark eyes pouncing on Miranda as if he had guessed she was the weakest link in their defenses.

Stunned, she didn't answer him.

Gabriel draped one casual arm about her shoulders. "She's my girlfriend."

"Can't she speak for herself?"

He shrugged. "She's shy. And probably a little afraid of you. Why shouldn't she be? You might feel the same way, if you'd lived in Cinco all your life and then found yourself facing *this*."

Indicating by a curt gesture that they should wait and not get back into the jeep, the corporal walked to his battered police car and activated his radio. As they watched, he appeared to engage someone in earnest conversation.

For several minutes he waited, tapping his toe and dragging nervously on a cigarette, as if he'd been put on hold. The discussion began again, with the corporal clearly trying to make some kind of point. To all appearances, he failed. With a disgruntled shake of his head, he signed off and came back to them.

"You're in luck, Sánchez," he said sourly, waving them back to their places. "You're still on Tío Hector's protection list, or I'd take you in for questioning. Go on... get the hell out of here before I run the risk of demotion and arrest you anyway."

Miranda's eyes were enormous as they drove away. Things had been touch and go and she knew it. Glancing at her, Gabriel reached over to pat her hand. "Not to worry," he said with a bit more assurance than he felt. "Except for the nail-biting, you did very well. That kind of harassment is typical."

The next half hour of their journey was without incident. Glancing at Gabriel's map, Miranda saw that the road to Batey Roncaldo, where they were scheduled to meet with labor leader Pablo Escobar that afternoon, led through Batey Venus, another small sugar-mill town. The site of a government-owned cane processing plant that had once belonged to the De Milos Sugar Company, it was also her former place of residence. She'd lived there from birth until she was five years old, playing in the dooryard of her parents' cottage by day and going to bed each night secure in the childish assumption that Juan Almeida, father, field boss and revolutionary leader, was a fixed star in her firmament. The closer she and Gabriel came to it now, the more memories that she'd shut out for years trembled at the brink of consciousness.

Inevitably they reached the town's outskirts. After an absence that had stretched to nearly a quarter of a century, she thought the place looked incredibly small. Its tiny houses were mere cubes of color, their peeling stucco walls and crude jalousies painted vibrant turquoise and gold and pink, and faded to softer hues by the merciless tropical sun. Children played, as they had in her day. As shabby and colorful as the houses, washing flapped in the breeze. Here and there, scrawny chickens scratched in the dirt.

"Do you want to stop?" Gabriel asked.

He'd put the question gently. But then he knew her history. Didn't everyone? It was hardly a secret to those Cariños who were old enough to remember. Gabriel would have been about fourteen when Juan was killed. It was a safe bet he'd seen her picture in *El Diario de Concepción*. She herself never had, and for that she was grateful. But she knew what it depicted—a screaming, terrified youngster spattered by her father's blood.

"I'm not sure I'll be able to stand it," she admitted, the fragmented recollections that had troubled her since she was small still powerful enough to wound. "But, you know, I might not have another chance. I suppose we'd better find out."

Without having to be told, he knew exactly where the house was. Parking across the street from the small, boxlike structure, he switched off the jeep's ignition and sat there quietly for a moment. As he watched in the rearview mirror, Raul and Emilio stopped a block or so behind them.

"Do you want to go inside?" he asked at last.

Though the January sunlight was pleasantly warm, Miranda had wound her arms about her upper body as if she felt a chill. Her eyes were like bruises as she stared at the place where Juan had been killed.

"I...that is, can we?" she responded in a small voice. "I mean, it's all boarded up."

"If you want to, we can probably manage it." Rummaging in the tool kit that had yielded the wires needed to start the jeep at the falls, he extracted a crowbar.

Miranda hesitated. There was no telling who owned the cottage now—probably the Santos government in its guise as heir to the De Milos sugar-processing facilities. She had a feeling it had been boarded up to keep it from being turned into a shrine. Probably all they needed to do in order to get themselves arrested would be to pry open one of the doors or windows and go inside.

If her true identity became known before the *guajiros* had been fully apprised of her presence, she could be in real trouble—the kind not even her United States citizenship could fix. You can't live your life as a coward, she reminded herself. Juan didn't. Neither does Gabriel.

"All right," she said. "I would like to see it again."

He didn't make for the front stoop, which would have exposed them to curiosity, but rather for a narrow alleyway that ran between her parents' former home and the *casita* next door. It was choked with weeds, and a host of burrs attached themselves to Miranda's trouser legs. She scarcely noticed. Halting abruptly, Gabriel had caused her to bump into him.

"Here, I think," he said, appearing not to find their collision too distracting as he inserted the business end of his crowbar under one of the rotting boards that barred their entry.

He'd chosen to tackle the window to her old room, a small, airless space except for the three-foot-square opening that faced a nearby wall. It was the setting in which Célia had heard her prayers and tucked her into bed, the place where Juan had come to kiss her goodnight. The boards Gabriel was prying loose reminded her of blinders being removed from the eyes of memory.

There was a wrenching sound as one of the boards broke in two. A jagged piece of it remained attached to the top of the window frame. Gabriel glanced toward the street. They'd made only a little noise. No one had shown up to investigate. If anyone did, he was counting on Raul and Emilio to give him fair warning and help him handle it.

"That ought to do it, I think," he advised. "Watch your head as I help you over the sill...."

It was dark inside. There hadn't been much furniture. Every stick of it had been carried off long ago, except for a rusting bedspring that seemed too large to have come from her little cot. Maybe she'd made a mistake. But no—there was the funny wall fixture she'd always stared at as she went to sleep, the arched doorway to the kitchen-sitting room from which a fringed and beaded curtain had hung.

"Are you all right?" Gabriel asked.

She nodded, too emotional to speak.

"Shall we take a look around?"

The kitchen alcove's terrazzo floor was crunchy underfoot with the shards of broken dishes and glassware. Its cupboards had been removed, as had the stove, sink and tiny, old-fashioned refrigerator. The saint who was the subject of a brittle holy picture gazed down sadly at them from one grease-stained wall.

As if drawn by the force of a powerful magnet, Miranda walked slowly to the single window beside the front door. Like the others, it had been boarded up. However, one of the boards was missing. There was evidence of moisture having blown in, an irregular chink of sunlight.

Gabriel's heart went out to her. "It happened..." he began, then thought better of it.

She pointed through the narrow opening. "There."

One after another, the memories her mind had locked away for her own protection were flooding back, bitter as gall in her mouth. With a little start, she realized Gabriel had come to stand behind her and offer his wordless presence. How she longed to turn and bury her face against his shirt!

"When I was growing up in the U.S.," she said, still staring at the patch of dusty street, "I couldn't remember much about that day. Just the gunfire and my father falling. My own screams of terror. I used to dream, sometimes, about the blood...."

From the depth of his being, he ached to heal the child Miranda had once been. Since that's not possible, I'd settle for comforting the woman, he thought. "And now?" he asked with an odd little catch in his voice.

"Now the scene is unfolding in my head as if it were a film loop in slow motion. I can almost see myself in a printed cotton sundress, digging in the dirt next to the stoop with my toy pail and shovel. My father coming out, calling the dog, lighting a cigarette.

"He smokes it, smiles at me, calls the dog again. Suddenly there's a black car, lurching into the street It's coming very fast. Juan yells at me to get in the house. I don't obey. He's about to make me. Somebody thrusts what looks like a machine gun out the open car window...."

She shuddered, huge tears slipping down her cheeks. Not stopping to think about whether it would establish an even closer link between them, Gabriel grasped her shoulders. "It's all right, *querida*," he soothed, his voice a low rumble beside her ear. "You don't have to talk about it."

"Ah...but you see, I must."

For several seconds, silence lay deep as the dust of decades in the shadowed room. Then, "The bullets came like rain," she continued. "*So many*. My father's chest and stomach...seemed to explode. There was blood everywhere. Some of it got on my dress."

"My God!" Gabriel's whisper was anguished.

In a way, it had been her fault. If she'd obeyed the first time Juan had ordered her into the house, maybe the gunmen couldn't have targeted him. With a sob, Miranda turned and sought the refuge she'd denied herself earlier. Like bands of steel shutting out calamity and guilt, Gabriel's powerful arms held her close.

He'd be her champion. Her protector. She sensed that and believed in it. She wanted more, though to get it she might have to open herself to more hurt. I could love you, she told him silently.

The realization that, vital and tough though he was, Gabriel's hard, masculine body was vulnerable to injuries like those her father had sustained caused a shudder to pass through her. I'd die a thousand deaths, she thought, if I let myself care and they did the same thing to him as they did to my father.

Was there still time to pull back with her separate self intact? Or was it too late? Had she fallen in love with him? Standing there with her arms tightly encircling his torso and her face pressed to the open neck of his shirt, she feared the latter question was the operative one.

"*Chiquita*..." he murmured, smoothing her hair.

It had been Juan's pet name for her. Thanks to the support and solid emotional strength of the man whose natural warmth seemed to flow into her very pores, she remembered that and a great many other things that had been lost to her. Not all of them were terrible. Many were bittersweet.

I shouldn't have brought her, Gabriel was flogging himself. The pain of what happened here must be almost unbearable. Stubbornly he refused to draw any parallels that might illumine his own precarious state.

"Can you forgive me for suggesting this?" he asked.

Raising her head, Miranda tried to smile at him. All she managed to produce was a trembling lower lip. Yet she was eager to reassure him. "Don't even think that way," she urged. "Coming here was right. I'm glad you were with me. Of all the people in this world, with the possible exception of my mother, you probably can guess at what I'm feeling best."

It was time to go. Glancing carefully about as they climbed back out the window, traversed the alleyway and returned to the jeep, they got under way.

A few minutes later, Gabriel mentioned that he'd brought food. "In case you were wondering, my imagination as a provider extends to more than chocolate bars," he said dryly, flashing her a grin. "I wouldn't blame you if you weren't terribly interested after what you've been through. But I didn't have time for breakfast."

He was always on the run. Miranda had to smile despite herself. "I suppose I could eat something," she said.

"*Bueno.* There's a little stream bordered by some shade trees a couple of kilometers farther along our route."

The trees were Cuban laurels, with graceful aerial roots. As for the stream, it contained more than a glint of water, though in the Caribbean winter usually brought the driest months. Pulling off the road, Gabriel got out and spread the army-style blanket he always carried on the grass. Soon, Raul and Emilio joined them. Eyeing Miranda politely but appraisingly as they helped themselves to the edibles, they claimed a spot a short distance away and turned on a portable radio.

As she and Gabriel basked in filtered sunlight after consuming their share of the bread, cheese and fruit he'd brought, she decided it might be best to put her memories of what had happened in Batey Venus on hold. For the time being, at least, Gabriel's cause was hers. She needed to know more about his thoughts.

"I hate to disarrange such peace but I've been wondering about something," she said. "How do the members of La Cábala and other enemies of Leander Santos hope to bring his government to its knees without the kind of pressure that can be exerted by a full-time military opposition equivalent to the former contras in Nicaragua?"

Gabriel realized afresh how intelligent and thoughtful she was. "That's a good question," he said. "For once, I can give you a fairly simple answer. With the Cold War over and the Soviet Union concentrating on its own very serious economic problems, it can no longer afford to back Caribbean and Central American communism."

She began to see. "Without Soviet help..."

"The Santos government is all but bankrupt. It has lost the people's confidence, just as many governments did in Eastern Europe. We're trying to do here what was done in Czechoslovakia, for instance. We don't deceive ourselves that it'll be completely bloodless. But with enough social and economic pressure, plus the occasional commando raid to show them we mean business, we believe Santos and his supporters will topple."

Miranda nodded. He made sense.

"We're fortunate to have a choice," Gabriel added. "Gaining our freedom that way will be far less destructive to La Caridad than a military campaign."

There was a lull in the conversation. Yawning, Gabriel stretched and bit into a blade of grass. A short time earlier, he'd taken himself to task for subjecting Juan Almeida's lovely daughter to the pain of her past and El Panal's uncertain political climate. Now, falsely perhaps, it seemed those things had only a limited power to hurt her.

How good it felt just to sit there with her on the blanket and savor a few moments' respite from his responsibilities. He was fully aware, of course, that to do so involved a different kind of risk. For the moment, at least, he was prepared to take it. Whimsically he quoted an old Spanish proverb—*Que dulce hacer nada, y después de hacer nada, descansar.*

Until then, they'd been conversing mostly in English and Miranda repeated the saying in that language. "'How sweet to do nothing and, after doing nothing, to rest.' Does the idea appeal to you, Gabriel?"

The glint in his eyes gave the lie to his sober expression. "What else would you prescribe for a wounded man?"

He'd switched back to Spanish and, as proficient as he was in that tongue, she barely noticed. All her attention was focused on the content of his words.

"You were *hurt* yesterday?"

There was so much concern in her voice that he was almost penitent. But not quite. "No... the evening you arrived," he answered.

She frowned. "I don't get it."

Lightly he touched her knee, which was decently covered by the tan cotton fabric of her trousers. "Have you forgotten, *querida?* The Spanish verb *herir,* to wound, doesn't just denote injury. In a poetic sense, it can mean to affect, to touch. Even to shine upon."

Chapter 6

They'd been careful. Still, someone, somehow, must have seen them and guessed Miranda's identity. The cane cutters and other laborers who toiled for ridiculously low wages in the province known as the Honeycomb had learned of her presence there.

As their caravan headed south from Gabriel's chosen picnic spot by the little stream with its grove of Cuban laurels, men in loose, threadbare clothing and crudely woven straw hats began to appear at the roadside. Some had women and children with them. When the jeep passed, they didn't cheer or even make a sound. They simply removed their hats in silent tribute.

It had happened before, at Josefina's house. But Miranda hadn't become accustomed to it. Chills raced down her arms. She felt as if destiny were breathing lightly on the back of her neck.

She knew the workers of El Panal honored Juan, not her. She hadn't done anything to merit their respect.

What caused her to shiver and marvel most was the enduring bond her father had forged with these people. It had survived twenty-four years through a time of great difficulty. Murdered, his revolution perverted by Cuban-backed communists, he was still a hero to them. Unable to present *him* with their homage, they offered it to her instead.

Yes, Miranda thought, a thousand light-years removed in spirit from her life on the concert stage. This is where I belong right now. These people need me. Because of Juan, they will listen to me. I have to make them realize how much they need Gabriel. Glancing at him, she surprised an almost hungry look on his face.

What would it be like, he wondered, to unite the country the way Juan once did? He wasn't sure he had the charisma and political savvy to accomplish it. Maybe someone else would be better suited to the task. Only time would tell. Meanwhile, he was deeply moved. When Miranda had padded barefoot onto the balcony at his aunt's house to meet a field full of strangers, he'd envied the mantle of trust that fell so effortlessly on her shoulders, even while he'd admired her courage. Now he felt no envy—just gratitude that she possessed the means he lacked.

"They're really something, aren't they?" he asked, raising his voice slightly above the roar of the jeep's engine.

She nodded, a lump in her throat. "It's no exaggeration to say I love them. Whatever I can do, I want to help."

He didn't doubt her commitment came straight from the heart. He ought to be overjoyed. *Wasn't* he? It was what he'd asked her for from the beginning. Now she was handing it to him. Ironically it made him worry.

News traveled fast in El Panal despite the government stranglehold of the press. The story of her involvement in their attempt to drive communism from the shores of La Caridad would spread like wildfire.

What if he'd been too optimistic, too casual in calculating the immunity the *guajiros'* support would give her? She'd put her safety and well-being in his hands. He hoped to hell she wouldn't have to suffer for it when the tale of her roadside reception reached Santista ears.

Despite the unrest in El Panal, they were as safe at Pablo Escobar's small, crowded home in Batey Roncaldo as they would have been anywhere in La Caridad. Tough, determined and, above all, practical, the burly union boss was far from appealing. He didn't command the laborers' hearts the way Juan once had. But he was a good organizer and he possessed formidable strength among the men he'd welded into a potent political force. Foremost among his weapons was the power of the general strike. Under the right circumstances, Gabriel believed, Escobar wouldn't hesitate to use it. Government leader Leander Santos and his henchmen had probably come to the same conclusion.

Gabriel and Escobar had never gotten along. A self-styled "man of the people," the union boss didn't completely trust Gabriel. As a well-educated son of a man who'd once owned vast sugarcane estates Gabriel believed he stirred up old resentments in the man's head.

Miranda, on the other hand, got an effusive welcome. Calling on his wife to bring coffee with plenty of *azúcar* and a plate of sticky, pineapple-filled pastries, Escobar shooed away flies, children and an errant rooster and begged Miranda to honor his table. She took the proffered seat with all the grace of a queen paying a state visit. Yet her every gesture indicated deference and the wish to sow accord. If he hadn't known better, Gabriel would have sworn she'd never set foot in a dwelling more elaborate than the one where they found themselves.

She had her father's touch. She drew Escobar out, making him feel special and important as she asked him all the right questions. Her back to a parrot-blue wall decorated with out-of-date calendars and family snapshots, and her slender, ringless hands resting gracefully on the fringed shawl that did double duty as a table covering, she also looked very desirable. With her shapely figure and tawny eyes, what man could resist her? God knew *he* was vulnerable.

He started paying closer attention to the conversation when Escobar asked if Miranda would be willing to speak at a meeting of his union members the following night. He hoped she would. If she and Gabriel appeared together, it would go far to cement relations between the former planters who'd fled to their summer homes in the mountains during the 1968 revolution and the field hands who'd stayed behind to labor in El Panal's vast cane fields.

Yet when she agreed, his immediate reaction was negative. The situation here in the south is too volatile, he thought. There could be trouble. She hasn't sufficiently established herself.

Is that the private man in you talking? he asked himself as they shook hands with Escobar and arranged to meet him at Batey Roncaldo's defunct Espíritu Santo Catholic church, which served as an unofficial union hall. Surely it's not the revolutionary leader who subordinates everything to the cause.

As Escobar walked them out, Miranda couldn't read Gabriel's thoughts. Yet by now she knew him well enough to guess he wasn't pleased. His air of dissatisfaction grew more pronounced when, with an apologetic nod to her, the union leader pulled him aside for a private talk just inside the fence. As she waited for Gabriel in the jeep, Miranda studied both men's faces. Each looked annoyed and mistrustful of the other. Talking as much with their hands as with words, they emphasized the points they were making with curt, forceful gestures.

Apparently they came to a meeting of minds, though Gabriel looked anything but happy about it. With a terse nod in Escobar's direction, he got in and started up the jeep.

"What was that all about?" Miranda asked as they drove off, with Raul and Emilio swinging into action a few hundred yards to the rear.

For her sake, Gabriel tried to shrug off his irritation. But he couldn't. That idiot! he thought. Planning something like that and then inviting Miranda to speak in the same town on the same night! Granted, her speech will provide a first-rate distraction and win us many new supporters. But there's no sure way of preventing the violence from spilling over onto her. Though it might dampen her enthusiasm, he had to find some way of persuading her to postpone her appearance. He'd talk to her about it at dinner, over a glass of *vino blanco* to relax her mood.

"Just a difference of opinion," he muttered finally. "Pablito and I have them all the time. They're a hallmark of our relationship."

He decided they should bed down in Reunión, a seacoast town that had once been a thriving resort but now had a fairly tawdry reputation. It would save time in the morning. He wanted her to meet with several resistance leaders there. Unlike some of their fellow Reuniños, the people he planned to introduce her to didn't have leftover mob connections.

They encountered no more workers lined up beside the road once they left the most extensive cane plantings behind for Reunión's semirural, truck-garden suburbs. As a result, Gabriel let himself relax a little. *Poco a poco,* he thought. We want her presence to become known. But not too precipitously. We don't want the Santistas to get a jump on us. Or a mob scene heating up in the city tonight.

The Caribbean was a broad, blue ribbon on the horizon by the time they found themselves approaching the third government checkpoint of the day. Though Miranda tensed at the sight of the tan-uniformed *policia* and their red-striped barricades, she'd faced them twice before. She decided she could handle the situation.

To her surprise, everything went smoothly. Allowed to proceed, they parked just beyond the first turning so their companions could catch up. As they waited, several minutes passed. The shadows cast by the concrete-gray trunks and feathery green thatch of several large royal palms lengthened a millimeter or so. Somewhere a bird sang. The waiting continued.

Unaccustomed to rising so early, Miranda stifled a yawn. Gabriel leaned back and laced his fingers behind his neck.

A moment later, he was sitting bolt upright. "Something's wrong," he said with conviction.

"Raul and Emilio?"

He was already out of the jeep. "Though they were well hidden, Mad Dog Hector's men may have found their guns. Stay here while I walk back and check."

Keeping to the underbrush beside the road, he returned before she had time to become too concerned about him.

"What happened?" she asked with bated breath.

Gabriel's expression was grim. "They've been arrested." He started the jeep's engine with a jerk. "As soon as we can find a phone, I have to call Manuel."

They were driving away from the checkpoint. "What are you doing?" she cried. "We can't just leave them!"

A muscle tightened beside his mouth. "What would you have us do? Go back and vouch for them? Do you want to be grilled by the *policia* yourself?"

He was being sarcastic—out of worry, she suspected. Surely he realized she didn't want anything of the sort. Yet she didn't feel she could forgive herself if they abandoned the two young men who'd come along on their journey for the sole purpose of protecting her.

It seemed the choice wasn't hers to make. Gabriel had already made it. To be fair, she was forced to concede that, if she hadn't been with him, he might have handled the matter differently—perhaps taking some immediate action himself.

"They may be young. But they knew what they were doing when they accepted this assignment," he added. "Since they've done nothing but carry arms illegally, chances are they'll be out in a few days. In La Caridad, money still talks. Meanwhile, we'll have to phone for reinforcements. You know, Miranda..."

"What?"

"We could have been the ones arrested, not them. Supposing we had. I wouldn't have expected Raul and

Emilio to keep us company behind bars if it didn't serve any useful purpose. Would *you*?"

She was silent a moment. "No, I don't suppose I would. Do we . . . have guns in the jeep?"

For a fraction of a second, she thought he might refuse to give her a straightforward answer. Then, "*Sí*, we have them," he said.

He phoned Manuel from a small neighborhood grocery. When he came out with a cola for each of them, he looked a little more at ease. He cares, she acknowledged, sipping at her soft drink and pushing her breeze-blown hair out of her eyes as they continued on their way, blending anonymously into city traffic. Raul's and Emilio's safety really does matter to him.

Suddenly another thought occurred to her. Without her bodyguards to act as chaperons, they'd be spending the night alone somewhere, unless Gabriel planned to take her to the home of friends or relatives. Her thigh just inches from his, she felt little brushfires of longing ignite in her blood.

She wasn't the only one thinking such thoughts. If the occasional, barely perceptible flicker of his gaze hadn't told her so, she'd have guessed anyway.

Limited though she was in her experience with the opposite sex, she found herself picturing their naked bodies entwined between breeze-scented sheets. From the moment Gabriel had kissed her beneath the waterfall, she'd craved him with an intensity that sprang from deep in the cell. Such craving was utterly foreign to her. The thought of being able to touch him the way she wanted almost swept her away.

"Will we be staying with people you know?" she asked, careful to keep the strong tug of desire she felt from surfacing in her voice.

He shook his head. "I don't think that would be a good idea. Santos and my father-in-law are well aware who their opponents are. They'd know just where to look for us. For tonight, at least, I think we're better off taking our chances in some second-rate hotel. We'll phone my contacts in the morning and arrange to meet somewhere."

Far from certain what his intentions were, Miranda felt rebuffed. You've got to get hold of yourself, she thought. Stop mooning over him like a sick calf and take in the scenery. You've probably misread his every look and gesture.

Doing her best to give it her full attention, she saw a Reunión very different from the scintillating, beautiful city her mother had described. According to Gabriel, in recent years it had become a center for the black market, prostitution and other crimes that had the government's tacit blessing.

In the downtown area, many of the beautiful old Spanish Colonial buildings desperately needed a coat of paint. The waterfront, once one of the handsomest in the Caribbean, had a distinctly shabby look that wasn't enhanced by the streetwalkers and other shady types who hung about on corners.

Buttoning up the jeep, Gabriel took her to dinner in one of the many waterfront restaurants. Run-down but still quaint, it contained exactly five tables. Three were already occupied. At one of them, an old man was reading a newspaper and talking to himself as he consumed his solitary meal.

The tiny eatery also boasted a flickering black-and-white television set with the sound turned off or out of order and a laminated lunch counter with three leatherette-and-chrome stools. The leatherette was peeling and the chrome was pitted from the seaside air. A tired-looking ceiling fan rotated slowly overhead. All the drinking glasses were cloudy. Behind the cash register, a blue-and-yellow-tile mural that had seen better days depicted a basket of fruit.

They sat at a table with a window view. Between them and the beach there was only the Avenida de la Revolución, a broad street lined with parked cars and overgrown date palms that bore panicles of showy, orange-colored fruit. Already the sun was down. Street lamps were lit. Sculpted by towering trade wind clouds that probably didn't contain any rain, the sky was deepening to soft indigo. Interwoven with the samba beat that emanated at low volume from a radio in the kitchen, they could hear the hush-hush of the surf.

At Miranda's suggestion, Gabriel ordered for both of them: yellow rice, salad and red snapper grilled with tomatoes, capers and olives. The waitress, a skinny, bored-looking teenager in a tight skirt, brought their wine right away.

If he'd known Miranda better, Gabriel would have realized any attempt on his part to get her to back off from her speech at the union hall was doomed to failure. To his credit, he did his best to convince her. His tanned, capable hands gesturing a hairbreadth from hers above the plastic-covered tabletop, he warned her about the possible consequences. Unfortunately he didn't feel justified in telling her about Pablo Escobar's plans.

"I thought speaking to the cane cutters and the other laborers was what this trip was all about," she complained. "I gave Escobar my word. And I expect to keep it unless you can give me a darn good reason for doing otherwise."

Figuratively speaking, Gabriel threw up his hands. He'd do his best to arrange protection for her. And to watch over her if he could. The rest was in God's hands. Or fate's. Yet that wasn't how he wanted it. What he wanted was her trust. The right to shelter her. As things stood, he didn't have either. The concern and caring he'd begun to feel for her were playing havoc with his peace of mind.

The hotel Gabriel chose was second-class only by a considerable and generous stretch of the imagination. Its reputation obviously wasn't the best and—to his way of thinking—that was all to the good. Despite her humble beginnings, he believed, Santos and his father-in-law would view Miranda as visiting royalty. Unless he'd lost his ability to read them, they wouldn't dream of looking for her there.

He could tell she guessed what kind of place it was when the clerk at the rabbit warren of a front desk blandly inquired if they wanted to rent the room "by the night or by the hour."

"By the night," he answered, leering at her. "Isn't that what we agreed upon?"

He felt her blush like an accusation as they mounted the thinly carpeted stairs to the second floor hall. So we're slumming, he thought. It's in our best interest. Playacting that we're a couple of lowlife characters doesn't mean I plan to coerce you into bed.

Miranda shot him a covert look as he unlocked the door and they confronted their shabby domain with its bare tile floor, sagging double bed and overstuffed chair with scratchy-looking upholstery. Where did *he* plan to sleep? Embarrassed by the way she'd longed for him earlier, she wanted nothing more than to shut her eyes and forget La Caridad's problems for a few hours. In the morning, maybe things would make more sense.

Gabriel pretended not to notice her discomfort. Of all the dives he could have picked, he'd chosen this one because it had phones in the rooms—probably so that the "working girls" who conducted their business there could communicate with their customers. Flopping down in the chair, he dialed Félix's number in Las Montañas. Though he let it ring a long time, there wasn't any answer. Next he tried Josefina. To his surprise, Angél picked up.

"Where are you?" his cousin asked.

"The Mirador Hotel in Reunión. I presume you've heard that Raul and Emilio were arrested. Manuel's taking care of it. I tried to reach Félix just now but he isn't answering. Will you ask him to send us replacements? If he can manage it, have them meet us at the Tres Hermanos Grocery on Poinciana Road."

Miranda was reluctant to appropriate the bed without settling their sleeping arrangements first, but weariness won out. She kicked off her shoes and sat down on the lumpy mattress with her arms wrapped around her knees and her back resting against the wrought-iron headboard. She did her best not to appear self-conscious as she and Gabriel went over the following day's objectives.

He was the first to broach the subject that weighed most heavily on her mind. "I think we ought to get some sleep," he said.

"How do you...propose we divide up the facilities?"

He grinned. "If you mean the bathroom, it's down the hall."

"Not the bathroom. The bed."

"You can have it."

She hesitated. "Where do you plan sleep?"

"Here in the chair."

"But that's so uncomfortable. It wouldn't cost that much, would it, to rent another room?"

"And blow our cover?"

He'd taken his shoes off, too. Stretching, he unbuttoned his shirt. Though she'd seen them before, Miranda had to admit the muscles of his shoulders, upper arms and chest were nothing short of magnificent. Against her will, her gaze traveled from his dark tangle of chest hair down the narrow seam of the same furring that connected it with the waistband of his trousers.

"You mean..." she faltered.

"Santos and company won't come looking for a lady of the evening and her paramour. But...just in case...I don't plan to let you out of my sight."

Borrowing the need for caution from him, Miranda decided to sleep in her clothes. She'd just pulled back the covers and plumped up a sorry excuse for a pillow when a loud disturbance broke out in the hall. Orders were being shouted. Doors forced open.

Santistas!

Gabriel raced for the window and swore. His worst fears were being realized. There were tan-uniformed police in the street, along with several police cars. Two or three of the officers were toting machine guns. To all appearances, he and Miranda were caught like rats in a trap, unable to exit via the balcony or use the hall to gain the back stairs.

"Quick...take off your blouse and get into bed!" Gabriel ordered in desperation, switching off the room's only lamp. "I want you to pretend you're having sex with me."

Frightened out of her wits but galvanized into action by her very fear, Miranda did as he asked. Flinging his body atop hers, he pulled up the sheet. She was still wearing her khaki slacks. Instinctively she cradled him between her thighs.

The deception came not a moment too soon. "Move! Act as if you're cooperating!" he urged in a hoarse whisper, causing the bedsprings to creak wildly as he took his own advice.

A second later, the door burst open with a crash. Miranda screamed, the most appropriate and natural response she could possibly have mustered. There was a harsh order. Then laughter and several lewd remarks.

"Your names!" a rough voice demanded.

In response, Gabriel came up for air, making sure her face and the gun he'd retrieved from the jeep when he'd taken out his shaving kit were well hidden. "Please, *señores*... we haven't done anything wrong," he protested in an accent typical of the island's working class. "Not unless lovemaking is against the law these days."

The order was repeated.

Quickly he stated a false identity. "I don't know *her* name," he added in apology, though without any seeming embarrassment.

"It's Isabel," Miranda croaked.

"You have papers to prove it?"

If she got up to retrieve them from her pocket and they saw she was partly dressed the game would be up. Gabriel had to do something. Fast.

"Can't a man spend his money in peace?" he whined in a subservient tone. "I'm *paying* for this, *señores*..."

As he'd hoped, the macho, vice-tolerant attitude of the National Police turned out to be their salvation. There was more laughter.

"What did I tell you?" another officer said after a moment. "Our tip was wrong. The daughter of Juan Almeida is a concert artist in America. She would never spend the night in such a place."

Before Miranda could quite believe they'd been let off the hook, they were alone. For several seconds, she didn't dare to move or speak. The side of Gabriel's gun still pressed, cold and metallic, against her ribs.

"Are they... really gone?" she whispered at last.

With a start, he realized she wasn't wearing anything above the waist. The soft, full breasts he'd cupped in his hands by the waterfall were crushed against his chest.

Outside their room, the policemen's booted feet could be heard, heavily descending the stairs. Though they'd found nothing, it was almost certain that they'd post a guard. Sitting back on his haunches, Gabriel looked at her. She was exquisite. His eyes well accustomed to the darkened room, he drank in every detail from upturned nipple bud to shadowy areola. Despite the inherent danger that still lurked in their situation, he went taut and heavy with desire.

I took an awful chance, he thought, willing his feelings to subside. If they'd tried to molest her, I'd have been forced to kill as many of them as I could.

"Id like to lie here in bed with you all night," he admitted, raising his eyes to hers. "Maybe even make it shake again. But we'd better not stick around."

Chapter 7

They weren't home free, though they were temporarily out of the woods. First they had to sneak out of the hotel and find a safe place to spend the night. Yet as they dressed in the dark, their fingers rapidly doing up buttons, they stared at each other in rueful fascination. For Miranda, the hard, sweet weight of Gabriel's body atop hers might be a memory. But it was achingly fresh. How would it be, she wondered, if suddenly there were no Santistas, no resistance movement to claim our attention? Would Gabriel and I spend the night together here, wrapped in each other's arms?

Shoes on, gun at the ready, he went to the window to watch Hector Ruiz's men leave. But at least two remained behind in an unmarked car across the street. They settled back to chew gum and monitor their radio. Had the officer in charge also assigned someone to the upstairs hall? What about the back stairs? There was only one way to find out. He wasn't afraid for himself.

What worried him was the woman who'd entrusted herself to his care—a woman he'd begun to care a great deal about.

Letting several minutes elapse, he stuck his head out in the hall. It was empty. At its far end, a bare bulb illuminated the door to the fire stairs.

"Let's go," he whispered.

As they dashed toward the fire exit, Miranda cringed in expectation of the stop order she expected to hear at any moment. None came. Apparently the guards posted out front were the only ones. Though the stairs creaked beneath their feet, the noise didn't seem to arouse any suspicion on the part of the management. For one thing, at the Mirador there was nothing to steal. For another, people who rented rooms in the disreputable little hotel paid in advance. Aside from incidents like the one that had just taken place, Miranda guessed, its managers had little to worry about.

Halting abruptly, Gabriel shielded her with his body as they reached a door set with small, square glass panes that led to the alley. He thought he'd seen something move outside. Maybe it was his imagination. Or maybe just a shadow. He decided not to take unnecessary risks.

"This way," he said softly beside her ear. "Believe it or not, there used to be a restaurant here. We'll go out through the kitchen. If you see anyone, pretend you've had too much to drink."

The bolt on the kitchen's exit door made only a faint scraping sound as Gabriel slid it open. Like the upstairs hall, the alley behind the hotel was empty. It backed up against some cheap apartments. Here and there, narrow chinks of light spilled from between half-open shutters.

True to the Fire

Firmly Gabriel took her by the hand. They started running toward the jeep, keeping to the alleys. Fortunately, they'd parked several bocks away. The men in the unmarked car wouldn't be able to see them approach. From what Gabriel could tell, the jeep hadn't been searched. They took off as unobtrusively as possible with the top up and the side curtains still buttoned into place. Nobody seemed to be following them.

Opting for the city's back streets and avoiding the suburban checkpoint location where they'd been detained that afternoon, they managed to get out of Reunión without incident.

"Where are we going?" Miranda asked.

By now, Gabriel was thoroughly berating himself for leading her into such a tight spot.

His answer was terse. "Back to Escobar's place."

They roused the union boss from sleep. Though his family was large and his house small, he made room for them. Gabriel slept on the floor while Miranda took the youngest Escobar daughter's bed. Unable to quiet her mind sufficiently for sleep after everything they'd been through, she lay wide awake, staring at the ceiling.

She couldn't stop thinking about Gabriel, or the way he'd looked at her. Uncertain though she was about what he really felt, she'd seen her own desire reflected in his eyes. I'm falling in love with him, she admitted. I know I shouldn't. He has the overthrow of the Santos government to worry about. And I've got commitments back in the States. Yet she'd made a promise to the *guajiros,* too. And she planned to keep it, though she knew by now her involvement wouldn't be any cakewalk. She'd stay as long as Gabriel needed her.

The following day, Gabriel was far from happy when he phoned the Tres Hermanos Grocery only to learn from one of the two young men Félix had sent that they were being watched.

"At least, I think that's what's going down, Señor Sánchez," the youth said. "The man I suspect isn't wearing a uniform."

Things were getting more difficult. "Hang out in Reunión for another hour and then head north to your uncle's house," he decided. "Watch carefully to see if anyone is tailing you. If anyone is, go home to Las Montañas. If not, phone." He gave the youth Escobar's number, and ordered him to memorize it rather than write it down.

Putting down the phone, Gabriel realized just how desperately the Santistas were trying to pick up Miranda's trail. He began to worry about what had prompted them to watch the grocery he sometimes used as a rendezvous point. We'd do well to remain at the Escobars' for the day, he thought. The various antigovernment activists we were planning to visit can come here to meet with us.

As it turned out, they were more than happy to. Over and over, Miranda was introduced to people who remembered her father well. Even those who didn't held him in high esteem. It made her feel good to hear Juan praised. The memories that were bandied about prodded hers, especially the happy ones. She also liked being in Escobar's house because it had the same feeling as her first home. Cramped but cozy, it was pervaded by the pungent, garlicky smells of Inez Escobar's cooking.

After a simple but satisfying meal that they shared with the Escobars, their children and six other adults, including the labor boss's top lieutenants, Gabriel made a last-ditch effort to persuade Miranda to forego her speech.

"I can't deny that, if everything goes without a hitch, the exposure will provide you with better immunity and freedom of movement than you have now," he admitted. "As we've discussed, the more widely known your presence is, the less likely Santos and his thugs will be to try something. Just the same, you're in the country illegally. I think you ought to wait... ease into the public eye a little more before you start making actual speeches on our behalf."

Confounded by what she considered a sudden and inexplicable attack of caution, Miranda refused to budge. "I told you before," she replied with a stubborn little shake of her head. "Unless you can give me a better argument than that, I plan to go ahead."

Her independence reminded him of his American-born mother, who'd died several years earlier. He couldn't help admiring it. Or wanting Miranda. He'd only known her a few days and yet his need for her had grown until it was a persistent ache. Would he be able to remember the way her hair curled, as if with an exuberant life of its own, when she'd left him and gone back to the States? What about her light-drenched eyes? The mouth that so sorely tempted him? Or would an emptiness simply open in his life, filled with haunting, diffuse echoes of what might have been if geography and politics hadn't stood in the way?

At least she'll be safe at the union hall for most of her speech, he thought. Bold as they are, the *policia* won't dare arrest her in front of so many who loved Juanito and sympathize with our cause.

Maybe the tension that's part of the constant battle he must wage gets on his nerves sometimes, Miranda thought. He wouldn't be human if it didn't bother him. At the moment, she knew, he had several things on his mind. He'd told her about the substitute bodyguards being watched at the little grocery and wondered aloud if he'd been under surveillance there in the past. Too, a remark by one of the police officers who'd burst into their room at the Mirador had given him pause. The man, who'd referred to Miranda by name, had mentioned a tip. Since then, Miranda was aware, Gabriel had been asking himself if they had an informant in their ranks.

At last it was time to go to Espíritu Santo Church. For safety's sake, they rode the short distance in a closed car with the union boss and several bodyguards he'd rounded up for her protection. Gabriel was wedged tightly against her in the back seat. Though physically they were touching, emotionally he seemed to have thrown up a wall. *Something's going on—something a lot more serious than bodyguards being followed and that policeman's remark,* she guessed. *It's as if he's bracing for a specific kind of trouble he knows is sure to erupt.*

Allowing herself the luxury of a glance at him, she visually traced his profile. How sexy he was! How strong and matter-of-factly courageous. Yet he also had a very human temper, as she'd learned at the waterfall. One quality stood out, endearing beyond the rest. Better than any man she'd met, he knew how to be a refuge. She'd wanted him to go on holding her forever in Batey Venus, when her father's death had crowded close.

A capacity crowd had gathered by the time Escobar's driver dropped them off in front of the union hall. Applause and shouts of welcome soared to the rafters as Miranda walked in the door. From Gabriel, her thoughts turned to Juan and the needs of his constituents, who had suffered so long without a voice. Even as she focused on them, though, she knew her feelings for the living, breathing man who'd protected her and fired her sensual imagination were inextricably a part of her deepening involvement.

Don't let me weep, Papa. Or blow this opportunity, she begged as she smiled and shook hands until she thought her arm would break. Let me remember every minute that I'm standing in your shoes, beside someone I've learned to admire and trust.

It was almost time for them to mount the podium when Gabriel drew her aside. "Since you're determined to speak," he said, "I'd like to ask a favor. Let me go on first."

They'd planned to do things the other way around. She gave him a puzzled look. "Of course, if that's what you want. But why? Any special reason?"

He shrugged. "Something's come up and I need to be part of it. I should be gone...maybe half an hour. If I'm detained, Escobar's cousin, Humberto Nuñez, will look after you. Your only concerns need to be to give your speech and stay out of harm's way. If anything unexpected happens, please...keep calm. And do as he says."

So I was right, she thought, pierced by a thin spike of fear. Something similar to the munitions-dump sabotage at Granja is in the offing. She tried not to let her worry show.

"Whatever you're doing," she whispered, "be careful."

Gabriel's speech was enthusiastically received, though Miranda thought she could sense a few questions on the part of his listeners. Probably those doubts stemmed from Gabriel's undeniable connection with La Caridad's upper class. Strung more tightly than the strings on her violin, she applauded when he'd finished and took her turn at the microphone Escobar had caused to be set up in front of the former church's communion rail. Even before she opened her mouth, she got a thunderous ovation.

These are Juan's people. And they're mine, she reminded herself, looking out at the sea of faces with love, though anxiety gripped her when Gabriel slipped out the vestry door.

She prayed God would keep him.

"*Señores y señoras,*" she began, her words all the more heartfelt because of her fears. "We're in this fight together!"

She was partway through her speech, already the recipient of numerous rounds of applause, when the audience was electrified by the sound of gunfire.

"*¡El Granero!*" someone shouted.

Immediately a hundred throats took up the cry. There was a mass exodus, with everyone pushing and shoving toward the exits. Humberto Nuñez materialized at her side. "We must return to my cousin Pablo's house... *now*," he urged.

Shrugging off his hand, which he'd rested lightly on her shoulder, Miranda started for the vestibule. "Not without Gabriel."

"You can't get out that way!"

It's obvious now why Gabriel didn't want me to speak, she thought, her footsteps quickening to a run. If he'd had his way, I wouldn't have come within ten miles of this place tonight.

Half frantic, Nuñez kept pace. "Señorita Burton!" he exclaimed.

The square that separated Espíritu Santo Church from the Granary, an erstwhile grain storehouse that had been converted to a jail for political prisoners, was in a state of mass confusion. Apparently a number of prisoners had been freed. Police seemed to be regrouping in an attempt to round them up. They were severely hampered by the surge of union members from the church. More shots were fired, this time into the air. Evidently some of the previous shots hadn't been. Several people had been hurt. She saw one man being led away who didn't look as if he could walk unaided. Another, in a police uniform, lay very still, a scarlet stain spreading on his shirt.

A second later, she saw Gabriel. And he saw her. To her consternation, he was holding a machine gun. He was clearly outraged by her presence.

Pushing his way toward them, he took her arm in a punishing grip and hustled her from the scene.

"What can you have been thinking of, to bring her to the Granary?" he taxed Nuñez furiously when they reached the relative safety of a sandwich stand several blocks from the disturbance.

The bodyguard was both angry and apologetic. "I *didn't* bring her. She wouldn't listen, I tell you!"

In the distance, tires squealed and lights flashed as more government troops arrived to quell the riot. Still holding Miranda's arm as if to force a manacle around it with his fingers, Gabriel tugged her into an alley behind several garbage pails and an old truck. He gave Escobar's cousin a disgusted look.

"You're relieved of your responsibility," he told the man curtly.

It was only then that Miranda realized he was wounded. Blood had begun to seep through a tear in his right sleeve.

"Gabriel... my God, you've been hurt!" she cried.

"It's just a flesh wound. *¡Vámanos!* Let's get out of here."

"But you've got to be treated!"

"In jail? I don't think so. I've got a first-aid kit in the jeep."

Keeping to the alleys, they made their way back to Escobar's house on foot. Miranda tried not to cry, though tears were stinging her eyelids. She almost stumbled several times in her effort to keep up with Gabriel.

His dusty, outdated vehicle was parked by the front gate. Ordering her to get in, he started the engine. He couldn't hide a wince of pain as he shifted gears. Nonetheless, he drove with considerable force as they lurched around corners and down rutted lanes in an effort to give the fracas a wide berth.

I can't take this, Miranda thought, fighting back an urge to beat her fists against the dashboard. He could have been killed. I don't want to live in a world where he *isn't*. Because of the dangerous life he led, the twenty-four-year-old trauma of Juan's death had come back to haunt her in a new and terrifying context.

Batey Roncaldo wasn't a very big place. They were quickly able to immerse themselves in the lush, agricultural countryside. By Miranda's calculations, they were heading southeast. "We're going back to Reunión?" she asked tentatively.

"No." Glancing in the rearview mirror, he saw no one. He let himself relax a little.

"Where, then?"

"My father's former estate. It's a collective farm now. In one of the more remote areas, there's a shed...."

Blood was still seeping through his sleeve. Given the way he must feel, she didn't want to burden him with her fears. Lapsing into silence, she regarded him with frightened eyes.

At last they reached their destination. A small barn with a weathered tin roof and thatched sides that looked like rows of straw smoking, it had a lean-to suitable for hiding the jeep. Parking the vehicle in the lean-to's shadows and throwing a battered tarp over it, Gabriel got out and gathered up the first-aid kit, the worn blanket they'd used for their picnic and a flashlight. Handing the blanket and first-aid kit to Miranda, he stuck a pistol in his belt and picked up the machine gun.

"C'mon," he said, face softening a little at the look of distress on her face. "There's a ladder to the hayloft. If we're in luck, there'll be some hay left over for our bed."

They were in luck. Spreading the blanket over the hay, which still had a faintly sweet, outdoor aroma, Gabriel stripped off his shirt. She couldn't tell for certain how badly his arm was injured because the flashlight beam wasn't directed at it. What she could make out looked a mess.

Seeing him hurt tore her up inside. But she knew her best gift to him at that moment would be a cool head and steady hands. "Is that rum I see?" she asked as calmly as she could, kneeling beside him and opening the first-aid kit. "Maybe you'd better have some before I get started."

Giving her the ghost of a smile, Gabriel unscrewed the cap on his leather-covered flask and took a healthy swig. "What was the name of that famous *gringa* nurse?" he asked. "Florence Nightingale?"

So he wanted to joke around. If it helped, she'd go along. "If I were you, soldier," she answered, returning the smile though her effort was a shaky one, "I'd watch my mouth. This is a field hospital. Your choices are limited."

Taking a deep breath, she positioned the flashlight so that it shone directly on his arm. Without being asked, he held the beam steady. Although she was repelled by the wound's bloody condition, she examined it more closely. *He's right*, she thought in relief and amazement. *It looks like a graze. I don't see anything remotely resembling a bullet hole.*

Still, his injury was far more serious than anything she'd ever had to treat. Relying on common sense, she cleaned the affected area with antiseptic and applied a sterile pad.

"Black market?" she inquired, trying to maintain the light tone he'd set.

He nodded, amused and grateful for her forbearance. Though his arm hurt, he was feeling much better emotionally. He wanted to be angry with her for disregarding his orders, but he couldn't. She might be a spoiled, headstrong *norteamericana*, but she was also quite a lady. She'd come through the evening's trauma with flying colors.

Miranda could feel his approval like a touch as she bent to secure the pad with gauze, winding it compactly enough to help stop the bleeding, though she was careful not to cut off circulation or cause him any unnecessary discomfort. She wasn't sure she merited praise from him, silent or otherwise. She'd panicked pretty thoroughly, connecting his injury to Juan in her head.

What he didn't guess, *couldn't* guess, was how much he meant to her. Though they'd known each other just a short time, he'd come to matter as much as life itself. I wouldn't be afraid to die with you, she told him without words, if that's what fate had in store. Living without you once my time here is over will be a far more onerous task.

"Maybe you should take another shot of rum," she said, putting the rest of the first-aid things back into the kit.

Raising the leather-covered flask to his lips, he downed a second, fiery swallow to please her. "Want some?"

"No, thanks. You might need it later."

"Don't worry, *querida*. I'll be all right."

Putting the rum away and snapping the first-aid kit shut, Gabriel leaned back on his good elbow to look at her. In the chiaroscuro created by the flashlight's yellow glow, her dark hair was in tangles, her lips parted, her mouth as bruised looking as if it had been kissed.

She'd been so worried about him, yet she'd managed to keep her cool. As she'd bandaged his arm, her fingers had been steady, even loving. It was a long time since a woman had handled him that way. His skin was hungry for it. *He* was hungry for her.

None of the women he'd known had ever made him feel what Juan's lovely daughter could so effortlessly. None had lit his inner fire the way she did. He wanted to take up permanent residence in the little hay barn, make love to her with no holds barred until they were both drunk with exhaustion and pleasure. He longed to know her body more intimately than she knew it herself.

Contrary to what his colleagues in La Cábala believed, getting involved with her could prove fatal to his commitment to the people of La Caridad. He knew she wouldn't—and probably shouldn't—stay in the island country of her birth. Yet once they were lovers, he guessed, he'd find it difficult to manage without her again.

Even as he tried to convince himself they should let the moment pass and try to get some sleep, his yearning to immerse himself in her sweetness intensified. Like his narrow escape at Granja, the bullet graze had made him want to live while he could.

"Know what I'd like?" he asked, not pausing to give himself permission to speak the words aloud.

She shook her head. Something additional to ease the pain, she guessed. By now his arm must be throbbing. Aside from the rum, there hadn't been anything in the first-aid kit, not even an aspirin.

"I'm still convinced it would be a mistake," he confessed, answering his own question. "But I'd like to do what we were only pretending to do last night."

He was saying he wanted to make love to her! The shock telegraphed erotic messages to her deepest places. Rekindled in an instant, the stunned anticipation she'd felt in the Reunión hotel room after the *policia* had left nearly swept her away.

They were alone, many kilometers removed from his aunt's *finca,* Pablo Escobar's cramped house, the prying eyes of his cousin Angél. No one would be able to contradict them if they chose to pretend nothing had taken place. Yet she knew exactly why he was cautioning her. The intimacy that could spring from what they might be about to share could make for a bitter parting.

For her, it was already too late to count the cost. I'll never love him any less than I do at this moment—only more, she realized. "It's what I want, too, Gabriel," she admitted, drowning in the hush that separated them. "But your arm...I don't want to hurt you."

"Making love to you would heal me," he said.

Chapter 8

They'd known each other exactly five days, yet they had a history together. And Miranda understood he wasn't referring to his wound, but to the ache of unsatisfied desire.

"Even revolutionaries have to feed their sweet tooth now and then," he'd told her as they drove away from the falls sharing a contraband chocolate bar. He'd probably been thinking that their bodies hungered for other things as well.

There wouldn't be any promises between them. Though she wished it could be otherwise, she wasn't too proud to ease his yearning or to seek surcease from her own. I want him to take me, she thought, her fingers going without hesitation to the top button of her shirt. Rock me until I shudder in ecstasy and wring from him his essence. I've been desperate for that from the moment we met and he took my hand in his.

Seconds later, her shirt was off and she was in his arms. "I want to tell you a couple of things," he said gruffly, nestling blunt little kisses against the curve of her neck and shoulder. "First, I like... the fact that you don't wear a bra, though it makes me hot and crazy sometimes. I keep watching... your breasts bounce and sway as you move... wanting to reach out and trace the outlines of your nipples with my fingers. Second, part of me was planning this."

Against the hair-roughened muscles of his chest, her delicate peaks firmed until they were hard, expectant buds. She wanted them in his mouth. God, how she wanted it! "I don't see... how you could have," she whispered, tilting her head back so that her neck curved like a swan's as she offered them to him.

Unable to resist such bounty, he took her first with his hands. The sensation was electric, nearly blowing her away. Already firm, her nipples stood erect.

"Remember this afternoon at Escobar's... when I went out for a while?" he asked, stroking her erotically with his thumbs.

"I... remember." Deep inside, she was quivering with heat. Her breath coming in little quivers, she tightened and released the place inside her where she wanted him most.

"I contacted a black market source." Gabriel kissed one nipple, drawing it partway into his mouth. "I wanted to make sure you'd have protection."

If he'd said he loved her at that moment, she wouldn't have been any more deeply moved or felt any greater internal knifing of passion. He wanted to devour her. To care for her. Abruptly they meant the same thing, in a way that connected her to love's most primal source.

"Gabriel, *querido*..."

"*Mi amor...*"

Muffled against her flesh, the endearment rippled through her like a blessing, though she knew Latin men were prone to flattery and exaggeration. Whatever its significance, they would have each other. Yes...*oh, yes*.... she affirmed. I'll never get enough. She wanted him to touch her, handle her everywhere.

Suddenly it seemed the grossest of oversights that she was still wearing her trail shoes and trim cotton cords. Straining to kick off the canvas hikers, she reached between herself and Gabriel to unsnap her waistband.

"Let me," he said.

Parting her zipper, he eased the cords down over the curve of her hips. She wriggled out of them, to face him in nothing but a tiny scrap of lace. In the half-light, her eyes were wide, their pupils huge puddles of velvet.

She was so utterly damn beautiful. Instead of removing his own trousers, which were bulging at the front with need, he hooked one finger inside her panties and pulled them down partway. Only a desire to prostrate her with rapture before indulging himself kept him from inserting his tongue into the dark nest of curls he'd uncovered. No novice, he knew what he liked. If he succumbed to that urge right away, he'd be inside her like a shot. Temporarily, he contented himself with slipping one finger into her liquid folds.

For Miranda, the glorious sensations that had flowed from Gabriel's attentions to her breasts were as nothing compared to what he was doing to her most private places. As he brought her to trembling life, she wanted just one thing—to open herself completely to him.

"I need..." she whispered.

"Tell me, *querida*."

"To take these panties off all the way. Lie down... spread my knees apart."

It was their first time. And he'd guessed she wasn't that experienced. To think she felt free to ask, to bare her craving to him in words that way! Sensation ricocheted through him as he moved over on the blanket and saw to it that she got her wish.

The hay was prickly beneath the blanket's thin covering, but Miranda didn't notice that. One of his knees was between her legs. Reinserting his hand, Gabriel had begun to kiss her ardently on the mouth. His tongue dueling lingeringly and erotically with hers, he worked his way down her neck and breasts to the taut, flat mound of her stomach.

A moment later, he satisfied his wish and tasted the core of her desire. Ah, but she was sweet. As he licked and caressed, his seed gathered to the bursting point. He'd protect her as he had promised; nothing could change his mind about that. But oh, how he longed to spill himself without restraint into her depths.

Her breath catching the rhythm of his ardor and accelerating with it, Miranda let the feast of feeling he evoked hold sway. As its spiral mounted, she bore down and gripped the blanket with her feet for purchase. Incredibly, this was *Gabriel*, touching her....

The acknowledgment pushed her past the brink. Crying out in astonishment because she'd never imagined her pleasure in lovemaking could be so profound, she dissolved in paroxysms of shudders. Heat rushed to her cheeks, to glow there with a thousand watts of candlepower.

Gradually lassitude overtook her. Settling in her thighs, it pervaded them with a delicious tiredness, though she was still quivering slightly at the point of light and heat.

"Gabriel..." she said. "You didn't..."

By now, his head was resting against her stomach. "Hush...don't talk," he advised. "We'll do that, too, I promise you."

It was as if they'd known each other forever and had been moving toward that night for years. She'd kept nothing back—not the smallest shudder of ecstasy or raggedly indrawn breath. He'd been privy to it all, every shiver, every telltale goose bump.

As he repositioned himself, guarding his injury as best he could and taking her fully in his arms, the frank, supremely trusting delight with which she'd offered herself made Gabriel lust for more. He longed to feel her against him, length to naked length. And that was only the beginning. The moment she was ready, he'd bury himself so deep....

Sated as she was, Miranda felt a little twist of fresh desire in her gut as he reached for his zipper. Her fingers brushed his. "Let *me*. It's my turn."

She was ready now. Or almost.

"Be my guest."

Seemingly inexhaustible when it came to him, her response escalated a notch as she helped him remove his trousers. He was fully engorged. So big and perfect for her. Wonderful in every way. She wanted to take him in her mouth.

Deed followed urge. It almost set him off to have her caress him that way. "Miranda, my soul," he pleaded, his Spanish more guttural than she'd ever heard it. "Let me come into you."

She didn't have to say it. As she relinquished him, waiting a moment while he availed himself of his purchase before straddling him and impaling herself on his need, the message was clear: *Take me... I'm yours, Gabriel.*

Bunching the powerful muscles of his buttocks, he thrust deeper. Sweet heaven, but she was limitless. The bond he'd yearned for since first setting eyes on her was blazingly complete.

That night, with all the forces poised to separate or injure them held at bay, and only their hearts to guide them, they scaled the footholds to paradise in a small, forgotten hay barn hidden away in a remote corner of what had once been his father's estate.

Overwhelmed by Miranda's passionate, giving nature, Gabriel didn't take long. Catching fire from him, she soared in tandem. Her release this time was deep and implosive, a helpless ritual of self-immolation and renewal powerful enough to shake the earth. Absolved of the need for control, he followed in seconds. Waves of gooseflesh spread over his back and thighs.

At last they quieted. Gently Gabriel eased her down beside him and, with his good arm, drew her against his body. They had only one blanket, and it was under them. Fortunately, they were in the tropics. Yet though it was balmy, the night air was already a little cool. He'd brought a clean shirt up to the loft for the morning; it would make a better coverlet than her blouse.

"Are you all right like that?" he asked after several minutes, reaching across her to switch off the flashlight and conserve his precious batteries. "Or would you like something to cover up?"

She nestled closer, charmed by the thought of spending the night in his arms. "I don't need anything yet. If it gets cold later, we can wrap ourselves up in the blanket like two caterpillars...."

* * *

Morning came, and with it the promise of rain though it wasn't the rainy season. Gabriel opened his eyes. A light sleeper who often had to make do with just a few hours of slumber, he'd been deeply immersed in dreams he couldn't remember.

He could sense Miranda was still asleep beside him. His arm hurt, but he seriously doubted he needed to see a doctor. Or that his wound would become infected after the way she'd cared for it.

Checking his watch, he was amazed to find it was nearly 7:00 a.m. They could have visitors at any moment if work had been scheduled in the area. They'd have to play it safe—get dressed and get the hell out before they were discovered.

He hesitated, unwilling to disturb the delicate balance created the night before. Yet by the sober light of day, it didn't seem wise to dwell on how wild and deeply fulfilling their lovemaking had been. Or to acknowledge that she was the reason he'd slept so well. Given their circumstances, he believed, he'd been wrong to propose they satisfy their desire for each other.

Reluctantly he glanced in her direction. She was still asleep, sprawled comfortably on her stomach. To look at her was to want her, though she was decently covered by his shirt from a point just below her shoulders to the tempting curve of her lower buttocks. He remembered waking briefly, to settle the garment over her nakedness and steal a kiss.

He couldn't have her. Not to keep, even if the entrancing thought had crossed his mind that they'd make beautiful children together.

Giving her up after what they'd experienced would be hard. Yet he couldn't convince himself that, for her, it wouldn't be best. Asking her to renounce her life in America and curtail her concert career for a man who might get himself killed tomorrow would be to demand too great a sacrifice—one she probably wasn't prepared to make.

His situation wasn't likely to improve with time, either. If they were able to force free elections, his friends in La Cábala would want him to run for president. It would be a difficult, dangerous and exhausting campaign.

Losing might mean there was a chance for them, but he hadn't entered the brutal arena of Cariño politics in order to lose. Winning, on the other hand, would increase his risk and commitment a hundredfold. In a turbulent, multifactional country like the one he was trying to liberate, getting elected to the top job wouldn't induce anyone to write him a life insurance policy. Or leave him with time to romance a woman the way Miranda deserved.

How ironic that she hadn't turned out to be the lightweight he'd taken her for. He knew now that she hadn't journeyed to La Caridad on a lark. Rather she'd come for deeply personal reasons that had to do with loyalty to her father and the tragedy that had marked her childhood.

He almost wished she *were* a "good-time revolutionary," dabbling in the effort to free his country simply for the thrill. Giving her up would have been easier. He only hoped their inevitable parting wouldn't cause her as much pain as the very idea of it was causing him.

Getting up quietly, he eased the shirt off her and tucked a corner of the blanket in its place. To be naked with her was both comfortable and erotic, and he hated to erect barriers again, though he felt he must. As he put on the shirt and zipped up his trousers, he imagined them waking together at his house to swim, nude, in the surf. To think about things like that wouldn't cost him anything but regret. He'd probably always feel it, whether he lived to be a hundred, or failed to survive his thirty-ninth year.

He was ready. It was time to wake her. "Miranda," he said.

With a soft little sound, she opened her eyes. She was wrapped in the blanket. Already dressed, Gabriel was a few feet away, his face in shadow. With his shirt on, it was impossible for her to tell whether his wound had bled through the bandage. Frowning and a little hurried, he was gathering up their things.

She wanted to luxuriate in his arms. Make love to him at least once more before they left the hay barn. Stubbornly she held out her hand.

If he pulled her to her feet, the blanket would fall away, revealing her beautiful breasts and the dark nest of curls that guarded the path to glory between her thighs. He'd caught a glimpse of those delights just minutes before and he knew his resolution would never stand another test. Aware she didn't like it when he handled firearms, he picked up the pistol and his machine gun as a way of putting distance between them.

"It's getting late," he said brusquely, feeling like a cad for failing to wish her a simple good-morning. "There might be farm workers about. Mind getting dressed while I carry these things downstairs?"

Without waiting for a reply, he started down the ladder. Still wrapped in the blanket, Miranda watched him disappear. A moment later, she heard him rummaging about in the jeep.

Her nipples brushed by the blanket's coarse weave, she recalled the sweet way he'd tugged at them with his mouth. From head to toe, her body felt supple, deliciously exercised.

Has something bad happened? she wondered. Yet how would he know about it, with us so isolated here? Maybe he just wants to forget our lovemaking ever took place. The blissful, cherished feeling with which she'd gone to sleep drained slowly out of her, leaving her feeling sick and confused.

For Gabriel, apparently, a one-night stand would be enough. Cold comfort though it was, she could lay one uncertainty to rest. Despite Angél's claim, he obviously had no intention of courting her for the cause. By the sullen, grayish light of a morning that matched her mood, he seemed anything but ready to include her in his future plans.

As they piled into the jeep and headed north toward some destination known only to him, it started to rain. Simultaneously, a news broadcast about the melee at the Granary came over the radio. According to the announcer, most of the prisoners who'd been freed had been taken back into custody. Two men had died. Another dozen or so had been injured.

"In related news, violence has again marked a dockworkers' illegal strike in Gerónimo," the announcer continued. "More strikes have broken out all over El Panal as well as in the province of Río Centro, in and around the capital. Police Commandante Hector Ruiz announced this morning that martial law will be imposed soon if order is not restored."

Miranda had come to La Caridad a little too late. Since her arrival, civil strife had caught fire the way they'd once hoped it would, and now it was burning out of control. Gabriel couldn't guarantee her safety any longer—at least not while she remained in the volatile province where her father had been killed.

I can't expose her to any more scenes like the one she got involved in last night, he thought, keeping his eyes firmly fixed on the road through the pouring rain and the slap of the windshield wipers. *Or* to the emotional trauma of dealing with a lover who backs off without giving her a decent explanation.

Briefly he considered sharing his feelings with her, trying to make her understand. But he knew where it would lead. Passionate, decent and fiercely loyal, she'd insist on sacrificing her career and remaining at his side simply because he needed her. Before long, they'd be back in each other's arms.

"Where are we going, anyway?" she asked in a small voice as they pulled up in front of a state-run pharmacy in the tiny village of Río de Oro. "And why are we stopping here? According to the sign, they aren't open this early."

He decided to answer her second question and ignore the first. "The pharmacist who runs this shop is a friend. He'll be in by now. I'm hoping he'll be able to 'resolve' some additional bandages for me, and take a look at my arm."

Gabriel also planned to make a phone call, though he didn't tell her that. While she perused the pharmacy's half-empty shelves, he rang Manuel from his friend's private cubicle.

"Can you meet us in Granja around noon and take Miranda back with you?" he demanded when Manuel answered. "It's too dangerous for her in El Panal right now. I thought she might go along on your planned swing into Enredadera later this week. In my opinion, she'll be much safer there."

Manuel agreed.

Breaking the news to Miranda was every bit as traumatic as Gabriel had expected. She was outraged. And deeply hurt.

"Why can't I come with you?" she asked, feeling his rejection like a kick in the stomach. "Is it because I showed up at the Granary over Humberto Nuñez's objections? Or is it..."

She couldn't make herself finish the sentence.

Distractedly Gabriel raked his fingers through his thick, dark hair. "Considering what I must do," he said, "you'd only be in the way. It's up to each of us to do whatever we can do best."

I wasn't "in the way" when you and La Cábala invited me to visit this country at considerable personal risk, she thought. Or when I spoke to Escobar's people last night. I probably won you a lot of converts. But that isn't the problem, is it? The problem is that you made love to me and now you regret it, for reasons you apparently don't want to discuss.

Whether or not they were the same reasons he'd stated at the falls, there wasn't much point in arguing with him. She wasn't about to force herself on a man who didn't want her. Still committed to helping her father's people, she'd continue to do that in whatever way she could.

"All right," she conceded, struggling to stem the tide of anger and hurt his decision had caused. "I'll go with Manuel if you think that's best."

Though the country was in disarray and the road bristling with checkpoints, people were being passed through quickly because of the rain. They made it to Granja in a little less than three hours. Manuel was already there, waiting in his ancient Buick at the appointed rendezvous, the weed-choked parking lot of an abandoned social club.

Carried out in the midst of a tropical downpour, the transfer took only a minute or so. Gabriel and Miranda were both so drenched that if she was crying he couldn't tell. About to get back behind the wheel of his vehicle after a hasty word with Manuel, Gabriel returned to the Buick's passenger side and motioned her to lower the window.

What good are words at a time like this? she thought. They'll only make matters worse. Reluctantly she did as he asked. Behind the wheel, Manuel waited. Rain and wind blew into the car and she shielded her face against them.

"Miranda..." Gabriel said helplessly, in a last-minute attempt to put things right.

Nothing could do that but his arms around her. "Goodbye, Gabriel," she whispered. "I'll be fine with your friends. Just make sure you take care of yourself."

As she traveled with Manuel among Enredadera's rural poor, Miranda had plenty of time to put things in perspective. It wasn't an easy task. Gabriel and their liaison in the hayloft were never far from her thoughts. Nor did she fail to worry over the danger in which he continued to place himself. Since stopping with him at the house in Batey Venus where she'd lived as a child, she'd remembered many more details about her father's death.

Reenacted in her head, her father's loss was no longer just a sad story that had colored her distant past. Instead it felt more like an open wound. Juan had been so young—only thirty-five, three years younger than Gabriel. Though she was reluctant to dwell on the connection, her fear that something similar would happen to the man she loved grew stronger with each passing day.

On Friday afternoon, while she and Manuel were meeting with resistance leaders in the back room of a bakery in the town of Ciudad del Campo, a man Miranda had met earlier that day rushed in and urged them to turn on a television set. Everyone hastily adjourned upstairs to the baker's cramped apartment.

To Miranda's amazement and distress, Gabriel was giving an inflammatory address on the campus of Asunción University. Incredibly, it was being televised! She knew such a phenomenon wasn't possible unless members of the resistance were operating the cameras, and had commandeered one of the powerful government transmitters.

With Félix at his side, Gabriel openly attacked the Santos government for its repressive tactics, and called for free elections. Immediately the students took up the cry, shouting for the elections to be held and chanting, *"¡Sánchez! ¡Sánchez!"*

"He's made a sitting duck of himself," Miranda whispered. "Not even the fact that he was once Hector Ruiz's son-in-law will help him now."

Within seconds, TV cameramen were focusing on uniformed officers of the National Police, who were arriving with dogs and clubs to break up the meeting. The camera bounced and tilted crazily as dozens of people were arrested, among them Félix and Gabriel.

Suddenly the screen went blank. Perhaps thirty seconds elapsed. Then a segment of a made-in-Cuba sitcom flashed in front of them.

The next few days passed in a blur. Escobar's union and La Cábala called jointly for a general strike, and it was very effective. As if a match had been touched to tinder, insurrection rapidly spread to most segments of the population. Demonstrations erupted in Asunción, the capital. Government television shut down, and people openly adjusted their TV aerials to pick up Puerto Rico and Miami instead.

Meeting in Josefina's dining room, those members of La Cábala who were still in Las Montañas voted to join the Asunción demonstrations in force. Miranda insisted on accompanying them. Urged by her Aunt Pilar to reconsider, she answered that it had become as much her fight as anyone's. Giving way, her aunt decided to accompany her.

With Ruben at the wheel they drove south, packed like sardines in his old van: Miranda, Pilar, Manuel, Angél, Josefina and Ruben's daughter Alicia, the severe-looking, dark-eyed beauty who had watched Gabriel with such longing the night of Miranda's arrival.

In Asunción, they found the balance of power up for grabs. Most of the shops in the city's pastel-colored buildings, frosted with stone-and-iron grillwork, were shut tight, though banners advocating the overthrow of the Santos government had been hung defiantly from some. Companies of the National Police in armored vehicles patrolled the boulevards, periodically clashing with, and sometimes retreating from, mobs of average citizens brandishing Molotov cocktails and machine guns. Every male in La Caridad—and some of the women it seemed—had secretly availed themselves of weapons.

Everyone in their group, with the exception of Pilar and Josefina, plunged into the thick of things with little regard for personal safety. Watched over by Angél, Miranda took part in a rush on the presidential palace that was beaten back only at the last moment. Following it, word quickly spread that Leander Santos had suffered a heart attack.

Chanting for La Caridad's "Little Castro" to "Free Sánchez!" and agree to "Elections Now!" the students whipped up by Gabriel's speech continued to apply the pressure. Cheers broke out when, the following day, Hector Ruiz appeared on a palace balcony to assure the crowd that it would get its wish: free elections within four to six months provided order was restored. Political prisoners would be released on a case-by-case basis.

The jubilation that greeted his announcement was deafening. Someone appropriated a sound truck and played a tape of the national anthem at top volume. It was followed by variations on the latest samba music. An impromptu dance got under way. When a Mexican TV reporter stopped to ask them for commentary, his cameraman accidentally tripped Alicia. In the confusion and crush of bodies, she turned her ankle.

"What about Gabriel?" Miranda asked Angél as they helped her to the car, where Pilar was waiting. "How do we go about getting him and Félix out of jail? I don't understand what Ruiz meant by a 'case-by-case basis.'"

Angél shrugged. "Just that a bribe must be paid commensurate with each prisoner's status. It's business as usual... a bit more blatant, perhaps, because of the situation. But business. Now that their power has been shaken, the Santistas will be all the more diligent about feathering their nests."

That afternoon, she, Angél and the others—including Alicia, who claimed her ankle felt much better—joined the throng of partisans converging on La Caridad's jails and prisons in the hope of freeing loved ones and compatriots. Diligent inquiry had revealed that Gabriel and Félix were being held in Asunción's municipal jail.

Perhaps because they were seeking Gabriel, people who were ahead of them in line offered to pass them through. The lean, mustachioed superintendent took their money with barely a flicker of interest. "Ricardo, here, will take you back," he said, negligently pocketing it. "We have a lot of prisoners in this place. If you can find Sánchez and Father Hill, they're yours."

Greasy and unkempt, the man called Ricardo opened one of the heavy cell block doors. "Have a look around, comrades," he suggested with a smirk.

Miranda couldn't help wincing at the crowded, kennellike cages where prisoners were kept like animals while guard dogs and their handlers patrolled the corridors. The cells had only one solid wall apiece, if that. The others were composed of heavy iron bars. Screened with wire on top so the prisoners couldn't climb out, the cells didn't reach to the twelve-foot ceiling. They offered little privacy or respite from the din of voices and other clatter that echoed in the cavernous space.

To Miranda, the cell block stank of sweat and unsanitary conditions. Men three and four deep stuck their hands through the bars as they passed, waving slips of paper and beseeching them to carry messages to relatives.

Promising to do what they could to help, they located Gabriel and Félix in a narrow cell by themselves at the end of a long row. There were shadows under Gabriel's eyes, though a little flame of pleasure leaped in them when he and Félix spotted their rescuers. Each man looked as if he'd lost weight, and each had several days' growth of beard.

"There they are," said Angél, pointing.

With a shrug, as if he'd hoped they would be unsuccessful, the jailer turned his key in the lock. Suddenly filled with misgivings about being there at all, Miranda hung back. Though she cared deeply for Gabriel, she didn't have any right to the man who'd made such exquisite love to her and continued to dominate her thoughts. She'd gone into his arms with no promises and her eyes wide open. He didn't owe her anything.

Briefly he caught her eye. And seemed to smile. His mouth formed the Spanish words for "I'm fine. Don't worry." A moment later, he was hugging Josefina. As they walked out, he was deep in conversation with Ruben and Manuel.

When they emerged into the plaza in front of the jail building, Gabriel and Félix were greeted with cheers. An instant rally formed. Gabriel was surrounded by dancing, exultant students. Overnight, it seemed, he'd become a hero to them. Miranda watched with mixed emotions as several pretty young girls threw their arms around him and kissed him on the cheek.

"I know how you feel," Alicia Camargo commented in a low voice. "I, too, find him irresistible. But he doesn't have anything to give an individual woman right now. For the time being, La Caridad must be his mistress."

Hard hit by Alicia's assessment, which she took to be sympathetic and probably accurate, Miranda tried not to spoil Gabriel's moment of triumph by letting her heartache show. *Maybe it's better if we don't pursue our attraction beyond one night of splendor,* she thought. *If we did, I'd only drag him down with my fears.*

From the beginning she'd known his friends in La Cábala wanted him to run for president. Though some sort of electoral process in La Caridad now seemed assured, his vulnerability to attack would continue. In addition to the Santistas, he'd probably have to deal with supporters of the former dictator, Octavio Blas. It was almost a given that Blas or one of his mob-connected henchmen would attempt a comeback. Reports were already circulating that several Blas enforcers had been seen in Playa Alta and El Pambril, on La Caridad's west coast.

Able to meet openly at last, their group rented a block of rooms at the National Hotel. During the joyous celebration and spontaneous planning sessions that followed, Miranda remained deliberately on the sidelines, watching and listening but saying very little as Gabriel was mobbed by people eager to jump on his bandwagon and get in a word or two about their ideas for his campaign.

At last, she couldn't take it anymore. Having wrestled with herself and settled on a course of action she knew would be filled with regret, she decided to go to bed early. With a last glance at Gabriel, she slipped out and walked down the hall to the room she'd arranged to share with Alicia. She was surprised to find Ruben Camargo's dark-haired daughter already stretched out on one of the beds, her swollen and discolored ankle propped on a pillow.

"Good heavens, your ankle looks terrible!" Miranda exclaimed. "You shouldn't have been walking around on it all afternoon. Is there anything I can do to help?"

Alicia gave her a little smile, as usual tinged with melancholy. "Do you think you could get me some ice?"

Miranda was filling a plastic ice bucket from the chest in the hall when suddenly Gabriel was beside her. Tired but obviously jubilant, he stood close enough to set off alarms in her blood. It was the first time they'd been alone since the rainy morning in Granja when he'd passed her like a piece of luggage to Manuel.

"How are you, *querida?*" he asked, lightly resting one hand on her shoulder.

Did he think he could touch her and call her "darling" and she wouldn't feel a thing? Maybe he did. She'd tried to accept that, to him, their night in the hayloft hadn't meant what it did to her. For him, its justification had been need, pure and simple—the physical release of tension, not love.

"All right," she answered with a sad twist of pleasure in the pit of her stomach.

"I've missed you. Today, in the crush of things..."

She stopped him with a little gesture. "There's no need to explain. It's understandable you've been preoccupied. I'd love to stay and talk, but I'm taking this ice to Alicia. She twisted her ankle when a TV cameraman bumped into us."

Ducking her head slightly in an effort to avoid his eyes, she started to turn away.

"Miranda...wait!"

Against her will, she paused. "What is it?"

"I don't blame you for being angry with me. That morning, in the hayloft—"

"Is history," she finished for him, trying to hide her anguish. "Just like the night before. I'm not angry at you, Gabriel. Far from it. I just don't think we should talk about what happened there."

She was telling him their intimacy was a closed chapter. His actions, he knew, had said as much to her. Yet that wasn't how it felt to him. Since handing her over to Manuel, he hadn't been able to forget the pain in her face as she'd looked up at him through the tropical downpour—or the sense he'd had of stabbing himself in the gut. Nights, as he'd lain awake, he'd tormented himself with the memory of her sweet, passionate response when they'd made love and with dreams of a future they couldn't share. He had nothing to offer her that any sane woman with a career like hers would accept. And yet...

"What do you say we start over, then?" he asked, flirting with temptation and selfishness.

Being "just friends" with Gabriel would kill her. But she couldn't tell him so. "If you like," she answered.

"Good." He planted a warm little kiss on her forehead. "In two days, we go back to Las Montañas. We have a campaign to plan. I'm hoping you..."

She wasn't going with him. "I've been thinking," she said in a voice not quite like her own. "And I've concluded the cause can do without me for a while."

He started to interrupt.

"No...please," she insisted. "Hear me out. Your support from Pablo and his union has solidified. And you've gained a strong following among the students. Meanwhile I have my composition for the NEA grant to finish. Since I won't have to sneak out of the country now, I can fly back with my aunt, through Mexico. I've decided to go home to Fort Lauderdale."

His bubble of euphoria bursting, he searched her face. He wasn't justified in talking her out of it. He just knew he needed her. His compulsion to have her was greater than ever, now that she was about to slip away.

On the verge of protest, he realized she'd mentioned her music. Except for Raquelita's birthday party, he couldn't remember her playing her violin since she'd landed at his secret airstrip. "Of course, you have to think of your career," he murmured, doing his best to put her needs first.

Miranda winced. Oh, Gabriel, she thought. I have four more months to write the damn composition. And the world won't end if I don't finish it. *That* will happen when I say goodbye to you. But she couldn't stay—not the way things were between them. It would be hell to live on the fringes of his life and worry constantly that, like Juan, he'd end up dead. The pain would be just too much.

Not knowing what to say, she didn't answer. As the silence between them lengthened, Gabriel longed to pull her into his arms. "When are you going?" he said at last.

"Day after tomorrow."

"You realize that, selfishly, I wish you could stay."

Had he changed his mind about them? Or was he just being kind? She let herself hope a little.

"It's only the fourteenth of January," she said at last. "That leaves plenty of time for me to come back and campaign for you before my concert schedule starts. If you feel I can help, please don't hesitate to get in touch."

Chapter 9

Six weeks later

The phone rang in Pilar Guzman's Mexico City apartment. Miranda's aunt was absorbed in a telecast detailing increased gangster-fomented violence in the campaign leading up to La Caridad's first free election in almost fifty years. She didn't answer the phone right away.

"In the view of many experts," the TV commentator was saying, "Antonio Haiman, the handpicked candidate of seventy-eight-year-old Octavio Blas, the island's former dictator, may outpoll both the former Communists and the Liberal-Labor Party headed by Gabriel Sánchez, if a threatened split among the Las Montañas rancher's supporters materializes...."

Pilar glanced at the phone in annoyance. Whoever was calling was being very persistent. "All right, all right. I'm coming," she protested, getting up from her favorite easy chair.

She answered on the fourth ring. To her surprise and pleasure, the caller was Gabriel.

"I thought I'd check to see how Miranda's doing," he said, after exchanging greetings with her, adding hastily, "You too, of course, *señora*."

She smiled indulgently. "Why not ask her yourself?"

There was a slight pause. "I've tried phoning her several times. But she's never at home. And though her stepfather always takes a message, she never returns my calls."

Pilar rolled her eyes. "Since you ask, I'm fine. But Miranda's another story, I think."

Gabriel felt a little prod of worry in his gut. Was she sick? Unsettled by the confrontation with her father's memory?

"Nothing's seriously wrong, I hope?" he queried.

"Physically, Miranda's fine. But she doesn't seem very content with her life. At least, that's been my impression whenever I've talked with her."

His thoughts were in a whirl. If she wasn't happy...

"I don't suppose there's any way you could have known," Pilar continued evenly, "but, since returning to the States, Miranda hasn't been home in Fort Lauderdale very much. She and her mother spent the past six weeks at a cabin her stepfather's family owns in North Carolina. She finished her violin suite there. Tomorrow evening, though technically she's still on sabbatical, she's scheduled to perform in the Tampa–St. Petersburg area—filling in for a sick colleague, I believe."

The line hummed empty for a moment as Gabriel considered the array of possibilities. "Please, Señora Guzman," he begged at last, making up his mind, "do you know where the concert will be held?"

* * *

On stage at Clearwater, Florida's Ruth Eckerd Hall, Miranda, three other string players and a pianist were performing their last number of the evening, Schubert's "Trout Quintet." One of Miranda's favorites, it made her think of flashing fins in sunlit depths.

They were still in the opening movement, the *allegro vivace,* with its bubbly keyboard phrasing and lively violin, viola and cello counterparts. Engrossed in the music as her bow flew over the strings, she didn't see the tall, dark-haired man in a business suit who entered the auditorium at one of the softly lit side entrances. An apron-clad usher whispered to him, gesturing toward a vacant seat on the aisle. Shaking his head, he remained standing. As if drawn by a powerful magnet, his gaze was fixed on the stage and Miranda's little frown of concentration.

Except for his daughter's birthday party, it was the first time Gabriel had heard her play. He was mesmerized. She's in her element, he thought. So beautiful. And so very talented. I shouldn't have come. But, though he could ill afford even a twenty-four-hour respite from the campaign trail, he hadn't been able to help himself.

At least they'd have a few hours together.

For Miranda, as they swung into the *andante,* with its more placid, autumnal harmonies that evoked images of diamond-bright reflections and leaves as yellow as gold doubloons, the music was like a drug, temporarily easing the pain of her loneliness. It was a month and a half since she'd seen Gabriel, and he hadn't called or written. Her sense of loss grew more poignant, more emotionally devastating with every passing day.

The third movement was bright and insouciant—ice giving way to freshets in a brook. Sedate but graceful, the fourth was enlivened by a sprightly maturity. At last the fifth, which they played *allegro gusto,* soared to its final, triumphant note. There was a moment's hush, followed by a storm of applause. In her off-the-shoulder, ankle-length black jersey gown, Miranda joined the three regular members of the quartet and their guest pianist in several curtain calls.

Walking back to the dressing rooms with her fellow performers, she turned down an invitation from the male cellist to join the group for dinner at a local restaurant. Exhausted both physically and mentally, she couldn't wait to return to her hotel. Once there, she planned to wallow in bubble bath, let her memories hold sway.

She didn't bother to change into street clothes or to shut the door when she reached the room assigned to her. She'd be leaving in a moment. Placing her violin carefully in its padded case and snapping the lid shut, she picked up the phone and dialed the house extension.

"This is Miranda Burton," she said when the concierge in the performance office answered. "Has the taxi I ordered arrived yet?"

"You won't be needing it."

The answer, spoken in a deep, subtly accented voice, came from the open doorway. "I have a rental car," her visitor added. "I'll be happy to take you anywhere you want to go."

One of the slender, ringless hands that had coaxed such dizzying crescendos of perfection from her violin flew to Miranda's mouth. The phone receiver went slack in the other. Her eyes widened to gold-rimmed pools of velvet.

"Gabriel!" she gasped.

With a shuddering little sigh, she came into his arms. Speechless at such unexpected good fortune, he gathered her close.

God, but he smells wonderful, Miranda thought. Like sunlight on freshly washed linens. And the musky aftershave he'd worn the night of his daughter's birthday. But mostly just like himself. She wanted to drown in him, worm her way inside his suit jacket and shirt. If she never experienced another moment of bliss, she'd count herself lucky after this.

"Ah, *chiquita*..."

Giving her a look that spoke volumes, he covered her mouth with his. Willingly her lips parted beneath the onslaught. He entered deeply, his tongue plumbing her moist privacy in a frank parody of the act of love.

He'd gone hard in an instant. Tangling one hand in her hair and lifting it away from her face, he slid the other down her back to grasp the tender flesh of her derriere through her dress's supple fabric. She moaned with pleasure as he fitted her lower body to his, the better to feel his eagerness.

What did it matter that she hadn't returned his calls? That he'd agonized over losing her permanently? They were together now. In his wild, reckless yearning, he forgot there had ever been scruples or uncertainties for either of them. Fusing himself to her, making her burn out of control like cane fields in autumn, was the only thing that counted. For him in that moment, it was all there was.

At last he drew back to look at her.

"What... are you *doing* here?" she asked, her words somehow fragile, as if she were a newcomer to the power of speech.

His mouth curved. "Holding you. Hungry?"

Ah, Miranda thought. Does he have to ask?

"Not for food," she answered, unwilling in those precious moments to lose even a fraction of what they could share by playing games with him. "Where are you staying?"

His hold tightened. "With you. I presume your hotel room has a bed."

He'd come all those miles, just to make love to her.

They kissed again, their hunger even more blatant than before. A moment later, Gabriel was picking up her violin case and small overnight bag and handing her the fringed black shawl she'd tossed casually over a chair. Impatient as he'd been on that rainy morning in the hayloft, but for a far different reason, he encircled her shoulders with one tautly muscled arm.

"*Vámanos*," he said, his voice discernibly husky. "The car's outside."

In response, she slipped one arm about his waist.

He'd left the spanking new Ford Mustang convertible he'd rented at the airport in a loading zone. The top was down. He helped her into the passenger seat and stowed her things in the trunk, then deftly removed a parking ticket from the windshield. Stuffing it into his pocket, he got behind the wheel.

At a turn of the key in the ignition, the Mustang's engine purred to life. "Where's your hotel?" he asked.

"Across the Courtney-Campbell Causeway."

Most of the concert traffic had already cleared. As they shot out of the parking lot, their hair whipping in the breeze, he reached for her. A console and the gearshift were in the way. But Miranda didn't let them stop her. Loosening Gabriel's tie and partially unbuttoning his shirt, she began to caress him in ways she'd never dreamed of touching a man as she buried her face against the hard warmth of his chest.

Somehow, he managed to keep his eyes on the road. But it wasn't easy. Distracted kisses against her hair and little groans of arousal told her what his diligence cost. As they sailed over the hump of the bridge and, a few minutes later, turned right at the softly lit entrance to the bay-front resort where she was registered, he tugged her ever more fiercely against him.

It was all they could do not to disrobe in the elevator. Her body bending into his like a willow as he ravaged her mouth, they let the door close again on her floor before remembering to get off. Still kissing outside her room with his clothing in disarray and her skirt hitched up to her thigh so he could stroke her leg, they scandalized an older couple who happened to pass them in the hall as Miranda fumbled with her key.

Shared laughter over the incident turned to erotic, half-whispered words and kisses once they were inside and free to seek the union they craved. They didn't bother to switch on the lamps. His mouth continuing to maraud hers, Gabriel divested himself of his jacket and half-open shirt. A shaft of moonlight penetrated the room between partially open drapes.

Seconds later, he was pushing down her off-the-shoulder bodice to uncover the first brassiere he'd known her to wear, a strapless push-up demi in black lace that hooked in front and revealed tantalizing glimpses of her nipples. She moaned softly as he stripped it away and cupped her breasts in his hands.

The helpless little sound goaded him on. *She's so beautiful*, he thought, gently kneading her. *Lush and full in contrast to her slender rib cage. And I love that. If our* circumstances were different and she let me give her a child someday...

He couldn't let himself think of that.

"I want you..." he whispered.

"Deep inside me."

"Taking everything."

"Yes. Oh, yes, Gabriel."

"I'm going to keep you awake until the dawn," he vowed, trailing kisses down her body as he removed her dress altogether and peeled off her panty hose.

When she was naked to his gaze, he invited her to finish undressing him. Less than an hour earlier, Miranda's heart had been aching at the thought that she probably wouldn't see him again. Now she was free to explore the rippling muscles of his torso at her pleasure, trace the dark, uneven seam of body hair that led downward to the focus of his desire.

The way she was touching him threatened to set off a maelstrom of passion he couldn't quench. He wanted the voluptuousness, the sweet initiation first, to tease her with every love trick in the book until she dragged him into her. But he didn't think he was going to make it. Hell, he *knew* he wasn't. They'd have to indulge themselves later. Briefly he pictured them getting started on the second round, taking things slow.

Since the first time they'd made love, his arm had healed. No longer was there the slightest ache where the bullet had grazed him. Or any deficit in his natural strength. Lifting her off her feet with virile, balletic grace, he held her up so that her hair dipped about their faces like a crinkled, silky curtain. In response, she wrapped her arms around him. Her knees clasped him in a scissors grip.

"This is like the falls," she whispered.

"I should have made love to you there."

"I wanted you to."

"I will now."

"In the shower?"

His mouth nuzzled hers. "If you close your eyes, it'll be the same."

She shook her head. Her insides had opened like a well to receive him. "I don't want to close them," she said. "I want to see everything."

Having yearned for him without ceasing, she'd store up every shudder and touch.

It was the deepest part of the night. The moon had waned, its silver presence stealing from the room. Only Gabriel's watch, which he hadn't glanced at since their arrival, insisted the Western hemisphere was tilting toward morning. There was still time, though inevitably Apollo's fiery steeds would catch up with them.

They'd slept little. True to his word, Gabriel sat in the straight chair by the dresser-desk that was attached to one wall, with Miranda astride his lap. Her forehead leaned against his. Her palms rested on his shoulders. Though they were barely moving—at one level swimming in weariness—he was buried in her. The room was rife with their sexual perfume.

She stirred, felt him swell inside her and tightened. He thrust a little deeper. She put his hands back on her breasts.

Positioning his thumbs to give her the maximum pleasure, he caressed her nipples lightly. "I don't want to hurt them with so much attention, *querida*," he said.

"You won't. Tomorrow, when I'm dressed, I want to feel the memory of this against my clothes."

Pierced with a wanton stab of pleasure at the mental image she evoked, he thrust again. She'd feel it in other places, too. As he would. On his way back to La Caridad alone, he'd ache for replication.

"Tomorrow's today already," he reminded.

"Not until the sun comes up."

"I'll want you twice more before then."

They struggled awake finally when someone from housekeeping rapped at their door. Light flooded the room. Gabriel was sprawled partway across Miranda in the bed, with the sheet pulled over them. The bedspread trailed drunkenly onto the floor, like a sail swamped in a tempest.

"Please . . . give us an hour or so," she managed, her voice muffled against Gabriel's dark hair.

Rolling off her, he stretched, plumped a pillow under his neck and drew her against his shoulder. She threaded one thigh over his as a matter of course. Her private, thoroughly ravaged nest of curls pressed against him.

During the night, between bouts of lovemaking, they'd talked. He'd told her about his ongoing troubles with Pablo Escobar, who was making noises about fielding his own candidate. But not about the Blas gangsters who were disrupting the campaign with increasing frequency.

"Tell me more about what's happening in La Caridad," she said as if she could read his thoughts.

Lightly stroking her arm, which rested on his chest, he spoke of the gangsters first. "It's as if they have a spy in our camp," he confessed. "They seem to know in advance about every move we make."

The incidents he went on to describe troubled her deeply. Was he taking enough precautions? What about hiring professional bodyguards? Or asking for United Nations protection?

Actually, Félix had fired off a letter to the U.N., he related. Supposedly some committee was studying their request. Again, he mentioned Pablo Escobar and the labor movement.

"He asks about you," Gabriel said.

Miranda tangled her fingers in his chest hair. Though every muscle in her body ached, the sensation was a pleasant one. She wanted to go on touching him that way forever.

"Does he?" she asked.

"Every now and then. He'd rather deal with *you*, you know."

There was a small silence. In it, his need for her arose again. But it wasn't an advantageous moment. First he had a question to ask. Or rather, a request to make. He might as well make it, though he doubted her answer would be yes.

"Come back with me," he whispered, having wrestled with his conscience and managed to silence it. "I need you."

She didn't answer right away. For the campaign? she wondered. Or as his lover? I couldn't stand it if he pushed me away from him again and we couldn't share these moments.

Gabriel could sense that she had unanswered questions. "I won't deny you're a valuable political asset," he admitted, groping for the right words to make her understand what he felt. "Or that you could help to heal the division in our ranks. But that's not why I'm here. The truth is, I can't do without you, *mi amor*... in my life and in my bed. I know it's selfish of me, wanting to take you away from your life and your work that way."

He wasn't offering her a future—just the temporary chance for them to be together. He hadn't even defined what together meant. Focusing on the endearment, she didn't really hear the guilt he'd expressed.

He'd called her his "love" just once before, the night they'd made love in the hayloft on his father's former estate. Then, as now, she hadn't taken him seriously, though she'd have given anything if she could.

At least she wouldn't have to worry about being shunted aside, handed over to Manuel's keeping in a driving rainstorm. Gabriel had admitted he wanted her with him. They'd be traveling together on a regular basis.

Afraid it would shake his confidence, she didn't share her worst fear. *If I do as he asks, I could learn to love him even more*, she thought—*only to have someone gun him down the way they did my father.*

It was a risk she'd have to take. It existed anyway. Octavio Blas's thugs could shoot him while she was performing in Jacksonville or Birmingham and it wouldn't wound her any less. Meanwhile, life without him had been shipwreck on a sea of loneliness.

"You haven't answered me," Gabriel prodded anxiously, searching her face.

She traced the shape of his jaw with one finger. "When do we leave? This morning?"

Joy crested in him like a tidal wave. *Did she mean it?* "Shortly after noon," he said, all but holding his breath.

She had two months left of her sabbatical. They both knew it wouldn't be enough.

"I'll call my agent," she decided. "Request he cancel my upcoming bookings until further notice."

The damage her career would sustain because of him was like a thorn in his flesh. But he wasn't selfless enough to forego her presence in his life. God help him, but he needed her. Delight and guilt mingling, he pulled her close.

"Sure that's what you want?" he asked.

Miranda nodded. "I just don't understand why you didn't call...ask me to come back to La Caridad a month ago if you felt this way."

She could feel his surprise even before he articulated it.

"But I did, *querida*," he insisted. "On several occasions. Each time I spoke with your stepfather. And he took a message. I had no idea you'd spent time in North Carolina until I spoke with your Aunt Pilar yesterday. She's the one who told me you were performing here."

Chapter 10

As if illumined by a bright light, the truth was suddenly evident. Obliging to a fault, Miranda's stepfather had passed on Gabriel's messages to his wife by phone when she and Miranda were in North Carolina.

And Célia Burton had deliberately withheld them. Still outraged by Juan's death and determined nothing should harm her daughter, Célia had obviously decided to insulate her only child from further involvement with Gabriel Sánchez and Cariño politics.

So what if that meant committing a sin of omission that was little short of a lie? And wreaking painful havoc with Miranda's heart? In Célia's mind, Miranda knew, her inaction had been justified.

Hesitantly, because she and Gabriel had only just healed the breach between them, Miranda told him what she thought had happened. Her hand on his chest, she felt rather than heard his faint sigh of regret.

"One can hardly blame your mother," he acknowledged. "To her, I must seem an opportunist of the worst sort, dragging her daughter back into the same volatile situation that resulted in Juan's death. I don't want to make trouble for you with your family."

Miranda loved her mother. But she couldn't let Célia rule her, not if that meant losing Gabriel. Stubbornly she kissed his jaw, which was scratchy with a night's growth of beard. In a way, she owned the beard. He'd grown it with her.

"If there's trouble with Célia, you didn't cause it," she insisted. "I'm twenty-nine...old enough to make decisions for myself."

Though he didn't respond in words, he hugged her close. She was so soft and delicious, yet she knew her own mind. And she was coming with him, though her mother would probably object. Given the constraints of his situation, he could hardly complain that her commitment was an open-ended one.

At the thought of her generosity, his need for her surfaced again. They'd made love off and on all night, and still it wasn't enough. Celibate for so long, he was insatiable now, for her. I'll wear her out with my loving, he taxed himself, nuzzling her mouth with his.

To his delight and amazement, she seemed equally obsessed with him. And they had time—enough time before they had to dress, drive to the airport and hurl themselves toward a life of speech making and public scrutiny. She didn't have to worry about buying a ticket. He'd already purchased one.

The call to Célia, placed while Gabriel was in the shower, didn't go well.

"What's wrong?" Miranda's mother asked immediately, her sixth sense, as usual, serving her well. "You never phone before flying home unless there's a problem."

Taking a deep breath, Miranda braced herself. The sweetness of Gabriel's lovemaking still permeated muscle and bone, making her feel as if she owned the world. But Célia, upset, could be formidable. "There's no problem," she hedged. "I'm just... not coming home to Fort Lauderdale right now as planned."

There was an ominous pause. "Why not?" Célia demanded. "What's going on?"

It was now or never. Miranda might as well admit the truth. "Gabriel Sánchez is here in Tampa with me, mother," she said. "We're going back to La Caridad together."

Shocked silence greeted her announcement. Then, "Over my dead body you will!" Célia exclaimed. "Risking your neck that way once was enough! He came up there and got you back into bed, didn't he? From the way you behaved when we were in North Carolina, I knew something of the sort had happened between you. But I thought it was over. How did he find out about your concert schedule? Did Pilar tell him? He couldn't have known, unless..."

He called Pilar when you didn't give me his messages, Mother, Miranda longed to retort. But she knew it wouldn't do any good to accuse Célia of wrongdoing. She'd never admit it. And her resulting hostility would only make matters worse.

"Mother, please..."

"He's going to get you killed, baby. Just like your father. Oh, God! You'll die too... just like Juan. Or *he* will, this Gabriel. And it'll kill you, if you let yourself care for him. I *know.* I've been there. You'll want to die yourself. *Please* say to me you'll be sensible and change your mind about this."

When Célia begged instead of issuing her usual orders, she was very difficult to resist. With effort, Miranda hardened her heart. She had to get off the phone before she betrayed too much. The foremost booster of her musical career, Célia would be utterly impossible if she found out about the concert cancellations. Give her a minute, Miranda thought, twisting the phone cord, and she'll guess.

"I can't do that, Mother," she said.

Maybe if she reminded Célia she'd loved Juan too much to leave him just because he was in danger, she'd understand. She was about to make the attempt when she heard the shower shutting off. A moment later, Gabriel came dripping out of the bathroom with his dark hair plastered to his forehead and a towel wrapped about his hips. Though they were closer now than she'd ever dreamed possible, she didn't want to admit her feelings—or her fears—in front of him.

"You're right...we have a relationship," she conceded. "We did when I was in La Caridad before, and we do again. I've missed him terribly. I promise...I'll stay in touch."

Riding on a commercial airliner bound for San Juan and Asunción with Gabriel as her lover and seatmate deeply satisfied Miranda's soul. Yet she knew the emerging shape of events was still stacked against them. In essence, Gabriel's obligations were unchanged. So were her fears.

They'd have to be discreet. Beneath the layers of amorality the Santista years had brought, La Caridad was a conservative, religious country. Friendship for Gabriel, expressed as devotion to his cause, would be acceptable to the voting public. Flaunting Miranda as his sweetheart would not.

Gabriel had phoned ahead from Tampa to say she was coming with him. In addition to Félix, Manuel and several other movers and shakers in his newly formed Liberal-Labor Party, a contingent of well-wishers and journalists met them at Asunción Airport. As they descended the portable metal steps from their plane, strobes flashed and TV cameras ground away. Gabriel waved. Standing at his side in a tailored red linen suit that was one of her favorite traveling outfits, Miranda wasn't certain what pose to strike. Hesitantly she followed suit.

Gabriel shot her a look of mingled apology and approval. "Looks like we're in for it," he commented under his breath.

The informal press conference began the moment their feet hit the tarmac. Their muzzles off, thanks to the recent relaxation in political climate, reporters from Cariño television and newspapers quizzed Gabriel mercilessly about the progress of his campaign, then turned to Miranda with a series of hard-hitting questions. They were joined by several members of the international press corps.

Had she returned to La Caridad to stanch the flow of labor support from Gabriel's campaign? one of the reporters asked. If so, did she think her presence would accomplish that? What about the danger? prodded another. By now, the presence of Blas enforcers in the country was well documented. So was the fact that the Communists hadn't given up. Neither group minded playing rough. Wasn't she afraid something might happen to her the way it had to her father?

Miranda fielded their questions as best she could without letting her feelings show. She wasn't worried about herself. She couldn't help breathing a sigh of relief when Félix managed to shepherd them into a closed car for their drive to the National Hotel, which had become Gabriel's campaign headquarters.

Her relief was short-lived.

"I wish we had the evening free since it's your first night back," Gabriel said, his knee pressing against hers in the back seat, though he refrained from putting an arm around her. "Unfortunately, I have to tape a panel discussion for the television. And give a speech at the university."

Less than twenty-four hours earlier, he'd walked through her dressing-room door in Florida and they'd embarked on a night of love. For Miranda, being back in La Caridad with the outside world rushing at them from all sides was like finding herself on another planet.

Gabriel was her man, her lover, though she was anything but sure of his affection. Public figure or not, he radiated the same warmth, intelligence and drive that drew her to him like a magnet. Sharing him with a nation was the last thing she wanted. Yet she cared about his country. In a way, it was her own. She'd settle for what he could give.

"Don't worry," she reassured him. "I expected things to be this way. Just tell me what I can do to help."

As they hit the campaign trail, Miranda found there was plenty to keep her occupied. In addition to making appearances before labor and women's groups, she often spoke in support of Gabriel before he addressed a particular audience. She also wrote radio and TV announcements and took her turn keeping his appointments straight.

Except for two occasions when he managed to arrange connecting rooms for them and spend part of the night in her bed, she slept alone. Though she longed for him, at least she got to see him every day. Compared to the way she'd felt in North Carolina, slogging away at her composition and grieving that he'd forgotten her, her misery was sweet.

As she'd guessed, her most poignant difficulty was her worry over Gabriel. They were all worried about him. There had been threats on his life and they were taking them seriously. With the Communists still firmly at the helm of the police and the supporters of Antonio Haiman, the Blas candidate, resorting ever more openly to violence, security had become an overriding concern.

At the end of Miranda's second week in La Caridad, Félix doubled their bodyguards. Though the additional protection gave them even less chance to be alone, she felt a little easier in mind. Convinced his former friends and political allies wouldn't harm him, Juan had operated without the kind of support that could have saved him. With the added backup, Miranda hoped, Gabriel stood a better chance.

Then one afternoon as they were traveling from a rally outside a Gerónimo packing plant to a dingy seaside resort farther up the coast, shots rang out. The report was like that made by firecrackers on the Fourth of July—a sharp, spurting *pop-pop-pop*. Instantly the rear window of their car exploded inward, showering them with broken glass.

Miranda screamed, realizing what had happened, though she hadn't heard machine-gun bullets being fired for many years. Simultaneously, Gabriel pushed her to the floor and covered her with his body. Behind them, more guns spoke as their bodyguards returned fire.

It had been raining and the roads were slick. Their car swerved, almost plunging down a steep embankment toward the ocean. A moment later, their driver righted it.

There was no third volley of shots. Apparently the attack had been hit-and-run. Yet, though they were traveling away from the scene at a high speed, literally hurtling through the rainy dusk along the lower west coast of El Panal Province, Gabriel didn't move. His fingers gripped Miranda's arm like a vise.

Had he been hurt? she wondered. Was that blood she felt? Something wet and sticky was dripping against her neck. A keening cry arose, frantic, terror-stricken. She realized it was coming from her own throat.

"*Querida*, stop!" Gabriel ordered, giving her a little shake.

"But you're bleeding...."

"Maybe I have a scratch or two, from the glass. Or maybe it's just the bottle of papaya juice I bought for Raquelita. One of the bullets passed through it."

The bottle of juice had been placed in a brown paper bag in front of the rear window—right behind Gabriel's head. If he hadn't ducked in time...

"You could have been killed," she answered in an agonized whisper.

"So could you. And for that, I can't forgive myself."

They remained in a crouching position until they reached the resort and Gabriel's bodyguards were in place. Her hazel eyes glazed with fear and misery, Miranda didn't demur when the man she loved put one arm around her shoulders as he walked her inside.

Though they could hear the surf, they couldn't see it. Warning them to stay away from the windows, Félix, who had been riding with them, drew the curtains. Somebody produced a bottle of rum and Gabriel insisted Miranda take a sip. Doing so to please him, she made a face. The rum burned her throat. Inside she was still shivering as if from the fiercest cold.

"Here," said Félix gently, settling her in an armchair and tucking a blanket around her. "You'll be all right in a minute. To the best of my belief, we're safe."

Sitting down on the edge of the bed across from her, Gabriel leaned forward and took both her hands in his. He could feel her shaking. The look of anguish on her face tore at his heart.

"I hate to say this when you're already upset," he told her, "but maybe we shouldn't travel together for a while. I can't allow you to suffer on my behalf."

It was happening all over again. "No," she protested, withdrawing her hands and hugging herself.

"We can double our protection twenty times over. And there could still be trouble."

"And you think that's a reason for *deserting* you?"

He winced. "I know it isn't. But..."

Shaken as she was, Miranda was adamant. "You invited me back to La Caridad to campaign with you, and that's what I'm going to do until the election," she said. "Afterward, if you don't want me around, I won't give you any argument."

Gabriel was at a loss how to answer her. With Félix and one of their bodyguards listening in, he wasn't free to say what was in his heart.

They'd brought food. But Miranda wasn't hungry. When her chill had eased, one of the bodyguards walked her to her room and took up a vigil beside her door. Another was patrolling the beach beneath her window.

Alone in the unfamiliar bed with its thin blanket and lumpy mattress, she let herself cry a little. I could have lost him today, she thought, oblivious to the danger she herself had faced. Célia was right. I'd die now if anything happened to him.

In the room he would share with Félix that night, Gabriel was struggling with his thoughts. I'd miss her terribly, he acknowledged. But if I imagined there was the slightest chance she'd listen to me, I'd order her to go. No matter how dangerous things got, he suspected, Miranda would refuse to leave him. Meanwhile she was stressed to the limit. Maybe, in addition to even more stringent precautions, a break from their routine would help.

"Considering what's happened," he said when Félix got off the phone after calling for another wave of reinforcements, "I think we should rearrange our schedule and go home for a few days. Miranda needs a rest. God knows we could all use one."

As before, in Las Montañas, Miranda stayed at Josefina's house for propriety's sake. After the crowds that had met them at every stop, the *finca* seemed unbelievably tranquil. Waking after a restless night and uneasy dreams to sunlight, birdsong and the shifting shadows of palm fronds against the walls of her room, Miranda missed Gabriel. We're lovers, she thought. And yet we're seldom together in that sense. I have no real standing in his life except a political one.

Just then, the phone rang downstairs. It was early still. Had something happened to him? From her bed, Miranda heard her hostess's part-time maid, Hortensia, answer it. A moment later, footsteps that matched the woman's short but hefty build trudged up the steps. There was a knock at Miranda's door.

"It's for you, *señorita*," the affable, middle-aged woman announced, opening it. "Señor Gabriel."

Snatching up her white eyelet robe and thrusting her arms into the sleeves, Miranda raced downstairs. "Hello?" she said breathlessly, picking up the receiver, which had been lying beside the phone on a polished, doily-clad table.

"*Mi amor*." His voice was warm, a caress in her ear. "Did you rest well?"

Not without you, she thought, certain he must be alone or he wouldn't have spoken to her that way. She pictured him at Las Brisas, his hair still rumpled from sleep, looking out at the ocean as he spoke. Since the attempt on his life, the idea that he could be hurt or killed was never far from her thoughts.

"Yes," she lied. "And you?"

"Well enough."

He was a man on the lookout for trouble with his head full of plans. Accordingly, his rest was uneven at best. Yet when he shared her bed, he claimed, he slept the way he had as a little boy.

"Will I see you today?" she asked, breaking a promise to herself to let him set the boundaries of their relationship.

His Spanish took on a husky note. "That's what I called about. This morning, as I looked down at the beach and watched the waves spread their wedding veils over the sand, I thought how wonderful it would be to make love to you there, half in, half out of the surf."

The mental picture he evoked pierced her to the quick. "Oh, Gabriel. I wish..."

The way she wanted him was the most powerful aphrodisiac he'd ever experienced. In his small, cluttered office at Las Brisas, Gabriel felt himself quicken with desire.

"I know a place," he said urgently. "Will you come to me there this afternoon, during the hour of siesta? For once, we can be alone. Here in Las Montañas, we don't need bodyguards."

Miranda's pulse beat faster as Gabriel described an abandoned sugar mill at the northeast corner of his estate and suggested she meet him there on horseback.

"It's on a low hill overlooking the beach," he added. "You can hear the breakers slap and pound as they race down the cove. I've let the vegetation around it run wild in the interest of privacy... made it into a sanctum of sorts."

Had he taken other women there? If so, she didn't want to hear about it. For now, at least, he belonged exclusively to her.

"How do I find it?" she asked.

"Old Roderigo, the man who cares for Josefina's stable, can show you. If you ask him, he'll be glad to ride with you part of the way."

As she put down the phone, Miranda was thinking of love, not bullets, for the first time in several days.

After the attack in El Panal, it wasn't easy for Miranda to convince Josefina that she didn't need an armed bodyguard just to take a simple afternoon's ride in the country. Arguing that, unlike Gabriel, she hadn't been targeted by anyone, Miranda managed it.

She didn't tell the older woman that she was meeting him. But she hinted as much to Josefina's elderly retainer. His wrinkled face creasing in a smile beneath his wide-brimmed hat, Roderigo agreed to help. Saddling up Josefina's mare for Miranda, he accompanied her across the fields as far as a path that led down toward the beach through a grove of coconut palms.

"Turn right when you reach the breakers," he instructed. "We're on a corner of Señor Roa's land here. *Pero,* once you pass the big flamboyant tree, you'll be on Señor Gabriel's estate. You'll see the old tower just ahead."

"And you? Are you returning to the *finca* then?"

Roderigo shook his head. "I'll wait for you here, *señorita,*" he said reassuringly, indicating a shady spot.

The beach was like brown sugar, packed smooth by the surf but crumbling soft above the waterline. As Gabriel had suggested, the waves were like *mantillas* flung flat, one over the other. Foam-edged, thinning to gossamer, they dissolved in a damp sheen that sparkled in the sun. To the north, she could make out the tiny fishing village of Cinco, its tin-roofed shacks ringing a crescent-shaped harbor and straggling up the hill behind it. To the south lay the stone tower, and Gabriel.

Turning her horse that way, Miranda quickly spotted the ruin he'd described to her on the phone. Squat, conical and flat-topped, it had been constructed some two hundred years earlier of heavy beige coral rock. Palms, sea grape and wild bananas surrounded it. Vines of every description had run rampant, clambering up its rough surface to form a shaggy green mantle. The spot was blissfully remote.

His horse tied in the deep shade of a grove of almond trees, Gabriel was waiting for her. He was wearing the black polo shirt she liked so much and faded tan shorts that exposed his muscular thighs. A forest fire of anticipation raged in his eyes.

Catching hold of her mare's bridle, he helped her dismount. A moment later, he'd tethered the animal beside his bay and pulled her into his arms. With no hesitation or false modesty between them, he grasped her buttocks through the jodhpurs she'd borrowed from Josefina and positioned her against his body. She gasped with pleasure to find him completely ready for her.

"Can you feel how much I've ached for you?" he asked, inserting his tongue in her mouth.

It wasn't difficult to guess. Hadn't she gone wild and wet inside at the evidence of his longing? Her tongue dueling and dancing with his, she felt unsteady on her feet.

They were alone—isolated in a remote corner of a private estate. Yet in La Caridad, the beaches were public. Someone could happen by, a *campesino* from one of the nearby ranches, and see the way they kissed each other. The message would be clear.

"Let's go inside," he said.

She nodded her assent.

The front of his shorts bulged as he helped her up rough, vine-choked steps. "I don't want to be discreet," he added fiercely, unlocking the tower's heavy wooden door. "I want to have you on the beach in broad daylight and to hell with anyone who objects. But we have to be careful."

With a strong tug from Gabriel, the door creaked open on its weathered hinges. He stood aside to let her pass.

Its thick walls slit by several square-cut windows, the mill's interior was surprisingly free of cobwebs. Gabriel had furnished it with a table and several mismatched chairs. A cot with a thin mattress and woven spread rested on a raised platform by one of the windows, atop a rickety flight of steps. Leaves and tendrils screened it from the beach below.

It would be their private world.

"You were saying?" Miranda whispered.

Putting his arms around her from behind, Gabriel teased the outlines of her nipples through her shirt. "If I were just a farmer, with no responsibilities beyond the planting of bananas and sugarcane, I wouldn't want anyone to see what we do together," he said. "What we have, *querida* . . . it's very precious. Just for us."

Swimming in a fog of desire, Miranda let him lead her up the steps. As they stripped off their clothing and with it the demands public life imposed, she didn't guess a man they both knew was walking the beach and had spotted their horses. Or that their secret wasn't safe with him.

Chapter 11

Gabriel was in the stable yard at Las Brisas the following afternoon, giving orders to one of his workmen when Félix drove up in a cloud of dust. Slamming the door of his ancient Ford sedan with uncharacteristic force, the lean, politically minded priest strode purposefully in their direction.

"¿Qué pasa?" Gabriel greeted him.

"I have to talk to you."

"Be my guest."

"Not here. Can we go into the house?"

Frowning, Gabriel searched his friend's face. "You look very serious," he said. "Is anything wrong?"

Félix evaded the question with an impatient gesture. "Let's talk in the house," he repeated.

Gabriel used the small office from which he'd phoned Miranda the day before to write speeches and do the estate accounts. Situated behind the kitchen, it contained a desk, two chairs, several bookcases and a heavily carved filing cabinet from Spain that had once belonged to his father. Its partly shuttered windows overlooked a sliver of ocean and a corner of the flagstone terrace where he and Miranda had danced the night of Raquelita's birthday celebration.

"Fix you something cool to drink?" Gabriel asked, pausing by the old-fashioned refrigerator as they were about to step inside the office.

Curtly Félix shook his head.

"So?" Ducking his head slightly as he passed beneath the low-hanging lintel of his office doorway, Gabriel half leaned, half sat against one corner of his desk. "What is it? Escobar again? I thought he told you last week he would stay the course with us."

"It isn't Escobar, though in a roundabout way it concerns him, I suppose. This is about you and Miranda."

Gabriel stared.

"You were seen meeting privately with her at the old sugar mill near the Roa estate," Félix added. "Forget the safety factor for a moment. According to my informant, the two of you were closeted there together for several hours."

Anger flashed in Gabriel's expressive dark eyes. "Damn your informant," he shot back. "He or she can go to hell. I want to know who it is."

"Sorry. I can't tell you that. I've given my word."

"Where? In the confessional?"

Félix ignored the dig. "If you say so, I'll believe you. But somehow I doubt you and Miranda were discussing campaign strategy yesterday afternoon."

More privately religious than church-going, Gabriel had known Félix for years. As a young man, the priest had been a good friend to his parents and an older brother to him. Not once had he lectured Gabriel on morality. Or—except for his suggestion several months earlier that Gabriel marry Juan's daughter to advance his cause—meddled in his personal affairs.

"What if we weren't?" he answered, forcing himself to some semblance of control. "We're both adults. What business is it of yours? Or anyone's?"

It immediately became apparent Félix was angry, too. "Don't look at me as if I'm some kind of crusader for chastity," he snapped. "I may believe in it for myself and for unmarried people generally. But that's not what this is about. As far as I'm concerned, your private life would be your own if you hadn't agreed to represent a movement and help govern a nation."

Stung by the undeniable logic of Félix's assertion, Gabriel was reluctant to given an inch. "Just because I'm a candidate doesn't mean I have to live like a monk," he argued. "God knows—"

"Hear me out." Félix's gaunt, ascetic face was just inches from his. "Despite some of the things that went on under Blas and during the heyday of the Santos regime, this is a very conservative country. Carrying on with Miranda could cost you the election."

Seized by perversity, Gabriel wanted to shout his hunger for Miranda from the rooftops. It was the final decade of the twentieth century, not the Dark Ages. People would understand. But he knew they wouldn't. This wasn't life he was living now. It was politics.

"Marry her," the priest-activist went on uncompromisingly. "Or give her up. If you don't, everything we've been fighting for will be lost."

For a moment, silence filled the room.

"I'm not sure Miranda would be *willing* to marry me," Gabriel finally answered. "Or that to do so would be in her best interest. However she feels, it wouldn't be fair to ask her until the campaign is over, and she has some idea of the sacrifices she'd be called on to make."

Félix's irritation softened visibly. But his essential position didn't change. "From what I can tell, Miranda cares about you... very deeply," he said. "I can't help thinking the feeling is mutual. You're a man of considerable standing and reputation in this country. What makes you think marrying you would be so disadvantageous for her?"

Before Miranda had stepped out of a borrowed jeep and into his heart, Gabriel had expected to spend the rest of his life alone. He'd been too burned by the travesty of his relationship with Raquel to think of laying himself open to more pain and humiliation.

Now Miranda's principled, giving nature had taught him to trust a woman again. Her sweet lovemaking had healed past hurts. He only wished it could solve the very real problems they faced. Maybe he'd made a name for himself in La Caridad, as Félix had said. But Miranda had been raised in America. Used to the privileges that entailed, she might find it difficult to give them up. In addition, she was very talented. Though she was only twenty-nine, she'd already achieved the kind of success most professional musicians only dreamed about.

Thanks to his mother's influence, he wasn't the kind of Latin male who thought nothing of insisting a woman relegate her career to second place. He'd tried not to think in terms of love for both their sakes. Yet he knew that was what they'd been making. If she left him when the campaign was over, his life would be like a desert. On the other hand, to have her as his wife...

With only burdens and risk to offer her, he didn't think it fair to ask.

"Like us, Miranda's committed to the liberation of La Caridad," he said at last. "She's all but put her violin aside in her efforts to help. But music isn't just a career to her. It's a gift... one she lives and breathes. Over the long haul, it would be 'death to hide,' as the poet says. If we were to marry and that gift were forfeited, we wouldn't stand the slightest chance of happiness."

In response, Félix ran long, slender fingers through his thinning hair. "Maybe I understand a little better why you've handled this situation the way you have," he conceded. "But I still think that, if you care for her and she feels the same way, getting married would be the right thing to do. There's no reason to suppose she can't resume her concert schedule after the election while continuing to support your efforts here. Besides, it's worked out the way we thought... she's a tremendous asset with Escobar and the laborers."

Nobody had to draw Gabriel a road map. Though they were friends, Félix's main concern was La Caridad, not his personal life. Because of the commitments he'd made, Gabriel knew, he was obligated to think that way as well.

If Miranda agreed to be my wife and I won the election, he thought, her responsibilities would be enormous. And if you *don't* win? asked a little voice inside his head. Will she be content making love to a rancher with failed aspirations and unrealized dreams?

Promising to think about what Félix had said, Gabriel accompanied him to his car. As the priest-activist drove away, he headed for the beach and a solitary walk by the surf. Though he hated to admit it, Félix's arguments made sense. It was just the mercenary aspect of the situation that troubled Gabriel.

Searching his soul as he skipped a handful of pebbles across the water, he came up with a plan. If Miranda could be persuaded to go along with it, they wouldn't have to part. Or make any decisions they might regret. Hopefully, they'd be able to quiet Félix's objections.

It was their best shot. Making up his mind, he strode to the stable, saddled up his favorite horse and rode across the fields to Josefina's place. He found Miranda playing dominoes with Angél on the patio. Greeting him with surprise and pleasure, she excused herself to fetch a pitcher of lemonade. Lazily Angél waved him to a chair.

Annoyed by his cousin's presence on that day of all days, Gabriel remained on his feet. "I'd appreciate it if you'd give us a chance to talk in private," he said.

Angél didn't move. "What do you and Miranda have to discuss that I can't hear?" he challenged in that forthright way of his. "I thought we were all in this campaign together."

A muscle twitched beside Gabriel's mouth. If he told his cousin about his intentions and then Miranda turned him down, Angél would never let him forget it. Yet, what did it matter, really? His cousin's opinion wasn't of paramount importance to him.

"If you must know," he said, "I plan to ask her to marry me."

He was alone on the patio when Miranda returned. "Where's Angél?" she asked.

"He had to leave."

Her dimples flashed as she poured a glass of ice-cold lemonade for each of them and slid back into her chair. "I can't say I mind. He was beating me pretty badly."

Gabriel's dark eyes gleamed with a hint of possessiveness. "Is that the only reason you're glad to see him go?"

"You know it isn't."

Upstairs, Josefina was taking her siesta. They wouldn't be disturbed. Sipping their drinks in silence for several seconds, they listened to the bees' soporific droning in the bougainvillea. In the antique wire cage that rested on a broad stone shelf beside the table, Josefina's finches were singing their hearts out. Though she and Gabriel weren't touching, Miranda was keenly attuned to him. The attraction between them had grown until it was almost a tangible thing.

It's so peaceful, just sitting here with her, Gabriel was thinking. No crowds. No danger to contemplate. I want this moment to last forever. But he knew it couldn't. Abruptly he covered her hands with his.

"Someone saw us at the mill yesterday."

"Oh, no..." Briefly shutting her eyes, Miranda absorbed the news. She didn't need to be told how damaging it could be. "Do you know who it was?" she asked.

"Félix wouldn't say."

If Félix had gotten involved, they wouldn't be able to shrug it off. They'd be held accountable.

"I don't suppose he's very happy with us."

In Gabriel's view, that was an understatement. "He didn't object on moral grounds," he answered. "He thinks what we've been doing could damage my candidacy."

A dull, sick feeling settled in the pit of Miranda's stomach. "Do you... agree with that?"

"I don't want to, *querida*. But yes. The truth is, I must."

The sick feeling intensified. "What does he want us to do?"

Gabriel couldn't think of any way to sugarcoat Félix's ultimatum. He might as well put it to her straight. "He thinks we should separate," he replied. "Or marry. Preferably the latter. He believes it would boost our campaign."

He hadn't mentioned his friends' original demand. Thanks to Angél, she knew about it. She was suddenly very still.

"Exactly what are you trying to tell me?" she said at last.

He tightened his grip, half-afraid she might get up and walk away from him. "I don't like being dictated to. Or told how to conduct my personal business. But, in light of my commitments, I think Félix is right. We can give each other up. Or we can wed. Since I don't want to lose you, I'm tempted to suggest we follow the latter course."

By now, there was a distinct lump in Miranda's throat. Desperately she tried to read him.

She didn't like what she saw. "But you're not suggesting that, are you?" she whispered.

He shook his head. "No, I'm not. At least, not yet. I hope you know I'd be pleased and honored to have you for my wife. It's just that, for both of us, there are a number of unanswered questions."

Were they back where they'd been that rainy morning when he'd transferred her to Manuel's Buick, putting her at a remove from him? The sunny afternoon stacked with trade wind clouds, two days after free elections had been announced, when she flew out of Asunción Airport alone?

She made herself say it. "Could you give me an example of what you mean?"

"For one thing, I'm worried about your career. We can't possibly know what the effect of my obligations will be on it until the election's over. I'd never want them to consume you."

Granted, her career was important to her. But compared to Gabriel, it didn't mean a damn. What bothered *her* was the possibility he might be killed the way her father had been.

"If you're willing," he added, "we could announce our engagement and postpone the wedding for a while. That way, we wouldn't have to part. We'd have a time buffer to work things out."

Was he asking her to marry him? Or wasn't he? He hadn't mentioned love. Or taken her into his arms. Where was the inventive, passionate man who, just the previous afternoon, had pushed her past the limits of reason as he'd pleasured her, body and soul?

Tempted to refuse him out of pride, Miranda cautioned herself to exercise restraint. True, he was asking because they'd gotten caught. And he'd expressed reservations. Yet he seemed to be urging her to accept. Unbidden, the memory of what they'd shared at the ruined sugar mill breathed softly in her ear.

Don't say no....

"Mind if I take a little time to think things over?"

His stomach clenching with the sudden fear he might be about to lose her, Gabriel answered that of course he didn't. "Come to Las Brisas and have dinner with us," he begged with sudden inspiration. "Just you, me and Raquelita. You can try us on for size as a prospective family tonight."

At Las Brisas, the three of them sat around one end of the oversize dining room table as Gabriel's housekeeper served an exquisitely prepared meal of rice, vegetables and roast chicken with papaya glaze. Conversation was light and inconsequential.

As if to make up for his restraint and awkward demeanor that afternoon, Gabriel was the soul of courtliness. Every word from his mouth, every light touch of his hand as he made a point argued the case that Miranda was precious to him. Each smoldering look promised bonfires of intimacy to come.

Shy in her role as hostess and clearly not used to her father inviting female guests home for dinner, Raquelita was smiling and eager to please. Seated at Gabriel's right in a white piqué sundress that made her look tanned, elegant and more desirable than she knew, Miranda attempted to draw the girl out. They ended up talking about school, the violin and Disney World. Never having set foot outside La Caridad, Raquelita expressed a strong desire to travel, particularly to the United States.

As they ate and talked, the salt breeze off the ocean caused the flames in the hurricane lamps to shudder and dance. Shadows leaped among the nooks and crannies of the dark, beamed ceiling. Light glinted off crystal and the family silver, which appeared to be very old. It puddled and flickered on the polished floorboards at their feet.

What would it be like to belong in this setting? Miranda thought. To fit in so comfortably that it was almost like breathing? Could the three of us make a life together? Though she'd seen very little of Raquelita, she was drawn to the girl. As a stepmother, she supposed, she'd be like a big sister to her.

Unsure what Gabriel really envisioned for them, she was pensive when, after a dessert of homemade guava ice cream, they strolled out to the patio. Her white dress a flag in the moonlight, she sat quietly in one of the wrought-iron chairs as he told stories from his boyhood, most of which his daughter seemed to have heard before.

Finally it was time for Raquelita to go to bed. Excusing himself, Gabriel went upstairs to hear her prayers. As Miranda waited on the terrace, listening to the hypnotic tug and pull of the ocean, she thought how different the secret life they shared was from the public roles they played. In the crucible of each other's arms, they were like one person. Nothing was forbidden. Nothing could come between.

In the public world, something had. As a result, she had a decision to make. Try though she would, she couldn't forget that Gabriel's suggestion they get engaged had been made under pressure. If we hadn't been seen at the sugar tower, she thought, he wouldn't have said a word.

One of their bodyguards had driven her over in Josefina's Chevrolet. He was waiting for her at the barn. "I suppose I'd better be heading back, now that our chaperon has deserted us," she remarked when Gabriel returned to her side.

As he'd kissed Raquelita good-night and descended the wide mahogany staircase that bisected his house, the man who'd swept Miranda's separateness aside with a look had been on the verge of abandoning caution.

If Miranda was my wife, Las Brisas would be her home, he thought. Raquelita's presence in the house wouldn't stop me from making love to her. I'd be within my rights to kiss her. Tease her. Coax her up to bed.

The image of them tangled up together between the sheets caused need to flow hot and helpless in his veins.

Not answering, he rested one hand lightly on her arm. "Have you been thinking about my proposal?" he asked instead.

Her lashes dipped slightly. "Yes."

"And?"

"I thought you were going to give me some time. So far, I haven't had very much."

Gabriel's strongly sculpted, charismatic features took on an apologetic expression. "Sorry," he said. "I didn't mean to push you. I just thought... well, that it would be criminal to let circumstances ruin things for us."

The disjointed explanation ended on a husky note. Closely attuned to him, Miranda could feel his arousal in the increased pressure of his fingertips. She knew he wouldn't indulge it with his daughter upstairs.

"I don't want that to happen, either," she confessed.

"Then say yes."

He was pushing her, the very thing he'd said just seconds earlier that he didn't intend to do. And she'd vowed after he left Josefina's that afternoon not to let him. Yet what purpose will it serve to draw things out? she asked herself. I could never bear to leave him now.

Though he hadn't said he loved her, his urging *was* a declaration of sorts.

Briefly, the possibility of a future they could share hung in the balance as she hesitated. But her decision was already made. Destiny and the fact that she was her father's daughter had brought her to that spot. Her love for Gabriel and commitment to his cause would keep her there.

"All right," she conceded, causing shivers of relief to skid down his spine. "I'll be your fiancée, if that's what you really want."

Chapter 12

In a bow to Cariño tradition, Gabriel announced his engagement to Miranda during a party at Las Brisas the following weekend. Pablo Escobar, his large family and several of his lieutenants, including Javier Fuentes, who was running for vice president on Gabriel's Liberal-Labor ticket, were among the hastily invited guests.

Only Félix and Josefina knew what was in the offing, until Gabriel decided to inform Raquelita an hour or so before the party started. Though she thought that was leaving it too late in the game, Miranda didn't argue. Telling Raquelita was his responsibility.

On the day of the party, she and the girl were in the kitchen, arranging cut flowers for the vases, when he came in and settled his hands on Raquelita's shoulders. Here goes, Miranda thought. She's had her father to herself for most of her life. I hope the idea of sharing him won't be too traumatic.

"I want you to know this is a very special occasion, *chiquita*," he was saying. "Miranda and I have some happy news for you."

Covertly Miranda glanced at the girl. It was obvious she didn't have the slightest idea what Gabriel was talking about. "Is it Miranda's birthday, Papa?" she asked in all innocence. "You should have said something. We don't have any presents for her...."

He gave Raquelita a little hug. "No, sweetheart. It's something much more exciting than that. Last week, I asked Miranda to marry me. And she said yes. Since we're going to be a family, we wanted you to be among the first to know. We plan to tell our guests about it this afternoon."

Raquelita was clearly stunned. Her mouth dropped open. "You mean..."

"She'll be your stepmother, *mi vida*. And my wife. It'll be good for both of us. You need a woman to talk to and help you pick out pretty dresses, now that you're almost a woman yourself."

He was making it sound as if their wedding would definitely take place. Partly obscured by an armful of jacaranda blossoms she'd gathered by leaning over the upstairs balcony and cutting them from a nearby tree, Miranda was rooted to the spot.

Raquelita looked from Gabriel to her and back again. "She'll be coming here...to live with us?" she asked, almost as if they were alone in the room.

He nodded. "Eventually. Not right away. You'll have time to get used to the idea first. We don't plan to get married until after the election."

Her dark eyes huge, Raquelita didn't seem to know what was expected of her. But she was Gabriel's child—

by upbringing if not by genetic inheritance. And she had exquisite manners. She was disposed to love and trust.

Reaching up to kiss her father, she turned and offered Miranda her hand. "I'm very glad to hear about this," she said with shy sincerity and a grace beyond her years. "I love my father and I want him to be happy. Though he's so busy most of the time, lately I think he's been a little lonely."

As they finished the flower arrangements and helped Gabriel's housekeeper set out the buffet, Miranda felt Raquelita studying her. Though the girl's scrutiny was clearly motivated by surprise and curiosity, not resentment, it only increased her nervousness. The hour of no retreat was fast approaching. She'd soon be on display as Gabriel's intended in the eyes of the world.

Since his proposal at Josefina's house and her acceptance at Las Brisas, they'd spent very little private time together. She still wasn't sure if the engagement they were about to announce was the real thing or a sham for convenience's sake. Gabriel had appeared to mean what he said in his remarks to Raquelita. Hanging on every word as he'd told the girl of their engagement, Miranda had been tempted to think he was playing for keeps.

I want him to say he loves me, she thought. Tell me he'd be lost without me if I went back to the States. From the bottom of my heart, I'm longing to hear that his unanswered questions don't mean a damn to him. Yet she had to admit her fears for his safety troubled her still.

A large part of her nervousness stemmed from the fact that she hadn't told Célia yet. As their guests began to arrive, first in groups of two or three and then seemingly by the carload, her tension mounted. I know why I haven't called her, she thought as she chatted with

Fuentes and several other colleagues of Gabriel's. I don't want her trying to talk me out of this. Once we've made our announcement, it'll be too late.

Because of his widowed state and the hardships imposed by La Caridad's worsening economic situation, Gabriel had told her, there hadn't been a party of that size at Las Brisas for many years. As guests circulated through the house and out to the patio, where the buffet and a number of tables and chairs had been set up, *sangria* and Caribbean-brewed beer flowed. The volume of talk rose amiably.

Gabriel had hired a group of musicians—two guitarists, a bass player, a drummer and a trumpet player who was also proficient on the marimba and the flute. With their heady blend of American pop, Brazilian classics and Cuban-Cariño folk tunes, and good-natured willingness to play almost nonstop, they enhanced the festive atmosphere.

All the guests seemed to be enjoying themselves immensely by the time Gabriel took up a position on the terrace steps with his back to the dining room windows. At a signal from him, the music faded. Raising his voice to the level he customarily used to address a large audience, he called for attention.

He's amazing, Miranda thought, noting his muscular physique and strongly sculpted features. The kind of man even the most deserving woman would feel lucky to get. He has his own special resonance.

"Contrary to expectation," he began when all eyes were firmly fixed on him, "I don't plan to make a political speech this afternoon. *Or* report on the progress of our campaign. I've invited all of you here to my home today for an entirely different reason...."

Miranda, who'd paused in the midst of a conversation with Angél, Ruben Camargo and his daughter Alicia, was all but transfixed. She felt as if she couldn't move or speak.

The crowd of guests waited expectantly.

"By now, you all know Miranda Burton, born Miranda Almeida twenty-nine years ago in El Panal Province, daughter of Juanito," Gabriel was saying. "You're well aware of her commitment to our cause and her incomparable generosity in putting her musical career on hold to campaign for us."

To Miranda's embarrassment, she received a spontaneous round of applause. "Don't be bashful," Angél whispered. "You've worked very hard. You deserve their appreciation."

For some reason, she got the impression Angél knew what was going on. Perhaps guessing where Gabriel's remarks might be about to lead, Alicia Camargo was staring at him in denial and surprise.

"Like you, I'm very grateful to Miranda for everything she's done," he added as the applause died away. "She's been a tremendous help to us. But I haven't asked you here today just to tell you that. I've asked you here..."

Gabriel sought her eyes. They exchanged a look.

"I've asked you here to tell you of an even greater generosity on her part," he said, his voice taking on a husky note. "Last Saturday, she did me the honor of promising to become my wife."

There was a moment of stunned silence followed by congratulations on all sides. "I never thought he'd do it," Miranda heard someone comment. "He's been a widower for ten years...the despair of every woman who set her sights on him."

Gabriel was holding out his hand. As if she were a sleepwalker in her white dress with her dark hair massed in curls about her shoulders, Miranda stepped forward to take it. A hush descended over the gathering as he drew her partway into his arms.

For a moment, she thought he'd kiss her on the mouth. But she wasn't surprised when he didn't. Though he had a hot, even passionate nature, when it came to the essential, the personal, he was a very private man.

The kiss was there in his eyes. He nodded at the leader of the little quintet. By prearrangement, the group struck up the venerable Spanish love song Josefina had played on Gabriel's phonograph the night of Raquelita's birthday. On that occasion, they'd danced on the terrace alone.

Their attraction to each other was public knowledge now. This time a crowd would watch. Their faces beaming with sentimentality and approval, his guests stepped back to make a circle for them.

"May I have the pleasure?" Gabriel said.

From beneath lowered lashes, Miranda answered in the affirmative. Uncertain where she stood, she felt surprisingly cherished. Even loved.

As they began to move, in graceful complement to each other, more applause broke out. Good wishes were showered on them in fond counterpoint to the music. In the background, that leitmotif of Las Brisas, the breakers that had acquired their original shape off the coast of Africa, echoed the crescendos of excitement in their blood.

Throughout the number, Gabriel's gaze didn't leave Miranda's face. He tucked her right hand against his chest in a tender, protective gesture. As dance partners or lovers, Miranda thought, swept away on a tide of feeling, we don't seem to miss a step. If they were to have a future together, their trust in each other would deepen. Only one thing could stop them if Gabriel wanted what she did: the failure of his bodyguards to foil another Blas attempt.

By the time she phoned Célia from his office that evening, most of their guests had gone home. Her mother's reaction was just about what she expected.

"Tom!" Célia Burton exclaimed, calling for her husband the moment she heard Miranda's voice. "Get on the extension, quick... it's Miranda! Darling... I trust you're *all right?* I can't wait to see you! Surely this phone call means you're coming home to us?"

"Hi, 'Randy." Tom Burton's raspy growl was in striking contrast to Célia's quick, high-pitched tones.

A glass of *sangria* in his hand and his tie comfortably loosened, Gabriel walked into the office from the kitchen and put one arm around Miranda from behind. "You can lean on me," he whispered affectionately, looking extraordinarily relaxed and pleased with himself. "That's what fiancés are for."

Now that the hurdle of announcing their engagement was past, had it turned out to be what he wanted all along? Grateful for his support, she was sorry for what he was about to hear. At least his knowledge of Célia's disapproval would be limited to one side of the conversation.

"I'm fine, Mother," she replied into the receiver. "Please try to understand. I'm not coming home just yet."

"But you must, sweetheart. Isn't that right, Tom? She's already done more than enough. If she stays in La Caridad much longer, her career will be damaged beyond repair...."

"Gabriel and I announced our engagement today," Miranda announced, her revelation cutting across the flow of words. "We plan to get married sometime after the election."

Fondly Gabriel's grip on her tightened.

Meanwhile, the shock had registered. Célia let loose a flood of invective in her ear. "You can't!" she wailed, the tide of her panic rising. "Oh, baby... you're making such a terrible mistake!"

More calmly but just as dogmatically, Tom Burton agreed. "It's one thing to play at being a revolutionary," he warned. "And another to spend your life with one. If you commit to this Sánchez fellow, you'll be giving up the only life you've ever known."

"Please say you'll come back to the States for a while and think things over," Célia begged, taking up the argument. "This grand passion between you and Sánchez... it's strictly hormones, plus a strong dash of political opportunism on his part, and you know it. It'll never last. For you to give up everything you've worked so hard to achieve, and go back to La Caridad..."

I hope to God you're wrong, Miranda responded silently, allowing herself to lean lightly against Gabriel. Because it isn't just hormones with me. I *love* him. And I always will. If I lost him, I'd be losing myself. It hurt to realize her parents' insistence they take things slow echoed Gabriel's.

A guest at Las Brisas, she'd phoned Fort Lauderdale collect. "This call is costing you," she reminded her mother, looking for a graceful way to end the conversation. "Besides, I can't afford to tie up the phone here all night. The fact is Gabriel and I have gotten engaged. We didn't do it just to irritate you. Or so we could throw a party. I'm hoping you and Daddy will try to accept the situation."

The day after their public betrothal, they hit the campaign trail again. Their first stop was the port city of Gerónimo. To their surprise, the news about their engagement had preceded them. As they made their way from one pier to another, introducing themselves and shaking hands with the dockworkers, they were greeted with avid cheers and good wishes. It seemed Félix had been right. Even burly, tough men who loaded bananas, copra and sugar on massive seagoing vessels were charmed by romance.

The ebullient mood of the morning was partly dashed that afternoon when opposition violence was reported in the province of Las Olas, on the island's west coast. They were headed that way, with a stop in the market town of Río Centro, where Gabriel was to address a newly organized federation of truck drivers.

His speech was scheduled to take place outdoors, in the town *plaza*, the only place large enough to accommodate the number of people who were expected to attend.

Miranda felt a flicker of worry when they arrived at the scene. The audience that had gathered appeared loud and unruly, and there were several access routes that appeared problematical to control. Numerous two- and three-story buildings with windows and balconies overlooked the speakers' platform. Despite the number of bodyguards they had traveling with them now, she could see that keeping a tight rein on security would be difficult.

Her premonition of trouble proved accurate, though not in the way she expected. Gabriel was barely a third of the way through his remarks when suddenly a fight broke out. Shouting epithets and inflammatory remarks, union members and a group of opposition supporters began trading punches. Women and children screamed. Blood began to flow.

With an alacrity that hinted they'd been tipped off in advance—if they hadn't actually engineered the brawl themselves—helmet-clad troopers of the Santista-controlled *policia* appeared with machine guns, dogs and clubs. Their usual enthusiasm for cracking heads and roughing up participants in the political process brutally in evidence, they began arresting people without regard to the part, if any, they'd played in the fracas. Several dark blue police wagons arrived to cart off to jail those who'd been taken into custody.

Abruptly the violence shifted direction and surged toward the podium. In Gabriel's split-second assessment of the situation, the disturbance and subsequent arrests were too much of a coincidence to be spontaneous. He was convinced the Santistas had masterminded them to discredit him. Meanwhile, Miranda's safety and well-being were at stake. They'd have to make a run for it.

His fingers bit into her arm. "Let's get out of here. Félix?"

The priest-activist was at his elbow. "This way..."

With their bodyguards, they managed to push through the shoving, combative mass of humanity to their car. As their driver negotiated the pedestrian-choked streets and they gained the main road out of town, Miranda's mouth was drawn with tension. Gabriel kept one arm positioned firmly about her shoulders.

The hotel where they planned to sleep that night was situated on the coast. A former luxury resort, it had catered almost exclusively to vacationing Americans before the 1968 revolution had turned Communist and La Caridad had been placed off-limits by the United States State Department. Now its clientele was mostly from South and Central America with a few intrepid Canadians and Europeans thrown in. Thanks to the uncertain political climate, it was more than half-empty when they arrived.

Now that they were engaged, Gabriel felt free to ask for adjoining rooms. Citing exhaustion and a need to unwind from the day's events, Miranda retired early. She'd barely managed to remove her outer clothing, shoes and stockings when Gabriel walked in and locked the door behind him.

About to slither out of her slip before an ornate dressing-table mirror that had been allowed to tarnish in the salt sea air, she paused to stare at his reflection with parted lips. Slowly she turned to face him.

God but she's lovely, Gabriel thought, feeling his blood race with anticipation. Every inch a woman and utterly desirable. Mine if I'm willing to forget her needs and push our engagement to the point of a wedding day. She'd been as courageous as any man in the face of the mob that afternoon, and he was very proud of her. If he could help it, she wouldn't be subjected to that kind of indignity again.

As she'd begun to get ready for bed, Miranda had been thinking parallel thoughts about Gabriel. Each time she let herself dwell on his vulnerability, she came face-to-face with the trauma of her father's death. The child she'd been so long ago wanted to run for cover and pretend they'd never met. Conversely, the woman she'd become yearned to seize the day—devour every passionate second allotted to them.

Though he'd kissed her hungrily the night before, after she'd completed her call to Fort Lauderdale, they hadn't made love. She'd gladly have put up with cramped quarters—offered herself to him on a desk instead of a bed and counted the discomfort a small price to pay. Yet neither of them had felt free to indulge themselves.

There'd been too many people about. In addition to Raquelita and Gabriel's housekeeper, both of whom hadn't been going anywhere, Angél and Félix had lingered interminably, talking about campaign plans. So had Josefina, who'd had a different reason: she'd been waiting to drive Miranda back to her house for the night. With its close proximity to the terrace and the likelihood his daughter would pop in at any moment to say good-night, Gabriel's little office hadn't been a very private place.

Now he was aching for her. He didn't try to hide it. Knowing him as she did, she guessed the day's kaleidoscope of events had exacerbated his need. There wasn't much doubt that their physical reunion, the first since their tryst at the ruined sugar mill, would be hard and swift.

Mad for him now, she went weak with anticipation. "I want you," she whispered. "In me. So deep..."

It was what he wanted, too, with a fervor that threatened to carry him away. Though they were engaged, they hadn't made an irrevocable commitment. She might not always be there for him. Unwilling to waste precious seconds, he didn't answer her in words. Instead, he dragged her slip's thin straps off her shoulders and down her arms. Its bodice followed within seconds, the lace cups skimming her nipples as he pushed it down to her waist.

The thought of being fully naked for his pleasure while he was still in street clothes prodded her to a fever pitch. As he lifted her breasts so that their fullness was exaggerated, and massaged their rosy peaks with his thumbs, she finished taking off the slip and its matching panties herself. Sharp knives of longing were piercing her to the quick.

Half-dizzy with anticipation, she let him ease her down to a sitting position on the edge of the bed. When he knelt between her legs to suckle her, she meshed her fingers in his thick, dark hair and wrapped her legs around him.

Taking first one nipple and then the other into his mouth, Gabriel licked and tugged as if he would devour her. The sensations he aroused were almost too exquisite to bear.

"Please . . . come inside me," she begged.

Before dawn, he'd be forced to leave her for convention's sake. She'd wake up alone. In the time they had, he'd devote himself to her utter abandonment.

As he stood to strip off his things and assume protection, Miranda sank back against the mattress. Her knees spread apart like wings and her feet firmly planted on the threadbare carpet, she invited him.

He was big and heavy, ready for her. A little moan escaped her when he knelt in her embrace again and thrust deep.

She longed to feel him even deeper. Whenever he filled her, the hidden throbbing drove her wild.

"Gabriel . . ." she pleaded. "I want . . ."

He already knew. Inserting his hands between her and the spread and grasping hold of her buttocks, he positioned her even more blatantly against him.

Chapter 13

Gabriel and Miranda's hectic, seemingly unending schedule had begun to take its toll several weeks later when he and Miranda returned to Playa Alta, the coastal city where they'd made love so passionately twenty-four hours after announcing their engagement.

Playa Alta and its sister cities of Playa Chica and El Pambril had long been a focus of mob-controlled gambling. Prior to 1968, the lucrative table games of blackjack, roulette and poker had enjoyed the protection of the government in exchange for a healthy cut of the take. Though they'd gone underground after the Santista revolution turned Communist, the casino owners continued to flourish with many of the same backers. The money men behind the scenes had simply bribed the new regime.

Through their international Mafia connections, supposedly, aging government leader Octavio Blas and his cohorts in Panama continued to make a handsome profit from gambling. The resort towns of La Caridad's Caribbean coast were still considered a Blas stronghold, and therefore somewhat dangerous.

Though she loved Gabriel more every day, Miranda had begun to chafe at the hard logistics of his campaign. They were always on the move, surrounded by a crowd of people. Wherever they turned, it seemed, there was someone underfoot. Too often, meetings and planning sessions extended far into the night.

True, on the concert circuit with its constant travel, daily practice and grueling performance time, she'd become inured to long hours and living out of a suitcase. But she wasn't used to serving as an adjunct to someone else's ambition, even if that someone was Gabriel. Her realization that the goal he hoped to achieve had come to mean a great deal to her only made her conflicting emotions about the part she was destined to play more difficult to resolve.

She reflected that she might feel a little less fractious and isolated if he, Félix and the others encouraged her to get more involved in policy-making. So far they hadn't, though they'd mentioned she was welcome to sit in whenever brainstorming sessions were held.

As it had gradually become defined, her role seemed limited to that of patron saint and consort. By her presence at Gabriel's side, she knew, she transformed him into a settled, family man in a way that being the single father of a twelve-year-old daughter never could. She also put the stamp of Juan's blessing on his activities.

From the standpoint of making a contribution that came from her *as herself*, neither role qualified. Essentially, she concluded, she was window dressing. Aside from making brief speeches linking Gabriel and his program for the country with her father's ideals, she didn't have any real function.

She was also edgy over her neglect of the violin. Though she tried to deny it, telling herself Gabriel's presence in her life ought to be enough, she missed the discipline of her music. He came first with her now, and she considered that appropriate. Still, the violin was food and drink to her, part of the rhythm of her breath.

Though it was their second visit to Playa Alta, Miranda had never really seen the place. At loose ends the morning after their arrival while Gabriel was closeted with party leaders from the surrounding area, she decided to go for a walk.

Donning dark glasses and a scarf, she slipped out of the hotel without telling anyone. In doing so, she felt a stab of guilt. Gabriel had made her promise she'd take an aide or bodyguard with her wherever she went, but she didn't really see the necessity. Unlike him, she wasn't the object of threats. She wanted some time alone with her thoughts.

Leaving the hotel compound and turning south along the boat harbor, she surveyed scattered cabañas, fast-food stands and a small boat-and-ski-rental concession without really seeing them as she mulled the situation over in her head.

What kind of life will it be if we marry and I end up abandoning the violin altogether to make room in my life for the ceremonial functions of being La Caridad's first lady? she asked herself.

The position would be an honor, she knew. In it, she'd have an opportunity to do a great deal of good for the country of her birth. Plus she'd have Gabriel in her bed every night. They could have children. Grow old together. Yet, wonderful as that prospect sounded, she feared her music would be a plaintive, jealous ghost.

Something else was bothering her, too. Though he was passionate and protective of her, Gabriel continued to shy away from any mention of love. He'd never given her so much as a glimpse of his thoughts in that regard. Is it his memory of Raquel with her excesses and infidelities that keeps his heart locked behind a fortress gate? she wondered. Or is that just how he is? Will he ever unbend and learn to care for me the way I care for him?

Absorbed in the complexities of her relationship, Miranda didn't realize that, as she'd set out on her walk, she'd made a very bad choice.

She didn't notice the men in a nondescript sedan who had slowed their forward progress and begun to follow her.

At the hotel, Gabriel's meeting was breaking up. He had half an hour before the next one was scheduled to get under way—enough time to drink a cup of heavily sweetened *café con leche* and talk with Miranda about a speech and two other appearances he'd tentatively promised she would make in Granja over the next few days.

If she agreed, she'd be delivering the speech that evening. A conflict had arisen involving Javier Fuentes, his vice-presidential candidate, and on the spur of the moment he'd suggested Miranda take Fuentes's place. He hoped she wouldn't mind too much. She did so much for him already. He really should have asked her first.

The trip would necessitate her being gone through part of the weekend. Though he wasn't happy about it, he thought she might enjoy doing some campaigning on her own. For several days running, he'd noted her restlessness. He realized her talents weren't being fully utilized.

"Where's Miranda?" he asked, pouring coffee for himself from a pot they kept going in their suite's sitting room and stirring in cream and sugar.

Félix shrugged. "She was here just a few minutes ago."

"If you're looking for Señorita Burton, I think she went out," a young activist from Partero said.

Gabriel frowned. "I hope somebody went with her."

Regretfully the young man shook his head. "I don't think so, Señor Sánchez. I didn't see anyone."

Gabriel's instincts told him the situation was a highly volatile one. With so many opposition strongmen about, anything could happen. Miranda was his fiancée and Juan's daughter. She was a major asset to the Liberal-Labor campaign. As such, she was a plum ripe for the picking. If the Blas underground got hold of her, she might never be seen nor heard from again.

Alarmed and furious with her for disregarding the precautions he'd imposed, he ordered his next meeting put on hold. "Félix, come with me," he rapped out. "You, Jorge, call Eduardo and have him bring the car around."

The ancient but well-preserved Oldsmobile they used for their travels was getting an oil change. Eduardo, who did double duty as a bodyguard and driver, rustled up a jeep.

"Which way?" he asked as they piled in.

Any instructions he gave would have to be based on a guess. Away from the hotels, Gabriel thought. By the yacht basin.

"South along the harbor," he said, fear warring with anger in his gut as they took off with a screech of tires from the hotel's porte cochere.

They drove perhaps three-quarters of a mile without seeing any sign of Miranda. Gabriel was on the verge of ordering Eduardo to turn around when he spotted the yellow marker of her dress. She was still some distance ahead of them, walking briskly into the wind. To his horror, a sedan with missing license plates was tailing her. The lack of an identification tag was a typical Blas trademark.

"There she is!" he said urgently.

As they gained on the sedan, eating up the distance that separated them from it with a burst of speed, they could make out its passengers: three rough-looking men in casual clothes, young to middle-aged. Gabriel had absolutely no doubt the three were Blas enforcers.

Abruptly, the driver of the sedan became aware of their presence. Glancing at Gabriel's jeep in his rearview mirror, he barked something over his shoulder. His *compañero* in the back seat turned around to look at them. A moment later he was pointing what looked like a gun in their direction.

"*Duck!*" Félix yelled as Eduardo swerved to the left, narrowly missing a vegetable truck that was bearing down on them.

Wildly inaccurate, the burst of gunfire intended for them spattered in the dust. It didn't look as if there would be another. Foiled in what would almost certainly have been an impromptu attempt to abduct Miranda or rough her up, the men who'd been following her drove away at a high rate of speed.

Painfully aware of what had taken place though she'd been lost in thought just a few seconds earlier, Miranda cowered by a sail maker's shack. I could have been shot or kidnapped, she realized, trembling. Because of me, Gabriel, Félix and Eduardo could have been killed.

The jeep skidded to a halt beside her. Not waiting for it to stop, Gabriel jumped out. Roughly he grabbed hold of Miranda's arms.

"Just what in hell do you think you were doing, going off by yourself that way?" he demanded. "You could have been taken hostage. Instead of trying to win freedom and justice for the people of La Caridad, we could have found ourselves negotiating for your release... making God knows what kind of concession!"

Shaken, furious with Gabriel for speaking to her that way in front of Félix and Eduardo and humiliated by her own bad judgment, Miranda didn't answer as he bundled her into the jeep. She felt as if a fist had plowed into the softest part of her stomach. To think that Gabriel was more concerned about damage to his campaign than he was about her! Yet that was how it seemed. Somehow she managed to control the quivering of her lower lip.

Backing up, Eduardo turned the jeep around. I don't belong here in La Caridad, Miranda thought miserably, shrinking from Gabriel's touch. She felt alienated and alone. A liability. Maybe she *should* go back to the United States.

The thought let loose a hornets' nest of unpleasant emotions. Staring at the back of Félix's head and refusing to look at Gabriel, she admitted to herself how little she wanted to see or speak to her parents—especially Célia. I'm not sure I'll be able to stand it if she's been right all along, she thought.

To his chagrin, Gabriel realized how overbearing he'd been. Like Miranda, he was still very angry and upset.

But he'd calmed down sufficiently to know recriminations would have a negative effect. What she needed from him at the moment was comfort.

Awkwardly he tried to think of a way to give it to her. On their return to the hotel, they wouldn't have a prayer of being alone. Several committees working on election day strategy had taken over their rooms. Meanwhile, if Miranda agreed to substitute for Javier Fuentes in Granja, she'd be leaving that afternoon. They'd be apart for several days.

With a little flourish that was characteristic of him, Eduardo drew up in front of the hotel's main entrance. Gabriel turned to Félix.

"Miranda and I have to talk," he said. "Would you go upstairs and make my apologies? We'll be back in a little while."

For once, Félix didn't quiz him about his intentions. Nonchalant as usual, Eduardo accepted his new orders as if he were called on to chauffeur a sight-seeing expedition every day.

Soon they were driving via a steep, sinuously winding but paved road into the residential foothills east of Playa Alta's harbor. From the heights, the view of red tile roofs, blooming flamboyant trees and the slender masts of sailing craft riding at anchor in the aqua-and-lapis Caribbean was breathtaking.

"Here?" Eduardo asked, slowing as they approached a *mirador* with room to park beside a planting of date palms and a low stone balustrade.

Gabriel nodded. "Mind giving us a few minutes alone?"

Since he'd ushered her into the jeep, Miranda hadn't said a word. Her gaze seemed to be focused somewhere in the middle distance, between the beach with its aging luxury hotels and a freighter out in the channel that appeared to be making for Puerto Rico.

Turning off the ignition and getting out of the jeep, Eduardo sauntered over to the balustrade and lit a cigarette. As soon as he was out of earshot, Gabriel turned to Miranda.

"Will you forgive me?" he said bluntly, catching hold of her hands. "I know I acted like a jackass back there. And I'm sorry. It's just that I was so worried about you...."

Don't you mean your campaign? Miranda wanted to retort. And the inconvenience I might have caused by being hurt or kidnapped? So far, she'd been able to stop herself from crying. Now, tears were stinging her eyelids, threatening to spill.

Gabriel could almost read her thoughts. "If anything had happened to you, winning this election would be a hollow triumph," he said. "Though I may not always show it, your safety and well-being are of the utmost importance to me. I lost control when I saw those hoodlums following you."

To her knowledge, he'd never lied to her. On the contrary, he'd spoken the truth, even when it wasn't what she'd wanted to hear. Maybe he *did* care, a little, in the way she wanted him to.

"Oh, Gabriel..."

"Come here, *chiquita*. Let me hold you." Sensing her resistance had faltered, he gathered her into his arms.

His favorite pet name for Raquelita, *chiquita* meant "little one." Abandoning her anger, Miranda hid her face against his chest.

"I didn't mean to cause so much trouble," she whispered. "It's just that I needed a little time to myself. I feel so pressured sometimes. As if we never have a private moment. And, at the same time, left out...more of a liability than an asset. I don't want my sole function to be filling a slot marked Juan's daughter. Or Gabriel Sánchez's fiancée. If I'm going to be part of changing La Caridad, I want to make a genuine contribution...."

Gabriel's grip on her tightened. "Ah, sweetheart. You have. You are...to the extent I've let you. I promise, things are going to change for the better. From now on, you'll be my full partner in what we're trying to do."

She couldn't be, of course. Not really. He was the one his supporters hoped the voters would choose. If they did, he alone would be responsible to them. But if she *could* put her talent to better use...

"I want you in on the planning sessions, the decision making," he was saying. "As for being a liability... our rooms at the hotel are occupied with meetings right now, or I'd show you just how much of a liability I consider you."

At his words, the last of the sadness that had threatened to engulf her dissipated. Gabriel's promise of a more important role had helped to vanquish it. So had the fact that he wanted to make love to her. Deep down, she still worried that physical intimacy was the only commitment he was prepared to make. But it was what she wanted, too. She wanted it very much.

"They won't be occupied tonight," she said.

To her astonishment, Gabriel swore. In his eagerness to set things straight with her, he'd almost forgotten.

"You're going to throttle me, *querida*," he admitted. "But I promised you'd fill in for Javier in Granja tonight, and attend some meetings there on his behalf tomorrow and Saturday. If I spoke out of turn, we can call and cancel. It won't be the end of the world."

* * *

She decided to go, though she didn't want to be separated from him so soon after the incident at the waterfront. But then, how could she refuse? She'd complained she wanted more involvement. In Granja she'd be standing in for Gabriel's vice-presidential candidate.

Félix and a bodyguard accompanied her. To her surprise, the trip restored a large part of her perspective. The audience she addressed was almost exclusively composed of Juan's *guajiros* and they gave her an electrifying welcome. Responding to it, she gave the speech of her life—one that called into full play the talent she'd exercised for the first time on Josefina's balcony the morning after her arrival in La Caridad.

The high it imparted carried over into the meetings that followed. Even Félix commented on her effectiveness. She began to realize that, while it might not be as profound as her musical ability, her talent for speech making and politics was considerable. She was Juan's daughter, after all. No doubt she'd inherited it from him.

Somehow, Gabriel and I will work things out, she thought as she, Félix and the bodyguard assigned to them drove to Reunión Saturday afternoon to rejoin Gabriel. When the campaign's over, I'll have time to practice again. In the meantime, I want to do more speech making. Expand my involvement with the farm workers and laborers. Maybe even visit some schools and hospitals. Besides giving the campaign feedback from a different segment of the population, she believed, such visits would net additional publicity on Cariño television.

Being in Reunión again evoked memories in Miranda of the seedy hotel where Santista policemen had burst in on her and Gabriel. Miranda found herself yearning to see the place again, but there probably wouldn't be time. They were scheduled to reunite with Gabriel shortly before a parade honoring the city's traditional spring fiesta got under way.

Crowds and the inevitable vendors were already lining up along the broad, waterfront Avenida de la Revolución. As they approached the beginning of the parade route, they were greeted by the cacophony of several bands tuning up. Gabriel was waiting for them in a cream-colored, pre-1968 Cadillac convertible.

The realization that they'd be riding in an open car caused Miranda's worries to soar. How could they possibly keep Gabriel safe? With their own candidate running in opposition to him, the Santista-controlled police weren't likely to offer much help.

Campaign workers and sympathetic onlookers cheered when Miranda moved to the Cadillac and Gabriel took her in his arms. So focused on privacy when they'd parted just three days earlier, she didn't mind. Today she had other concerns, other thoughts. Gabriel was solid, real. And so precious to her. She'd go mad with grief if anything happened to him.

"Surely this can't be a good idea," she confided in his ear. "Like Playa Alta, Reunión has a strong Blas element."

Recent polls had shown Gabriel pulling ahead. With Miranda back at his side and the election just a few weeks away, he felt euphoric, as if he led a charmed existence. Releasing her, he threaded one arm about her waist.

"Nothing can touch us, *querida,* now that we're together again," he responded. "With God's help, we'll win. And for the first time in recent memory, the people of La Caridad will have democracy... a government they can call their own."

For Miranda, the parade passed in a blur of color and sound and light. Incredible as it might seem, in a city where once they'd been forced to remain anonymous if she was to escape Santista clutches, they were being welcomed. Even acclaimed. Though her vigilance on Gabriel's behalf didn't slacken, pride was uppermost.

It's conceivable we could carry this off, she thought in amazement, catching Gabriel's eye and sharing his exhilaration for a moment before turning again to wave at bystanders. His dream could truly be realized. And a people liberated.

Chapter 14

Following a rainstorm that had passed in the night, election day dawned breezy and clear. It was the kind of unbelievably perfect morning when the air is like crystal. Every palm frond and leaf was clean-washed and licked with light. Even the water was a study in brilliance. As Gabriel, Miranda and the others drove to Cinco so that Gabriel and Josefina could vote in their home precinct, wavelets in the little harbor with its brown-sugar beach and colorful fishing craft appeared to be crosshatched with diamonds.

Voting early, just after the polls opened, Félix had driven to the capital to keep tabs on the election process there. In his absence, Manuel Roa accompanied Gabriel and his friends. Though neither was eligible to cast a ballot, both Raquelita and Miranda had accompanied him.

Since Miranda and Gabriel had announced their engagement, they'd spent very little time in Las Montañas, as the province was generally conceded to him. The opportunity for Miranda to deepen her acquaintance with Raquelita had been slim at best. Still, it seemed to her that the girl had begun to accept the idea of having a stepmother—perhaps even to discover some benefits in the situation. Before setting out from Las Brisas, where Miranda and Josefina had driven shortly after sunup, Raquelita had consulted her on which dress to wear.

"I want to look my best for Papa on his special day," she'd acknowledged shyly, noting Miranda's light blue summer frock. "Concepción, our housekeeper, says there'll be many reporters present. Is it true that blue photographs best on the television?"

From Gabriel's perspective, the morning seemed hyperreal. With the campaign over, he was at loose ends, tentatively balanced between the past and a future that hadn't yet revealed itself. Essentially his life was up for grabs. Its pieces were poised to fall in one of two patterns, either of which would be vastly different in texture and content from the struggle he'd just waged.

When the election results were in, he'd be a farmer—or he'd be president. There was no in-between. However things turned out, he feared, he stood to lose the lush, fine-boned woman with freckles like gold dust who had ended the drought of passion in his life and given him at long last the feeling that he wasn't alone.

Over the long term, he believed, she'd never be happy buried amid the somnolent cane fields and copra plantations of Las Montañas or as the wife of *el presidente,* with all the social engagements and stress that entailed. Neither option called into play her incredible musical talent. It wasn't every woman who could coax the song of angels from a violin.

He wasn't ready to give her up, though it would probably come to that, because he didn't want to hurt her or fail at marriage again. First he needed more nights in her arms. While they were still together, he could go on pretending La Caridad wasn't just an episode to her, that she'd always be there for him. Without calculating the gesture, he laced his fingers through hers—hollow to hollow so that each hand protected the other's vulnerabilities.

Cinco's modest cream-and-ocher town hall, which bore only a trace of the Colonial splendor that marked so many Cariño public buildings in the larger towns and cities, was the designated polling place. They piled out of the car like a family, though if the suspicions Gabriel had voiced about Raquelita's parentage were correct, only he and Josefina were connected by a blood relationship. As his housekeeper had predicted, a swarm of reporters, photographers and television cameramen were waiting for them.

"¡Señor Sánchez!" they shouted, attempting to elbow his security personnel aside in their effort to get close to him. "Any predictions about how the voting will go? What about the United Nations poll watchers you requested? Do you think they'll be able to keep the opposition from stealing the election?"

It was a loaded question—one that had concerned them for weeks. In addition to the U.N. election task force, which counted a former United States president among its members and had finally agreed to oversee the balloting, they'd assembled their own army of poll watchers. Tough-minded and courageous, several hundred volunteers had fanned out to designated areas to help guard against vote fraud and intimidation.

Throughout the day, Gabriel would be getting phone reports from them.

Smiling and expressing confidence, both in the U.N. team and his own prospects, Gabriel ushered their little group inside. Curtained voting booths had been set up inside the scrubbed and flag-draped council room, where as recently as a week earlier the Santista-appointed *alcalde* of Cinco had met with his so-called advisers in a travesty of the democratic process.

All three booths were occupied. Declining to take precedence over the long line of prospective voters though the opportunity was offered them, Manuel, Gabriel and Josefina took their place at the rear, where they chatted with the people ahead of them. Well-known and liked in Las Montañas, aunt, nephew and neighbor had known most of them for years.

More people entered to shake Gabriel's hand and wish him luck. At last it was his group's turn to vote. He indicated with a nod that Manuel and Josefina should vote first. Finally, while they, Miranda and Raquelita waited, he ducked into one of the booths and filled out his own copy of the standard paper ballot, which included the names of candidates for La Caridad's Cortes, or parliament, as well as those for the island country's top offices.

When he emerged, charismatic and energetic-looking in his pale gray suit, light blue shirt and tie, he hugged his daughter and gave the victory sign. He, Miranda and Raquelita were videotaped and photographed with their arms about one another.

As she smiled for the battery of cameras, Miranda couldn't help wondering if Célia and Tom Burton would see the result on the evening news at their home in Florida. If they did, she imagined, they'd commiserate with each other. Though she'd written them several times since their ill-fated phone conversation the day she and Gabriel announced their engagement, they hadn't answered her.

If Gabriel lost, they'd expect her to come home. And if he won? She couldn't predict what their reaction would be. Doubtless it would be the same. She only wished she knew what Gabriel wanted.

After pausing to field a few additional questions from reporters and thank local well-wishers for their support, they drove back to Las Brisas to wait. The campaign was over. Now the voters would have their say.

Around 1:00 p.m. Concepción brought out a light lunch to the terrace and they picked at it, talking little and eating even less. Tall cumulus clouds that resembled white irises in shape bloomed on the horizon. Inexorably, the breakers rolled to shore—wedding veils thinning to transparency on the sand, as Gabriel had once suggested.

One by one, the other members of the original La Cábala group who weren't involved in poll watching arrived to wait with Gabriel. Somebody rolled out a portable television, complete with extension cord. Somebody else mixed up a batch of *sangria*. Now and then the phone rang. Aside from two incidents of violence, the election seemed to be going well.

It was still too early to tell what the final outcome would be. Though the Liberal-Labor Party was conducting its own exit poll, so far no clear pattern had emerged. As for an official count, La Caridad lacked the modern vote-tabulation equipment that was readily available in the United States. Ballots had to be trucked to the capital and counted by hand. Gabriel had warned the process might take several days.

Increasingly restless with so many loose ends in her personal life on the verge of being tied up, Miranda excused herself and went into the house. After using the quaint upstairs bathroom with its claw-footed tub and old-fashioned, column-style sink to powder her nose, she didn't return to the terrace right away. Except for Concepción, who was stirring something garlicky and aromatic in the kitchen, the house was deserted. Wondering if she'd ever actually live there, Miranda had an irresistible urge to look around.

She got no farther than Gabriel's room. Large and sparingly furnished, it had floor-to-ceiling French doors that opened onto a balcony overlooking the water. With its wide-planked mahogany floor, cream-colored walls and heavy, plain four-poster and dressing table, it was totally lacking a woman's touch. There's no trace of Raquel left, Miranda thought. And no hint that another woman might someday take her place. I wonder if we'll ever sleep here together as husband and wife—wake to make love beneath the swath of mosquito netting in the privacy of a room that belongs to both of us, then shower and join Raquelita for breakfast.

With only moderate success, she tried to picture her perfume bottles on Gabriel's dresser, her negligees and sheer summer dresses hanging beside his clothes in the tall, mirrored wardrobes that lined his adjoining dressing rooms. Like dwelling on the possibility that he might be La Caridad's new president in a matter of hours, it seemed a risky exercise in conjecture.

"Miranda?"

It was Gabriel's voice, snatching her from her reverie as he called her from the foot of the stairs.

"Be right with you," she answered, a trifle self-consciously.

Gabriel didn't appear to notice that she'd been in his room. "Come walk on the beach with me awhile," he said, holding out his hand. "I need something to do. The waiting is getting under my skin."

Evening dragged on, a compendium of the day's anxieties and speculation, though on the surface everyone was relaxed and affable. When 11:00 p.m. rolled around, Gabriel insisted Raquelita go to bed. Worn out from all the excitement, she'd already been up an hour past her usual bedtime. Nobody else made a move to leave. Without exception, the friends, relatives and political cronies who had gathered to wait out the results with Gabriel were still pacing, snacking, making predictions and watching what returns were available on television when Félix called shortly after midnight.

Answering on the second ring, Manuel listened for a moment. Then, "He wants to speak to you," he said, motioning to Gabriel and holding out the receiver.

A number of meaningful glances were exchanged. As expected, the provinces of Las Montañas and Enredadera seemed to be in Gabriel's pocket. Despite his team's best efforts, however, Las Olas appeared to be going for the Blas candidate. Still in doubt were Río Centro, with its volatile mix of students, professionals and laborers and El Panal, the traditional Communist-Labor stronghold where Miranda had campaigned most extensively. Either could swing the balance in Gabriel's favor. Perhaps some new figures had been released.

"This could be it," Josefina whispered.

"Hello?" Gabriel said.

As usual, Félix was terse and to the point. But he couldn't hide his jubilation.

"It's looking good," he advised. "After being touch and go, El Panal is headed into your column. The Cariño correspondent from ABS-TV just phoned and tipped us his network is going to call the victory for you. Our exit polls agree, though the count is still only twenty-three percent complete. I think you should drive down here as soon as possible in order to be on hand when the final tally is in."

Though he'd been hopeful, even reasonably confident, Gabriel was stunned. Unless ABS, Félix and his own pollsters were wrong, it looked as if he'd been chosen to bear the burdens of a country. Was he equal to the task? Complex and steadfast enough to navigate the shark-filled waters that lay ahead? He'd committed to them long ago, but it would take time for him to get used to the responsibilities that were about to be thrust upon him.

"Apparently I'm it," he told his friends with a slightly dazed expression as he put down the phone. "One of the American networks is calling the election for us. And our pollsters agree. I don't know what to say except how grateful I am to each of you. It's been dangerous, difficult work, and you've risked your lives to do it. Because of you, La Caridad will be free. The fire we've started will go on burning...."

It was actually happening! With a whoop of joy, Manuel flung both arms around him. Tears running down her weathered cheeks, Josefina did likewise. Jaime Roa, Manuel's oldest son, broke out several bottles of champagne. Soon everyone was hugging everyone else and proposing toasts. Caught up in Gabriel's embrace, Miranda felt as if her feet had ceased to touch the ground. I'm so proud of him, she thought, her own tears starting to flow. I've never loved him more than I do at this moment.

They decided to travel in a caravan to the capital after getting what sleep they could. With a drowsy Raquelita in tow and Eduardo driving, Gabriel called for Miranda and Josefina at the older woman's *finca* shortly after 5:00 a.m. From the shadows beneath his eyes in the subtle, predawn light, Miranda could tell that he'd barely shut them.

"Are you okay?" she asked as they exchanged a quick embrace.

Alone in the quiet hours, he'd longed to reach for her. And berated himself for her absence. If he'd followed Félix's advice and asked her to marry him right away, she might have said yes. They wouldn't be playing this hole-and-corner game. Yet the questions that had bothered him earlier still nudged at his consciousness. Soon, he and Miranda would have to talk.

"*Sí*, I'm fine," he answered. "Too wired, I guess, to feel the exhaustion much. I want to thank you in advance for being at my side today."

Gently Miranda smoothed his lapels. Since Félix's call, he'd been on a gratitude kick, as if he didn't deserve the honor that had been accorded him. "Where else do you think I'd want to be?" she asked.

They were mobbed by a cheering, ecstatic throng when they arrived at their campaign headquarters, Asunción's National Hotel. Increasingly charged up as they'd traveled southward, Gabriel seemed to enjoy the attention. Importuned repeatedly by the chant of *"¡Sánchez! ¡Sánchez!"* from the street beneath their windows, he stepped out onto the balcony and gave a fiery, off-the-cuff address. Though Miranda was worried about his safety, she had to admit the crowd's enthusiasm gave her goose bumps. Gabriel's promise to call a constitutional convention, made repeatedly throughout the campaign and stated again, drew the most applause.

Final results in the presidential race were announced at the Cortes late that afternoon, with several United Nations mediators looking on. As they'd been led to expect, Gabriel was La Caridad's new president—the youngest in the Caribbean basin.

At the news, the city exploded in a vast celebration that swept from the hotel to the Cortes steps and the gates of the presidential palace, where ousted strongman Leander Santos was said to be in seclusion. It looked as if the dancing and fireworks would go on all night.

"Remember in Reunión when the *policia* almost caught us?" Miranda asked Gabriel much later, when finally they were able to break away from a Liberal-Labor Party bash in the hotel ballroom and head upstairs.

He nodded. "It's as if that happened a hundred years ago."

There were several people in the corridor outside their rooms. Again they shook hands, accepted congratulations. Pausing outside Miranda's door, Gabriel unlocked it for her and gave her a good-night kiss. "Be with you shortly," he whispered. "I want to look in on Raquelita first." For the time being, his daughter was sharing a room with Josefina at the end of the hall.

Stepping into her own room and shutting the door behind her, Miranda managed to remove the jacket to her red linen suit before the phone rang. Surprised, because they'd asked the desk to hold all calls except for emergencies, she answered.

It was Célia, phoning from Fort Lauderdale.

"Baby... I've been trying to get you all day!" her mother exclaimed. "If you'll let me, I want to offer you and Gabriel Sánchez my congratulations. *And* my apologies. I was wrong about him and I freely admit it. He's managed to accomplish what Juan only set out to do."

Taken totally by surprise, Miranda sank onto the arm of a nearby chair for support. "Of course I forgive you, Mother," she said after a moment. "I was never angry at you and Daddy in the first place. Just... *sad*, I suppose, that you didn't approve of someone I care about."

Now that she'd decided to accept Miranda's involvement in Cariño politics and, apparently, her engagement to Gabriel as well, Célia characteristically went all the way.

"You can be proud of the help you gave him," she said with a ring of conviction in her voice. "I can't help but think it was one of the deciding factors. If we haven't burned our bridges, Tom and I would like to travel to La Caridad for the inauguration... *and* your wedding, of course, if you plan to hold it soon. In the meantime, now that it's relatively safe, I'd like to show Tom around the island."

Without realizing it, Célia had touched a nerve. Though Gabriel's future as La Caridad's new president was assured, Miranda was anything but certain when—or if—there would be a marriage ceremony.

"Speaking for Gabriel, we'd both be very pleased to have you present when he's sworn in," she replied, hedging as best she could. "As for the wedding, we've been rather busy. We haven't had time to set a date."

She'd just returned the receiver to its cradle when Gabriel entered from his room.

"Time for our celebration...yours and mine," he said with narrowed eyes, locking their connecting door and closing the shutters at her windows to cut the noise from the street. As he did so, more fireworks went off. Someone raised the chant, *"¡Sánchez! ¡Sánchez!"* yet again.

They'd had so little time alone in recent days. And she loved him so. Why couldn't he tell her he felt the same way, if that was how it was with him? Following his inauguration, he'd move into the presidential palace, taking Leander Santos's place. When that happened, what was she supposed to do? Rent a room at the National? Hang around until he had an evening free and was feeling amorous?

She hadn't bothered to switch on a lamp. With the shutters closed, the room was dark—awash in shadow. What little light there was illumined the milky curve of her upper bosom and caught the questions in her eyes.

Not knowing what those questions were, Gabriel couldn't answer them. He wasn't even sure if he was ready to ask several of his own. He only knew he couldn't bear to lose her yet.

If she had a small sadness, he'd erase it—comfort her with the most profound pleasure his body could give. For himself, he wanted to drink in the perfumed texture of her hair. Suck at her honeyed nipples. Lose himself in her depths. When he was sheathed in her, he felt as if nothing could separate them.

"Let me love you," he begged.

From their first incendiary kiss beneath the Cascade of the Angels, Miranda hadn't been able to refuse him anything. By the very act of wanting her he made her knees go weak. Stepping out of her skirt and peeling down her slip, she went into his arms like a blind woman.

"Sí, Gabriel," she whispered.

Scooping her up in his arms, he carried her to the bed. As the tumultuous celebration of his victory continued outside, she strove beneath him, lifting her hips and dragging forth his ecstasy before dissolving in her own culmination.

Motionless, they were absorbed in the peaceful flow of existence their release always brought. Warm and familiar, Gabriel's weight pressed her into the mattress. She loved to feel him that way—matching her length for length, partway in her still.

They were just getting started. Though it wasn't physically possible for them to maintain that state, Miranda wanted him in her all night. She knew Gabriel craved the same thing. Before dawn broke, they'd come as close to achieving it as they could.

The shadows had deepened and the commotion outside ebbed a little when at last he rolled off her and stretched out on his back, with his head against the pillows. After the previous night's lack of sleep and the momentous events of the past two days, he should have been tired. But he wasn't.

"Come here, *chiquita*," he said.

Like an experienced dancer who instinctively knows what move is being requested of her, she straddled his thighs. Her hair a tangled, fragrant cloud about her face and her breasts high and full in his hands as he kneaded them, she stroked him back to readiness.

Chapter 15

The hectic pace began anew. Instead of Gabriel campaigning from one end of La Caridad to the other, the country came to him—specifically to the temporary suite of offices he'd set up at the National Hotel. His election ratified, he was busy assembling a cabinet and meeting with his old enemies, the Santistas, to effect a transition. He also tried to get the jump on constitutional change by working with a blue-ribbon committee he'd appointed.

Any discussion of the future he and Miranda had officially pledged themselves to share seemed to get lost in the jumble of press conferences, consultations and meetings. Deeply involved as she was in his preparations to assume the nation's top office, she couldn't help but think about it now and then.

Did Gabriel expect to follow through on his proposal that they wed? Or was it inevitable that—over time—they'd drift apart, separated by the wedge of his responsibilities and her career? Already the latter was tugging at her, in the form of regular phone calls from her agent. So was the strong attachment she felt to the United States. If they married, would Gabriel view it as disloyalty when she spent time there, performing on the concert circuit and visiting friends and relatives?

She'd give up her career, even her citizenship, if that was the only way they could be together. But she didn't see why it should be necessary. She'd lived long enough to realize an important truth. Love enriched you. It didn't try to separate you from important parts of yourself.

At least the physical danger to Gabriel seemed to have lessened. She didn't know of any incidents or threats since he and Félix had intervened in what could easily have turned out to be her kidnapping by the Playa Alta boat harbor.

Gradually the strain of wondering how their relationship would work out began to tell. When she was alone, she had trouble falling asleep. She suffered from restless dreams. The week before Gabriel was to be sworn in as president, she decided they needed a break from each other. Maybe if she was absent for a few days, he'd miss her and think about setting a date.

Raquelita was feeling the pinch of his schedule, too. Happy for her father and extremely proud of him, she'd begun to mope a little as a result of losing him to so much public attention and acclaim.

With Gabriel's blessing, Miranda flew with Raquelita to meet Célia and Tom Burton in Puerto Rico, where they'd stopped over at the vacation villa of friends before continuing on to La Caridad. While she and Raquelita were there, she'd decided, they'd do some shopping. They both needed new clothes for the many functions and parties they'd be required to attend. In Cariño boutiques and department stores, the pickings were depressingly slim.

Because of the constraints on travel that had been imposed by the Santos regime, Raquelita had never been out of the country. As their plane circled over the pastel frieze of luxury hotels that rimmed Isla Verde Beach and landed at nearby San Juan International Airport, the twelve-year-old's excitement grew.

"Is there really a big choice of dresses in the stores here?" she asked, obviously thrilled with the chance to see unfamiliar sights and shop in a capitalist country—an actual possession of the United States.

"Dresses, shoes, jewelry...you name it," Miranda answered with an indulgent smile. "Your father is a very important man and you must do him proud. Among other things, that means a closet full of pretty new clothes."

The villa where the Burtons were staying was situated at Puerto del Rey, near Fajardo—part of a marina, shopping and condominium complex. It was owned by Jack and Carmen Fairchild, their best friends in Fort Lauderdale. Renting a car at the airport, Miranda drove into the city of San Juan first for an afternoon of shopping that catapulted Raquelita into ecstasy.

When at last they'd finished, with tired feet and a satisfactory heap of purchases lovingly nestled in tissue paper and designer shopping bags, they headed east on Route 3, parallel to famed Luquillo Beach. Célia, Tom and their friends were eagerly awaiting them. All four took to Raquelita at once, fussing over her as if she were already part of the Burton family.

It wasn't any secret to Miranda, as they relaxed over aperitifs on the Fairchilds' porch with its view of the marina, that her mother and stepfather were doing their best to mend fences. She tried to keep that in mind a few days later when, in a private conversation between the two of them, Célia pumped her about wedding plans.

Almost in the same breath, Miranda's mother worried aloud about her career. "No matter whom you choose to spend your life with, you can't abandon your music," she declared with authority. "I presume you'll be returning to the concert stage shortly after Gabriel Sánchez takes office—certainly after your marriage to him, whenever that takes place."

It's entirely possible I'll be returning to it on a full-time basis because there'll *be* no marriage, Miranda thought. But she couldn't make herself believe Gabriel wanted to end things. The bond that united them was too strong, too deep now to be easily broken. When they were together again, they'd have to talk—even if that meant setting their personal record straight on the eve of his swearing-in ceremony.

The afternoon before they were scheduled to fly back to Asunción, Miranda left Raquelita in Célia's care and drove in to Old San Juan to visit the Pablo Casals museum and have lunch with an old friend who lived in Puerto Rico. Settled comfortably at a corner table for a meal of Spanish-Caribbean cuisine, they concentrated on catching up with each other's lives.

Just as it always did whenever they were together, time got away from them. Finally the pair said reluctant goodbyes. Miranda wasn't thinking about anything in particular a few minutes later as she strolled toward her car, which was parked three-quarters of a block away.

Suddenly she gasped, unable to believe her eyes, and ducked into the alcove entrance of a shop she was passing. But the object of her amazement was real enough. There, emerging from a local hangout known as El Patio de Sam, was Gabriel's cousin, Angél. With him was one of the gangsters who'd shot at Gabriel and Félix the day she'd gone walking by the Playa Alta waterfront.

He and Angél *were* definitely together. There could be no mistake. As she watched, an envelope changed hands. The two men paused for an additional moment's conversation.

Abruptly, Gabriel's cousin bade his unsavory-looking companion farewell and started in her direction. *I can't let him see me,* Miranda thought. Hurriedly putting on her dark glasses, which with her unaccustomed chignon and the wide-brimmed hat she was wearing rendered her all but anonymous, she turned and stared into the shop window. A chill seized her as Angél's reflection brushed past hers.

Gabriel had continued to claim a spy had invaded their camp. Could it be that, while in Puerto Rico, she'd discovered the identity of the man who'd tipped off police they were staying in that questionable Reunión hotel? The informer who'd given opposition supporters advance details of their campaign schedule?

Angél has sold us out for money, she thought. She strongly suspected that was what the manila envelope had contained.

Shakily inserting the key to her rental car into the lock on the driver's door, Miranda realized how much his cousin's treachery would hurt the man she loved. Wounded herself, because she'd liked Angél and had trusted him, she shrank from having to tell Gabriel the truth. Though her feelings weren't strictly rational, she was vaguely afraid that being the bearer of bad news about someone he'd been close to all his life might cloud their relationship at a critical juncture. She decided to confide in Félix and let him do the dirty work. Thank heaven Raquelita wasn't with me this afternoon, she thought.

Miranda and Raquelita flew back to Asunción early the next morning. Tom and Célia Burton were to join them the following afternoon, in time for the inauguration ceremony. Miranda's Aunt Pilar, who would begin her journey in Mexico City, had to change planes in San Juan, and would arrive on the same flight as the Burtons.

Busy as he was, Gabriel wasn't able to meet the two at the airport. Instead, he was waiting for them with open arms back at the hotel.

"How are my best girls?" he asked, hugging them in tandem. "Raquelita, my angel, you look positively stunning. That's a new dress, isn't it? I take it some of the credit goes to Miranda for this."

He was so pleased to see them. And Raquelita was glowing with his praise. Miranda didn't have the heart—or the courage—to tell him about his cousin. She'd let Félix do it, the way she'd planned.

Her chance to talk privately to Félix came almost too quickly, when he called her aside to discuss the various formalities of the following afternoon.

"Could we go over this in your office, Félix?" she proposed, wishing she could forget the whole thing. "There's something else I want to talk to you about, too."

Ushering her into his cubbyhole of a converted hotel room, Félix crooked one brow. "What's this about?"

Succinctly Miranda described what she'd seen. Though his features were very grave, she got the strong impression Félix wasn't totally surprised. Perhaps he'd never quite trusted Angél. Whatever the case, she couldn't help thinking he had regrets. And it was true. If he'd had reservations and pursued them, they might have spared a great deal of risk.

"Well, that's it," she said with relief. "If you don't mind, I'd rather *you* tell Gabriel. As close as we are now, we met just a few months ago. He's known Angél all his life."

To her surprise, Félix gave her a swift, brotherly hug. "Don't worry, Miranda," he said. "I wish you felt free to tell Gabriel about this yourself. But I'll be glad to act as your intermediary. If I can lay my hands on some photos of known Blas gangsters, would you mind looking at them and trying to make an identification?"

Though the prospect wasn't a pleasant one, Miranda agreed to help. She'd just walked out of Félix's office when Alicia Camargo approached her.

"The doctor who showed you around that clinic you visited just before you went to Puerto Rico called," Alicia said. "He asked me to tell you the hospital in Miami has agreed to treat his young patient free of charge. All the boy needs is a plane ticket."

Setting aside her worries over Angél and the hurt Gabriel would feel when he found out about his cousin's treachery, Miranda focused on the children's clinic that had been sadly neglected during the Santos years. During her tour of the facility, a small boy with a rare bone disease had caught her attention.

According to the doctor who'd been charged with managing his case, there was no hope for little Juanito Alvarez if he remained in La Caridad. But with the new techniques and drugs available in the United States, he might have a chance.

Promising to see what she could do, she'd phoned a Miami contact of her stepfather's, who was on the board of a large hospital there, and requested assistance. Now that phone call had borne fruit. If a plane ticket was all that stood in the boy's way, Miranda would be happy to provide it.

Javier Fuentes's office was empty. Stepping inside, she used his phone to dial the clinic. When a nurse finally located the Alvarez boy's physician in one of the treatment rooms, he couldn't thank Miranda enough.

"You're so generous, Señorita Burton," he gushed. "I hope you know I'd have gladly paid Juanito's way. But I have six children of my own. And unlike my colleagues in the U.S., I make only a small government stipend...."

Jotting down the date Juanito's treatment was scheduled to begin, she ended the call and placed another to the airlines in order to make the child's reservation. As she was reciting her credit card number, she remembered that little Juanito was an orphan. He probably hadn't been on a plane before. And he had no one to travel with. Sick and afraid, he'd be shipped off to Miami with a placard around his neck.

There's no reason I can't accompany him myself, Miranda thought, since he won't be leaving until a week and a half after the inauguration. "Make that *two* tickets, with a second in my name," she told the reservations clerk. "I'll be traveling with the boy and returning the following day."

As she was correcting a possible mistake in her northbound reservations, she heard a faint click on the line. Phone connections in La Caridad were notoriously bad. When the click did not happen again, she didn't give the matter another thought.

Her call completed, Miranda unpacked and then joined Gabriel for a formal luncheon honoring his chosen cabinet members. Several toasts were proposed and a great deal of wine was drunk. With the inauguration to take place the following afternoon, everyone was in a festive mood, including Gabriel.

"I've missed you, *querida*," he whispered in her ear. "What would you say if tonight I proposed setting a date for our wedding?"

Was he serious? Or only teasing her? The moment he found out about Angél, she feared, his lighthearted mood would vanish.

Though she tried to respond, he wouldn't let her. "Hold that thought," he urged, keeping his voice low so they wouldn't be overheard. "Before we discuss this topic in any detail, I plan to put you in the proper frame of mind."

Miranda was in her room, writing a thank-you note to her parents' hosts in Puerto Rico, when Jaime Roa knocked. "Father Hill said to tell you he has the photographs," the handsome twenty-four-year-old reported when she invited him to enter. "He wondered if you'd mind coming downstairs."

Frowning, she put her writing materials away. Unless it had gained something in the telling, Félix's message sounded urgent. Her impression that something serious was in the wind only deepened when she presented herself in his cubicle of an office. A uniformed lieutenant of the National Police was there with him, leaning against a filing cabinet.

At Félix's request, Miranda took a seat and began to go through a stack of grainy, black-and-white photographs, which were encased in plastic sleeves. As she did so, she realized she was suffering an intense feeling of dread. Yet she couldn't identify any of the pictures. She'd almost reached the bottom of the pile when the pockmarked face of the man who'd been driving that day in Playa Alta and who had met with Angél in San Juan was suddenly staring back at her.

"That's him! I'm positive," she said, a sensation of fear and nausea rising in her throat.

Félix nodded, grim but satisfied. "Okay. Go on about your business and don't worry. I'll take care of it."

Miranda shuddered. She was unable to let go that easily. "Do you... know who he is?"

"The man's name," said Félix, "is Enrique Echevarria. He's a known assassin, suspected of several recent gangland-style killings in Panama City."

"You don't think..." Miranda could barely frame the thought that assailed her in words.

Félix supplied them. "That Angél would plot Gabriel's death? No, I don't think so. But Blas would. And Echevarria would do his best to carry out the old man's verdict. We'll have to look into this at once."

Miranda hugged herself, unable to speak.

"I do think Angél would sell information," Félix added. "Though it went underground during the Santos regime, gambling has continued to exist in La Caridad. Angél is a gambler. It wouldn't surprise me if he owes the Blas gang his skin, let alone his shirt."

Within minutes, Félix was facing Gabriel in his temporary office at the hotel. Explaining that Miranda felt awkward about broaching the news, he described the scene she'd stumbled across in Puerto Rico: Angél consorting with the enemy. He added that a few minutes earlier she'd identified Echevarria from photographs as one of the gangsters who'd followed her in Playa Alta.

At first, Gabriel didn't want to believe the truth. He'd known Angél since they were boys. But he couldn't avoid the truth, or the pain that accompanied it. With a moment's reflection, he had to admit the pieces fit.

"I've called in the *policia*," Félix added when Gabriel didn't speak. "Echevarria is a known assassin and we need their help on this. To my surprise, they've offered to search for him with something approaching enthusiasm."

Gabriel's former father-in-law, police commandante Hector Ruiz, had left the country a week earlier. Apparently the officers Félix had contacted were pragmatists who hoped to cement a working relationship with the new regime.

While Gabriel and Félix were talking with the police lieutenant, Miranda was huddled over a cup of strong, sweet coffee in the hotel coffee shop. Once again, Gabriel's life was in jeopardy. Maybe she'd be standing next to him when the shots rang out, just as she'd been playing in the dirt near Juan so many years ago. Frozen in horror, she'd see Gabriel fall. Watch his life's blood drain out of him. Maybe it would happen while he was swearing his oath of office. As if trying the unthinkable on for size, she imagined him crumpling at the podium.

"No... *no!* Please, God, I couldn't bear it!" she whispered, moving her lips as if uttering a preventive incantation.

Her panic increasing by the moment, she cast about desperately for ways to prevent the tragedy she was suddenly convinced was about to take place. We can't let him take the podium in Plaza República tomorrow, she thought. We'll have to hold the ceremony indoors, with a cordon of armed bodyguards around him. If they want their newly elected leader to stay alive, the Cariño people will have to watch his inauguration on television.

As Miranda sipped at the scalding coffee, which didn't seem to alleviate her chill, Gabriel was sending for Angél. When his cousin arrived, he asked Félix to leave the room. Though it was clear he'd have preferred to remain, the priest-activist complied without an argument. There was only a flicker of surprise and dismay in Angél's eyes as Gabriel leveled his charges without identifying their source.

When he fell silent, Angél shrugged. "*Sí*, it's true," he admitted. "I gave them information for money... mostly the money I owed them."

Gabriel studied him for a moment, a look of aversion on his face. "There's something I don't understand," he said at last, remembering a phone call he'd placed in January to Josefina's house. The call had been an attempt to locate Félix. Angél had answered. It had been to Angél that he'd delivered his message.

Caught, his cousin appeared relaxed, even nonchalant. "Ask," he suggested.

"You owed money to the Blas syndicate. But you informed on me to Santos as well, didn't you? You're the one who told them where to find us when Miranda and I were at that hotel in Reunión."

Angél's guilt looked back at him from eyes very like his own. "They offered me money," he said. "I *needed* money. If I didn't get it, Blas's apes would have broken my legs."

Gabriel felt sick. Miranda could have been raped or killed because I trusted my boyhood companion, he thought. "Both sides against the middle," he said fiercely. "Was that it?"

Angél nodded. To Gabriel's disgust, his cousin didn't seem to feel any shame or regret.

"Principle didn't enter into it," Angél said, as if explaining an equation to a child. "I was in a tight spot and I did what I had to do. Why should I let them savage me? To protect you, cousin? You who've always had everything you wanted... including the one woman who's truly appealed to me in years?"

He was referring to Miranda! How *dared* he? "Leave my fiancée out of this," Gabriel lashed back. "You put her in great danger. And if you think she has any sympathy for you, you're mistaken. She's the one who saw you in San Juan and informed on your activities."

For the first time, Angél was clearly stung. His eyes took on a dangerous glitter. "I wouldn't be so sure of *her* loyalty, either, if I were you, cousin," he retorted.

Though he'd tried to mold himself into a statesman, Gabriel couldn't always keep his passionate nature in check. Propelled as if by the force of nature, his fist connected with Angél's jaw. His cousin reeled backward, crashing into a chair and slamming against the wall. A trickle of blood was visible at one corner of his mouth.

"*That's* what I think of your filthy insinuations," Gabriel said, his chest heaving with the effort of regaining control. "Say what you will, I'll never believe Miranda's been unfaithful... certainly not when the accusation is leveled by a traitor like yourself!"

Being Angél, his cousin fought back with words. "Who said anything about infidelity?" he countered. "All I know is that she's about to leave you. Just this morning, she ordered a plane ticket to Miami. She plans to return to the States once you've taken office. Who can blame her? She's probably tired of taking a back seat to your pious crusade."

In response, Gabriel swore, stringing together epithets he hadn't used in years.

"If you don't believe me, call American Airlines," Angél persisted, dabbing at his mouth with his handkerchief. "Ask them if she has a Miami reservation." He named a date.

Gabriel felt as if he'd been punched in the stomach. Burdened with vast, new responsibilities and determined to make sure that, if he and Miranda married, it wouldn't turn out to be a mistake for either of them, he'd put off any mention of a wedding date until an hour or so earlier. What must Miranda have been thinking during these past weeks, he asked himself, suddenly seeing them from her point of view. That I'd forgotten about the whole thing? Yet he couldn't believe she'd bow out of his life without telling him first. As his last perfidious act, Angél was attempting to drive a wedge between them.

Gabriel's voice went cold. "You'll leave La Caridad at once. And you won't return. If you do, you'll be arrested and tried for conspiring to subvert the political process. Possibly for abetting an assassination attempt. Is that clear?"

After Angél was escorted out, Gabriel told Félix shortly that he didn't want to be disturbed. Grief-stricken over his cousin's treachery and angry that his relationship with Miranda had been dragged into their confrontation, he covered his face with his hands. Gradually, though he tried not to let them, doubts crept into his head. What his cousin had said about Miranda couldn't be true, could it? It wasn't hard to think of reasons she'd want to go. And Angél had seemed so sure of himself.

Maybe the whole damn world is full of traitors, Gabriel thought, longing for a punching bag to hit. Yet, though he hated himself for it, he looked up the American Airlines number and dialed it himself.

Announcing he was phoning for "Señorita Burton," Gabriel asked the ticket clerk to confirm Miranda's flight to Miami on the date Angél had mentioned. To his dismay, the cheerful agent read back the information from her computer just as Angél had given it to him. Devastated, Gabriel hung up without thanking her, thus missing the added details she started to volunteer about the time, date and number of Miranda's return flight.

What I first suspected is true, he thought in anguish, shutting his eyes. Miranda has no true sense of my mission. No staying power. All she cared about was the thrill, the revolutionary mystique. Now that most of that's behind us and the backbreaking work of putting this country on its feet is just beginning, she wants no part of it. The fact that he'd been forced to learn about her planned defection from Angél made him feel doubly betrayed.

Miranda didn't see Gabriel until dinner. As usual, they planned to take their evening meal with friends, members of his staff and political associates in one of the hotel's banquet rooms. Closeted with a special ambassador from the United States who'd arrived to talk with him about reestablishing diplomatic relations, he came to the table late.

Her insides churning with fear for his safety, she'd all but forgotten her earlier concern that he might be angry with her for informing on Angél. To her shock and dismay, as Gabriel took the chair next to hers, his demeanor was like ice. Answering her tentative greeting with a curt nod and speaking to her only in monosyllables, he refused to look in her direction.

With no idea of the misunderstanding Angél had caused, Miranda could come to only one conclusion: he was angry with her for carrying tales about his cousin. Damn his Latin pride, she thought. What did he expect me to do—hold my tongue? If I had, we wouldn't have known Echevarria is probably stalking him and wouldn't have taken preventive measures. She decided to confront him the minute they were alone.

It turned out to be something of a wait. Pushing back a plate of food he'd barely touched, he excused himself and walked out of the banquet room deep in conversation with Manuel. After returning to her room, Miranda read awhile. But it was useless to think she could distract herself that way. Her mind simply refused to concentrate. Ultimately she closed her book, a biography in Spanish of British composer Ralph Vaughan Williams, with the feeling she hadn't comprehended a word.

She was in her nightgown, seated before her dressing table to brush the tangles from her hair, when Gabriel entered. Glimpsing the look on his face in the mirror, she jumped up and turned to face him.

"What's wrong?" she asked. "You look terrible. Shouldn't I have told Félix about Angél? If I hadn't..."

She broke off, wincing, as Gabriel grasped her by the arms. His strong, capable fingers bit into her flesh.

"*Querido*,, please...you're hurting me!" she exclaimed.

Though he softened his grip, the expression on Gabriel's face didn't alter. With all the force of his being, he willed her to tell him the truth. *I could respect you if* you leveled with me, he thought bitterly. And keep on loving you, too, though we're fated to live in two different worlds.

It didn't appear that a confession would be forthcoming. Instead, she acted as if she didn't understand what he was talking about. His anger pushing past the limits of reason and civility, he lowered his head to bruise her mouth with a punishing kiss.

God help her, she thought, but he planned to make love to her without resolving anything. "No, Gabriel... not like this!" she pleaded when he gave her a chance to speak. "Making love in anger isn't loving. If you're upset with me, let's talk."

Struggling for control, he dropped her wrists. His temper was like a dangerous wild animal, temporarily collared but certain to make a break for it. He had to get out of the room before he did something he'd regret.

"Thanks to the choices you've made and haven't seen fit to discuss with me the time for talking is past," he said, his voice going cold and hard as obsidian.

Turning, he headed for the door.

Confused and upset though she was, Miranda wasn't willing to let their discussion end that way. "Gabriel, wait!" she exclaimed, running after him and catching his sleeve. "I don't understand!"

Grimacing, he shook off her touch. "The odds have been stacked against us from the beginning," he answered, his dark gaze drilling into hers. "Without honesty, they're insurmountable. Thanks to my confrontation with Angél, I've realized in time that we don't have a future together."

Chapter 16

Gabriel had gone. Weeping, Miranda flung herself across the bed. Out of the blue, he'd ended their relationship. She hadn't known it was possible to feel such pain.

None of what he'd said about honesty made any sense. She hadn't lied to him, just asked Félix to be her go-between. Yet apparently the business about Angél was the root of their troubles. What was I supposed to do—keep quiet about what I saw? she asked herself again as tears stained her pillow. If I had, we'd never have known about Echevarria and the likelihood of an assassination plot.

One thing was certain. At the moment, Gabriel was in no mood to listen to her. In the morning, she'd give him one last chance to explain. If he continued to refuse, she wouldn't have any choice. She'd probably regret the necessity of leaving La Caridad for the rest of her life. But she couldn't bear to stand on the inaugural platform at

Gabriel's side and endure the travesty of having him smile at her for the television cameras when she knew how he felt. If people remarked on her absence, he could tell them the truth. Or make up some excuse.

Though she was convinced it would be impossible, after a while she slept. Gabriel didn't try. Instead of remaining in his room, he went downstairs and called an unscheduled meeting with his vice president elect and several cabinet members. To their chagrin, it had run extremely late.

A short time after it broke up, Manuel found him stretched out on an old-fashioned velvet sofa in his office. His eyes were shut, his expression bleak.

"Come, *Presidente*," his old friend said, mistaking the reason for his mood. "We haven't left the task of looking for Echevarria to the police. If he tries something tomorrow, we're ready for him. But it's better if you don't sleep here. Doña Miranda will worry if you don't go upstairs."

Gabriel opened his eyes. It was clear from Manuel's comment that they hadn't fooled anyone with their adjoining but separate rooms. The greater my shame, then, he thought. "Let her worry," he replied.

Manuel was taken aback. He almost stuttered. "I... don't understand, *amigo*."

"You don't have to."

This wasn't the generous, loving man Manuel knew. "Is this about Angél?" he asked.

Gabriel shook his head. "Not really. He's just the one who told me what to expect."

Manuel had the expression of a man who knows he must tread carefully. "What did Angél say?" he asked in the most tentative of tones.

Gabriel grimaced. "You might as well know. Everyone will, soon enough. After the inauguration, Miranda plans to break our engagement and return to the States."

Manuel was dumbfounded. "I don't believe it," he said after a moment. "Just because your cousin—"

Upset and unaccustomed to baring his soul that way, Gabriel quickly lost patience. "Angél knew what plane she's planning to take. And on what day," he interrupted. "I checked with the airlines. For once my cousin was telling the truth."

Miranda awoke with puffy eyes and a sick feeling in the pit of her stomach. She flinched as the events of the previous evening came back to her in a little rush. As soon as possible, she had to confront Gabriel and demand an explanation. The inauguration ceremony would start at 2:00 p.m. Keenly aware she had family members arriving in advance of that time to help them celebrate, she bathed, dressed and hurried downstairs.

She found Gabriel in a breakfast meeting with his advisers. He didn't see her come in and, briefly, she was able to study him. He was haggard, unsmiling on what should have been one of the happiest, most triumphant days of his life despite their worries over the opposition hit man who was still on the lose.

As if he could feel her gaze on him, he looked up. Their eyes met. His were as hard as onyx. A moment later, he was looking away, dismissing her as if she didn't exist. Hot tears stinging her eyelids, she fled the room. Expecting it to be unoccupied, she ducked into Gabriel's office to compose herself.

Manuel was there, going through some papers. An impulse seized her. "May I speak to you in confidence?" she asked.

The older man's discomfort was plain. "Doña Miranda," he said at last, as if resigning himself to an awkward scene. "What can I do for you?"

Miranda hesitated. But she had to know the truth. "I beg you to tell me if you know the answer," she said. "Why is Gabriel so angry with me? Is it because I informed on Angél?"

Manuel's obvious embarrassment grew.

"I was afraid he'd feel compromised if I brought his cousin's activities to his attention myself," she explained, hoping irrationally that, if she could make Manuel understand, she could convince Gabriel. "That's why I asked Félix to tell him in my place. Gabriel and Angél were boys together. They've known each other all their lives, whereas Gabriel and I only go back a few months."

The more she said, the more confused Manuel seemed to become. It was as if she were speaking some language that didn't exist.

"What does Gabriel think I should have done?" Miranda asked in desperation. "Keep that sort of information to myself? If I had, the man I love might have been assassinated!"

Apparently her strong declaration of love for Gabriel decided him. "You mean... that's all there's to it?" he asked. "You're not breaking your engagement to him?"

She stared. "What on earth are you talking about?"

"Gabriel says Angél told him you were planning to leave him... go back to the States permanently after he takes office."

Stunned and furious that Gabriel would believe such a thing without hearing it from her lips, Miranda didn't connect his cousin's tale with her plan to help Juanito Alvarez. Nor did Manual mention Gabriel's call to American Airlines.

With a supreme effort, Miranda got control of herself. "Thank you, Manuel...you've been very helpful," she told him in a strained voice. "Apparently Gabriel doesn't plan to share his cousin's accusation with me...just to believe it. Perhaps I *should* go. Considering the way he feels, there's nothing left here for me anyway."

Miranda wasn't the sort of person to swallow that kind of insult. Gabriel's made a fool of me, she thought. From the outset, he had no intention of setting a wedding date. He just wanted to use me politically. Now that he's impaled his pride on his own mistrust, he's ready to throw me to the wolves.

Her fears for his safety subsumed by her anger, Miranda decided to leave before the inaugural festivities started. Gabriel could tell the press she was sick or something. Later the news of their breakup would have less impact.

It was essential she arrive in San Juan before her parents and Pilar took off for Asunción. She didn't dare phone them from the hotel for fear of being overheard.

In a furor to be gone, she raced upstairs. She didn't need clothes. Or luggage. Just two things—her violin, which had been gathering dust while she devoted herself to Gabriel, and her purse with its credit cards and American passport.

Realizing she'd be recognized unless she disguised herself, she put up her hair in a chignon and donned the hat and glasses she'd worn for her lunch in Puerto Rico.

For a fraction of a second, she hesitated, her gaze resting on the bed where, on so many occasions, she and Gabriel had slept lovingly together.

At least those occasions had *seemed* loving. Maybe they hadn't been. Maybe the closeness she'd felt had been wishful thinking. With a little wrench, she turned away. Fighting back fresh tears, she hurried down a rear stairway and hailed a cab.

In the hotel banquet room, the breakfast meeting was breaking up. Félix and Gabriel remained behind for a few moments to talk. It was there that Manual approached them. A careful man, usually wary of personal confrontation, he had a determined air. Behind wire-rimmed glasses, his eyes were flashing with conviction.

"Gabriel, my friend, I think you're making a colossal mistake," he said. "Miranda wasn't planning to leave you after the inauguration. She loves you. She told me as much, just a few minutes ago."

Gabriel's mouth closed in a hard, uncompromising line. "I don't need this from you, today of all days," he said.

Félix rested one hand on his shoulder. "Take it easy. Let's hear him out."

"She's very angry that you would think such a thing," Manuel continued, as if neither of them had spoken. "Considering her mood, anything might happen. She might actually *go.*"

Obviously amazed that there should be any question about Miranda's feelings and loyalty, Félix demanded a full accounting. Reluctantly, Gabriel gave him one. The priest-activist who'd been at his side throughout the campaign was aghast.

"Do you mean to say you believed your cousin without hearing Miranda's side of the story?" he demanded.

Gabriel didn't answer. His silence was response enough.

"From what I've been able to determine, Miranda cares deeply for you," Félix said. "If you have even a smattering of the sense God gave you, you'll find her and straighten this out right away...before you really *do* lose her."

With a painful jolt, Gabriel emerged from his waking nightmare. He was bathed in guilt and self-condemnation. *Of course* Félix was right. Angél had simply wanted to hurt him. As for the ticket the airline confirmed, there had to be a logical explanation.

For a moment, it was as if both his cousin and his late wife, Raquel, were beside him, laughing in his face. Angél's vengeful stab had found an easy target. Because of his treachery, and the pain Raquel had once caused him—a pain Gabriel had believed safely buried in the distant past—he'd been far too willing to believe Miranda uncommitted and selfish. In so doing, he'd wounded her deeply, maybe even lost the only woman he'd ever truly loved.

"God forgive me, but I've been a fool," he groaned, raking his fingers through his thick, dark hair. "I'm not fit to lead a country, let alone be Miranda's husband."

"Go to her," Félix advised. "Tell her how you feel. Miranda loves you. She knows, better than anyone, what kind of strain you've been under these past months, because she's shared it. You'll be able to make things right with her."

The swearing-in ceremony was just a few hours away. But Gabriel didn't think of that, or of the opposition hit man who was supposedly stalking him. Taking the stairs with their iron grillwork two at a time, he ran to Miranda's room, only to find it empty.

With a sinking feeling, he noticed her violin was missing from its usual place. But he didn't think she was off practicing somewhere. She'd hardly had time to touch the instrument since returning to La Caridad with him.

She's left me, he thought. *And I don't blame her. But that doesn't mean I intend to let her go without a fight.* Causing heads to turn, he raced back downstairs and called for his car and driver. A jeep with two armed bodyguards moved into position behind them as Eduardo threw the Oldsmobile into gear and they took off with a squeal of rubber for the airport.

At the ticket counter, Miranda had just learned there wouldn't be a flight to San Juan for several hours. First, the plane that would carry her parents and Pilar from Puerto Rico to La Caridad had to arrive and discharge its passengers. *Maybe if I call them,* she thought, glancing distractedly about for a public telephone.

Though she dialed the Marina del Rey villa several times, she kept getting a fast busy signal. Apparently all the long-distance circuits out of the country were already in use. Even if she could get through, she realized, her mother and stepfather had probably left for the airport.

If I wait and Gabriel decides to come after me, there could be an awful scene, she thought. *I don't want my family to be caught up in that. It would be too painful, too utterly humiliating.*

Casting about for an alternative, she fastened on the idea of a charter. If she couldn't engage a pilot, she'd fly the plane herself and pay someone to return it. Picking up the phone again, she dialed the charter service. The man who answered sounded sleepy.

"*Sí, señorita*, we have someone who can fly you to San Juan if you're willing to pay," he said. "Wait by the main entrance. I'll send someone around to pick you up."

Without a single hour's flight time to her credit in recent months and only a brief history as a licensed pilot, Miranda was relieved—doubly so when the charter manager agreed to put her fare on a credit card. Quickly her credit was checked out. M. L. Burton had a history of paying her bills. The name didn't excite any particular interest.

Gabriel was just a few minutes behind her. He wasn't recognized either as, in white polo shirt, tan slacks and dark glasses, he turned up at the airport ticket desk looking for her. Learning that a woman answering to Miranda's general description had been transported to the charter area by one of that company's employees, he jumped back into his car. They were off to the charter area like a shot.

Miranda's violin was already stowed aboard the charter plane, a red and white Piper Cub. Clasping her hat to her head with one hand to keep it from coming off in the breeze, she was about to get a hand up from the pilot when suddenly she realized the gravity of the situation. She was abandoning Gabriel when he was in danger of being shot by one of Octavio Blas's hoodlums, not to mention giving him up for good.

Dear God! she thought. I can't do that—no matter how angry he is at me. I *love* him. Even now he could be in danger. "I've changed my mind. I'm not going," she told the startled pilot. "Please, hand me back my violin. I'll be glad to pay you for any inconvenience I've caused."

Just then, a dark sedan lurched to a halt in front of the plane, effectively blocking its path to the runway. It was the Oldsmobile that had seen them through so many harrowing miles during the campaign. Seconds later, Gabriel emerged. A jeep with two armed men had halted in his wake.

"Do you know this man, *señorita?*" the pilot asked nervously. "Or shall I call for airport security?"

She didn't seem to hear. Striding toward her, Gabriel removed his glasses.

"*¡Presidente!*" the pilot greeted him in astonishment.

Briefly Gabriel acknowledged him. But he had eyes for only one person. "Please don't leave," he begged Miranda, by sheer force of will keeping himself from reaching for her. "No matter how I behaved last night and again this morning, I love you and trust you. Without your love, I'm lost."

How long had she been aching to hear those words? At least half of forever. Yet he hadn't even apologized. Miranda wanted to shake him, somehow to make him feel the pain she'd felt. What stopped her was the fact that she loved him, too—not just the hero, but the man who'd been under so much stress and taken so many burdens on his shoulders. I've never stopped, she thought. Not for a single second.

"I'm so furious with you," she answered with a little shake of her head.

Gabriel regarded her steadily. "You should be. I deserve it."

A small silence rested between them.

"Maybe I shouldn't admit it," she said. "But I changed my mind just now. I decided not to leave you. The truth is, I planned to come back and give you hell. If need be, to stand between you and any...any...would-be assassins...."

Her voice broke. If anything happened to him, she'd die. Tears were trembling on her lashes.

"Ah, *querida*...." he whispered.

A moment later, she was in his arms. Her hat twirling off in a gust of wind and the shoulder strap of her handbag slipping down her arm, Miranda let him crush her to the hard length of his body. For the first time, she felt it: the complete and utter bliss of knowing he belonged to her, and she to him. With Gabriel, she was home free at last. Only the fact that Enrique Echevarria was still on the loose cast a shadow.

They had things to discuss. Arrangements to work out. In the car, Gabriel's kisses on her mouth, her neck, her eyelids, prevented either of them from saying anything for several minutes.

At last. "I have no excuse for the way I behaved, my darling," he said as Eduardo whisked them past the colorful but tacky suburbs of Asunción toward the city center with its glistening modern buildings and wonderfully preserved Spanish Colonial district. "But I do want you to know what prompted it. With so much going on, I've felt terribly guilty for neglecting you. Angél played on that. When he said what he did, I was an easy mark."

Kissing the little groove beside his mouth, she snuggled closer. "It can't have been easy, finding out your cousin was a traitor."

"You're right. It wasn't."

"I don't see how you could have believed him, though."

Gabriel shook his head. "I don't, either, *mi amor*. I invite you to abandon me if I ever do it again."

Another kiss found its mark. But he still hadn't answered her question. A moment later, he did. Rueful at his bad judgment, Gabriel told her how he'd called the airport to confirm or refute Angél's accusation.

"At the time, the ticket clerk's reply seemed like airtight evidence," he said. "Now I realize there's been some mistake, though I still don't know what it is."

The truth of what had happened was dawning in Miranda's hazel eyes. "That part wasn't any mistake," she answered. "I am going...with Juanito Alvarez. But I'll be back the very next day!"

Gabriel frowned, thoroughly confused. "Who's Juanito Alvarez?"

Lovingly, Miranda explained. "We were so busy I forgot to tell you about it," she concluded.

Moved by her genuine, unassuming concern for a sick child, Gabriel hugged her close. If he'd looked for a million years, he couldn't have found a better first lady for La Caridad. Or a smarter, sexier woman to ease his soul. And she could play the violin like one of God's most talented archangels.

They'd have to talk about the violin. He didn't want her to give up her career.

The subject of his safety came up first. "Now that I have the right," Miranda whispered, tracing a pattern on the back of the tanned, capable hand that rested on her knee, "I'd like to say something. Unless Echevarria is caught and placed behind bars, I think we should curtail this afternoon's ceremony...namely, hold it indoors where you can receive adequate police protection. Like me, the people of La Caridad stand to lose a great deal if anything happens to you. With that in mind, they ought to be willing to watch you sworn in on television."

Gently, Gabriel explained that what she was suggesting wasn't possible. "Today marks a new start for La Caridad," he said. "In my opinion, its citizens have a right to see their new president sworn in firsthand. I hate to bring it up, but aren't you the same enticing woman who, that afternoon on the mountain ledge above the falls, told me any movement she joined had to have as its aim a free and open government, one that was accessible to *all* the people?"

Reluctantly, Miranda admitted she'd said something of the sort. At the moment, however, it wasn't principle she was concerned about. Rather, it was Gabriel. Now that she was sure of his love, she'd find it doubly difficult to lose him.

For the first time, she let him see the full extent of her fear. "Each time someone threatens you, I think of my father and imagine you bleeding to death in the dirt the way he did," she confessed with a little shudder. "What worries me most isn't the assassin we know about, like Echevarria. It's the one we don't. Juan didn't expect to meet his maker that day in Batey Venus. He didn't have the slightest inkling he was in danger."

Kissing her forehead, Gabriel admitted she had a right to worry. "It's sensible to be afraid," he said. "And understandable, considering what happened to your father. But I can't spend my life in hiding, even for you, *querida*. If I did, the opposition would win by default. Insofar as my office will permit, we're going to *live*."

She hadn't quite given up on her plan for him to take office in the Cortes chamber. But she was wavering. "And that means?" she asked.

"Getting married as soon as possible, if you'll have me. Enjoying to the fullest the incomparable blessing of being alive in this world together."

Of course she'd have him. Had he ever entertained the slightest doubt? Kissing his mouth, she told him as much. Yet her fear persisted. Because of the mission Gabriel had undertaken, it would be an inevitable part of loving him. Thanks to the tragedy she'd witnessed as a child and the depth of her feelings, the price would be steep. Life without him was out of the question.

"I'll... do my best to live with the situation," she vowed as their car entered the city's historical district.

In return, Gabriel promised not to take any unnecessary risks. "As for your career," he said, changing the subject. "Surely you miss it?"

Miranda smiled, touched by his concern for it. "It's true, music's a part of me," she said. "But I was hoping that, once we were married, we could start a family..."

He just didn't want to be selfish. "We were talking about your career," he said stubbornly. "If we skate by now, I promise... I'll give you a baby when the time is right. First I want you to pursue your profession to whatever extent will satisfy your soul."

With every minute, he became more indispensable to her. "Oh, Gabriel..." She buried her face against his neck. "I love you so much."

For a moment, he hugged her so tightly she thought her bones must break.

"I'll want your sweet presence in my bed as often as possible and your help with my duties here in La Caridad whenever you can give it," he said. "But I also want you to fly with your own wings. I'll always be waiting for you when you return from your concert engagements."

She'd always come back to him. Now that they were one in every sense, neither of them doubted it.

At the hotel, they went directly to her room. "No calls," Gabriel told the hotel operator. "Not even if there's a revolution. Or a hurricane."

They didn't have much time. As usual, they took all they could. To Miranda's ineffable delight, while the rest of La Caridad prepared for his inauguration, Gabriel sealed their reunion in her bed. Soaring out of control in his arms, she felt bonded to him and the universe. Surely, even with the shadow danger cast on their lives, she was the luckiest woman in the world.

They didn't have a chance to talk afterward. Or drift down in lazy contentment. While they'd been indulging themselves, the hands on Gabriel's watch had crept steadily forward. Suddenly it was a scramble to shower and get dressed.

They barely made it down to the lobby in time to collect Raquelita and hug Miranda's relatives as they arrived before they were required to get into a state-owned limousine with Eduardo behind the wheel and drive to the Plaza República, where the Cortes was situated.

Miranda's fears returned when a scuffle broke out in the crowd beyond the barricades. With great presence of mind and the smoothest possible execution, Eduardo made a rapid and unscheduled detour of several blocks before drawing up at the inaugural platform. Somehow, the veritable army of bodyguards and uniformed motorcycle police that accompanied them managed to keep pace.

Tense, nervous and ready to shield Gabriel, Miranda was greatly relieved when Félix greeted them with a walkie-talkie in hand and some wonderful news. Within the past few minutes, Echevarria had been taken into custody. Though henceforth vigilance would be an everyday affair for them, there'd be no shots to disrupt the ceremony. Or their lives.

It was only as Miranda stood beside Gabriel to watch him swear his oath of office that she fully realized her own breach of faith. He was wrong, terribly wrong not to trust me when Angél tried to create doubt in his mind, she thought as the man she loved began his address to an enthusiastic citizenry. But I was wrong too, not to force a showdown with him. By running away, I was true only to my pride. Not to our love. Or to the torch of freedom we've carried to this place.

No such lapse would occur again. As the crowd cheered Gabriel's tribute to Juan Almeida and the inspiration he'd provided for their struggle, Miranda knew with the deepest kind of knowing that her father would approve. Juanito, man of the people whose mission had been cut short, would be very proud and happy for them.

* * * * *

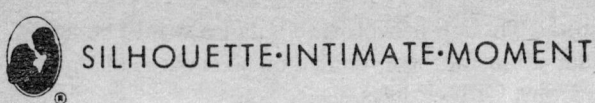

COMING NEXT MONTH

#437 SOMEBODY'S LADY—Marilyn Pappano
Zachary Adams and Beth Gibson were as different as chalk and cheese. Zach knew the beautiful attorney could never be interested in a country lawyer like himself. But when an important case forced him to seek Beth's help, he took advantage of the opportunity and pleaded *his* case. After all, what better place for a courtship than a courtroom?

#438 ECHOES OF ROSES—Mary Anne Wilson
Music was everything to Sam Boone Patton—until he met Leigh Buchanan. Sam thought Leigh was the perfect woman. She was beautiful, sensitive and creative. But then he learned that she was also deaf. Sam cared for Leigh, but he couldn't imagine life without sound. Until he realized that life without love was even worse....

#439 WHOSE CHILD IS THIS?—Sally Tyler Hayes
Kate Randolph was a woman with a secret—J. D. Satterly knew that much. What he *didn't* know was whether her foster child was the baby he was searching for—his baby. He'd already had his share of dishonest women, and he didn't want another. Unfortunately, his body kept telling him otherwise....

#440 PAROLED!—Paula Detmer Riggs
Dr. Tyler McClane had lost so much—his medical license, his daughter, his freedom. And the one person he'd thought would help him had been instrumental in convicting him. Now Caitlin Fielding was back, asking for forgiveness. True, they had once shared something special. But as much as he wanted Cait, could he ever learn to trust her again?

AVAILABLE THIS MONTH:

#433 UNFINISHED BUSINESS
Nora Roberts

#434 WAKE TO DARKNESS
Blythe Stephens

#435 TRUE TO THE FIRE
Suzanne Carey

#436 WITHOUT WARNING
Ann Williams

Summer romance has never been so hot!

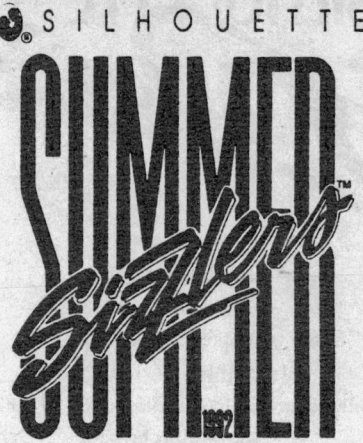

SILHOUETTE SUMMER Sizzlers

A collection of hot summer reading by three of Silhouette's hottest authors:

Ann Major
Paula Detmer Riggs
Linda Lael Miller

Put some sizzle into your summer reading. You won't want to miss your ticket to summer fun—with the best summer reading under the sun!

Look for SILHOUETTE SUMMER SIZZLERS™ in June at your favorite retail outlet, or order your copy by sending your name, address, zip or postal code, along with a check or money order for $4.99 (please do not send cash), plus 75¢ for postage and handling ($1.00 in Canada), payable to Silhouette Books to:

In the U.S.
3010 Walden Avenue
P.O. Box 1396
Buffalo, NY 14269-1396

In Canada
P.O. Box 609
Fort Erie, Ontario
L2A 5X3

Please specify book title with your order.
Canadian residents add applicable federal and provincial taxes.

SS92

Something old:
Love and Marriage

Something new:
June Grooms—six sexy heroes!

Something borrowed:
Silhouette Desire, for the month of June

Something blue:
The reader who misses even one of these sensual, sassy love stories

You are cordially invited to attend the romances of our June Grooms—six handsome hunks who have met their matches!

#715 THE CASE OF THE CONFIRMED BACHELOR
by Diana Palmer
#716 MARRIED TO THE ENEMY by Ann Major
#717 ALMOST A BRIDE by Raye Morgan
#718 NOT *HIS* WEDDING! by Suzanne Simms
#719 McCONNELL'S BRIDE by Naomi Horton
#720 BEST MAN FOR THE JOB, June's *Man of the Month*,
by Dixie Browning

JUNE GROOMS: Six sinfully sexy heroes say goodbye to their single status—forever!

Also, watch for the Silhouette Desire 10th Anniversary Collection, with stories by three of your favorite authors. You'll want your own memento of this joyous occasion.